Butterface

Butterface

AVERY FLYNN

This book is a work of fiction. Names, characters, places, and incidents are the product of the author's imagination or are used fictitiously. Any resemblance to actual events, locales, or persons, living or dead, is coincidental.

Copyright © 2018 by Avery Flynn. All rights reserved, including the right to reproduce, distribute, or transmit in any form or by any means. For information regarding subsidiary rights, please contact the Publisher.

Entangled Publishing, LLC
2614 South Timberline Road
Suite 105, PMB 159
Fort Collins, CO 80525
rights@entangledpublishing.com

Amara is an imprint of Entangled Publishing, LLC.

Edited by Liz Pelletier
Cover design by Deranged Doctor Designs
Cover photography by GettyImages/iStock

Manufactured in the United States of America

First Edition August 2018

AMARA

To women everywhere who've had to deal with the BS of society's expectations of what they should look like or do or want simply because they are women. You, my dear, are fabulous just the way you are.*

*And yes, I totally heard Mark Darcy in my head when I typed that.

Chapter One

Gina Luca knew one thing right down to the very marrow of her wedding-planner bones: brides were the devil. And a bridezilla on her fourth round of tequila shots during the reception? A highly flammable devil capable of anything, including hijacking the videographer and projecting an impromptu Kiss Cam on the movie theater–sized screen behind the bridal party dais.

The screen was supposed to be showing guests in real time celebrating the happy couple's nuptials. Instead, it was showing one of the bridesmaids going octopus on a startled guy in a brown suit holding a shrimp cocktail in one hand.

She stood on the outer edge of the crowd, watching the beautiful wedding she'd planned get turned into an episode of trash reality TV. "There is no way this is going to end well," she muttered to herself.

"With as many of my co-workers as are here tonight?" a man next to her said. "It's an HR nightmare."

Startled, she turned and took in the man who spoke. Tall. Dark hair. Green eyes. The scruff of a trim beard. The tie on his tux was undone and hanging loose around his neck. She recognized him immediately.

Ford Hartigan.

The name fit. He was a cop. He was built tough—muscular, without looking like he couldn't actually put his arms down. He looked hot, solid, and totally out of her league—not a shocker. Her league was microscopic, which she'd accepted and moved past because she had other things that were amazing in her life that had nothing to do with the size of her dating pool. She owned her own business and had great friends. The moral of the story? She wasn't the kind to ever turn a hot guy's head, but who the hell cared? Not her.

At least that took the pressure off trying to sound cool, which she most definitely was not.

"Aren't you just a total romantic." She softened the snark with a smile.

"With a Kiss Cam? At a wedding reception with an open bar? With about fifty-three percent of the Waterbury Police Department in attendance?" He snorted and somehow managed to make the rude noise sound sexy, because that's the magic good-looking people had. "Romantic isn't the word I'd use for it."

She crossed her arms and stared up at him with amusement. The glittering lights in the ballroom must have flickered at that moment, because she could have sworn his gaze dropped down to her mouth, then to her breasts—totally covered in her high-neck green dress—before snapping back up to her face. And what she saw in his eyes then? It wasn't the casual dismissal she was used to.

Obviously, something wonky was happening with the lights. She'd have to follow up with the hotel staff about it.

"How *would* you describe the situation?" she asked.

His intense focus turned back to the wedding guests hooting and hollering as the Kiss Cam zoomed in on a new couple. "Inadvisable."

"Agreed." She turned and stared at the couple on the screen. They'd been bumping and grinding on the dance floor an hour ago, the woman having matched the bride shot for shot earlier. "But at least we're not them."

The couple leaned into each other, mouths agape. Sloppy didn't even begin to describe the resulting kiss.

"Oh man," Ford groaned. "You can see their tongues. I should never have to see Partridge's tongue. That's gotta be a violation of something."

Gina smiled up at him, calling his bluff. "You don't use your tongue when you kiss?"

"On a Kiss Cam?" His eyes went wide but couldn't seem to stop watching the horror unfold on the big screen. "Hell no."

She laughed, she couldn't help it. Something about his hot and uptight vibe got to her. "Have you been on many Kiss Cams?"

His jaw tightened. "Just *this* one."

Her gut dropped to the center of the earth, and she looked away from him and back at the screen. The sloppy kissers were gone from the screen. Instead, it showed Gina and Ford.

While they stood there as if turned to stone, the crowd began to chant, "Kiss! Kiss! Kiss!"

And if that wasn't bad enough, she got to watch in live high-def as embarrassment turned her entire face a blotchy red and her already-large eyes did the whole bugging-out thing that made them protrude even more than they normally did. *Great.* Add that to the big nose and the stress zit on her chin from organizing this wedding from hell—all shown in great detail on the huge screen—and she was so not the kind of woman a guy like Ford would kiss. Even in the dark. Even after *eight* tequila shots.

She forced her mouth to form as much of a smile as she could manage at the moment and shook her head.

Of course, that didn't stop the chanting and catcalls from the rowdy guests. And here she'd thought planning a wedding of a Waterbury cop to a nurse at St. Vincent's would be a low-key, everything-according-to-procedure type of event. Wow had she been wrong.

"Kiss! Kiss!" the crowd continued.

A guy in the back yelled, "Give her a smooch, Hartigan."

"We're celebrating love, you gotta kiss," the bride called out as she lifted another tiny glass filled to the brim into the air as if she was giving a toast instead of making a drunken demand.

Yeah. There was a reason why Gina planned weddings for a living. One, she hated—no, loathed—being the center of attention, which a bride always was. Two, she got off on color-coded spreadsheets, checking things off to-do lists, and organizing like nobody's business. Three, she was really good at it. *Love*, however, didn't have a single thing to do with her career choice.

"Kiss!" the bride's grandmother yelled out.

Again, Gina shook her head. Her voice seemed to be disappearing along with her last shred of dignity the more time that damn videographer kept his camera in a tight shot on her face. Taking the if-you-ignore-it-long-enough-it-will-go-away philosophy that sometimes worked when her washing machine started making that clunking noise that always eventually stopped, she dropped her attention to the very pointed toes of her tan kitten heels.

A whir of sensation tickled her ear and made her pulse pick up half a second before the man stuck in the Kiss Cam spotlight with her leaned in close.

"Let's just get it over with," Ford whispered, the low timbre of his voice edged with tension.

Her gaze snapped up to his too-handsome face, with its perfect square jaw, dark green eyes, and high cheekbones, and her flush of humiliation deepened. He'd probably never been teased a day in his life about anything and had no idea what being laughed at by a group of people was like. Meanwhile, she'd spent her formative years getting called rabbit because of her buckteeth. She'd thought that after the braces came off, all of that would be behind her, but that's when she'd gotten a new nickname that was even worse: Butterface. Why? Because her body was okay, "but her face?" Not so much. Annoyance at the unfairness of it all made her prickle. Just get it over with indeed.

"Aren't those the words that every woman is just dying to hear," she shot back, keeping her voice quiet enough that only he could hear and not letting her fake smile slip a millimeter. "I'm not kissing you."

Unlike her, while the wedding guests continued to call for a kiss, he didn't bother to hide his scowl. Of course, that just made him look even sexier. "Why not?"

Reasons! She clamped her mouth shut before that inanity escaped and called it a victory. Knowing the right thing to say at the right time had never been one of her gifts, so the fact that she managed to keep her trap shut was a total win. When he raised one dark eyebrow in question, she scrambled to come up with something besides *because you're too hot*.

"I'm working," she said.

Ford cocked his head and gave her some premium cop face, that blank suspicious stare that all but screamed *you're full of shit*. "You don't think our fine groom, Porter, was on shift when he met Meg at the emergency room after a guy he was arresting took a swing at him with a two-by-four? It's just a kiss, and then they'll move on to the next victim."

She turned her attention back to the big screen display of this horribly awkward moment rather than meeting Ford's unwavering gaze.

"Do *not* disrespect the Kiss Cam, Hartigan!" someone bellowed out as the chanting crowd grew more restless. And louder.

"One quick kiss," he said, his tone grim with a thread of something more vulnerable underneath. "Then, they'll leave us alone."

That's when Gina's gaze moved from her own face, blotchy with embarrassment on the screen, over to him. The tips of his ears were scarlet, and he was tapping the tips of his middle finger and thumb together like he was keeping rhythm for a ska band.

He was hiding it better, but the reality was he wasn't enjoying this anymore than she was.

Glancing from the screen to the actual man himself, her lungs tightened. He was a big guy, and she wasn't just talking about his broad shoulders that filled out his tux to a mouthwatering degree. He had to have at least four inches on her own five foot ten.

He glanced down, making eye contact, and for a second they weren't the hottie and the nottie. They were two people stuck in a completely socially awkward situation that they had no control over.

She nibbled the inside of her cheek and considered her options before deciding that Ford was right. A quick peck would get the videographer out of their faces and divert the boisterous crowd's attention to another couple happier to indulge in this bit of insanity. Then, she could finish up the last of her duties and go home to her peaceful, if totally messy, mid-renovation Victorian.

She let out a shaky breath, not sure she was making the right decision. "Fine. A kiss. Whatever."

Gina had barely gotten the words out when his large hands cupped her face, sending electric shock waves through her that made her lips part slightly with surprise. He dipped his head down—and he kissed her.

The roar of approval from the crowd faded to almost nothing when he seemed to groan involuntarily. Her body approved and made an answering sound of its own. At her encouragement, his tongue slicked across her bottom lip, and her mind lost all reasonable thought. Teasing her senses and sending her heartbeat into overdrive, she softened against him, practically melting against his hard, muscular chest. Somewhere in the back of her mind she registered that people were cheering. She just couldn't for the life of her care. The world turned electric and the air practically vibrated against her skin as he deepened the kiss. His tongue swept against hers in a brief but oh-so-potent move that had her clutching his lapel before she'd even realized she'd lifted her hands.

Then, almost as soon as it began, he lifted his head and stepped back, breaking the connection.

Dazed, she released his tuxedo jacket and looked around, catching sight of herself on the giant screen. Her face was flushed and her eyes hazy. She pressed her fingers to her still-tingling lips. She looked like a woman who'd been kissed senseless, which made sense because that was exactly what had just happened.

Thankfully, the videographer—whom she would *not* be subcontracting out to again—moved on to another couple.

Just when she thought the whole situation couldn't get any more awkward, she and Ford were left staring at each other after the crowd's attention turned to the next couple being projected onto the screen. Ford's tux lapels were wrinkled, which just made the fact that his bowtie hung undone from around his open collar hotter, as if he'd just had a quickie in a linen closet. He'd probably done that at some point in his life. Gina had read about it. Did that count?

Nope. Not at all.

Ford cleared his throat. She tried to smile, but her mouth was so dry her lips sort of stuck to her teeth. Oh God, this wasn't completely uncomfortable *at all*.

She should say something, preferably something smart and witty, like…her brain went totally blank. She had nothing. Who were these women who always said the right thing at the right time, and how could she learn their ways? Maybe there was an online class for the socially inept?

Ford rubbed his hand across the back of his neck. "Sorry about that."

"What?" *Oh, brilliant, Regina. You should be teaching a snappy banter class.*

He shook his head. "I should have known something was up when Ruggiero and Gallo slipped the video guy money and then hightailed it out of here."

"Well, it's over with now," she said, pulling herself mentally together. "Thank God."

"Can I buy you a drink to make up for it?"

And there went all the work she'd done to get her brain back online. A drink? With her? This hot guy *and her*? In a heartbeat, her brain waves were all static and nothingness. Of course, that's the exact moment when words came out of her mouth anyway: "It's an open bar."

His half-smile faltered.

Shit. He'd probably been trying to not be an asshole about the whole thing, and she'd given his peace offering the middle finger. *Smooth move, Regina.*

She took a quick step back, desperate for escape before she made a bigger idiot of herself. "I've gotta go finish up some things."

His gaze dropped to her lips as he started to tap his finger and thumb together again. "Maybe another time."

Like that was gonna happen. Women who looked like her didn't end up with hot guys like him—especially not when the him in question was a cop and her family had ties to the we-never-met-a-law-we-didn't-want-to-break Esposito family. Her overprotective brothers would lose their shit if she even hinted at dating a cop. Yeah, Ford Hartigan was straight up *only* jilling off material.

"Doubtful," she said, turning and not running but walking away from the scene of her latest humiliation as fast as her kitten heels could take her.

...

What in the hell were you thinking to slip her the tongue, Hartigan? Have you totally lost it?

Finally escaping the never-ending wedding reception and still wondering just how bad his kiss must have been for the wedding planner to have blown him off without a second thought, Ford walked through the hotel lobby, searching for the chuckleheads who'd made the whole Kiss Cam thing happen.

Shocking absolutely no one, he spotted detectives Johnnie Gallo and Tony Ruggiero at the hotel's bar, sipping amaretto sours through cocktail straws like sorority girls at happy hour.

Like the jackasses they were, Gallo and Ruggiero raised their glasses in salute as he approached.

"Feeling all hot and bothered there, Hartigan?" Ruggiero asked, his shit-eating grin as wide as his ass, which had seen four thousand too many doughnuts. "Or did you come for some bleach Chapstick to sterilize your lips?"

He and Gallo bent over on their barstools and slapped the shiny bar as they laughed. And this was the brain trust that ran point on the Esposito case for the organized crime task force. Or as he liked to think of it: bear claws versus cannolis.

"She's not bad-looking," Ford said, hoping like hell this conversation would end with that.

And she wasn't. She wouldn't be winning any beauty contests, but neither would most folks. Plus, Hartigan was trained to never trust only what he saw. The truth of a person was rarely on the surface. And that kiss... It'd been a while since someone had surprised Ford.

She'd seemed all-business, in her just-perfect dress and shoes. But damn, the heat under the surface still rattled his senses.

"The wedding planner chick?" Gallo sputtered. "Did you see the size of that nose and the general ugh of that face? Do we need to let the captain know it's time to pull you in for a physical so you can get your eyes checked?"

Ford cut a deadly glare at the detectives who, technically, were his bosses. "Shut up, Gallo."

The comments pissed him off. Of all the people in the world, *they* should be the last ones to fall for the whole hot-equals-good bullshit. They were cops, after all. They spent every day neck-deep in cases of people who might be beautiful on the outside but were a fucking radioactive cesspool on the inside. Yet these two morons still only saw the surface, which probably explained why the organized crime task force was circling the drain.

"Come on, you gotta admit the wedding planner is harsh on the eyes, not like that one." Ruggiero glanced over at the boutique hotel's reception desk. "You know, she asked about you when we came out here."

Ford didn't mean to look over at the hotel clerk, but he did anyway. She was a sexy blonde with big tits and an ass that would bring a sinner to church—the kind of girl his brothers would be chatting up by now. But him? Not a chance.

He wasn't the charming Hartigan. He was the boring, rule-following nerd who'd become a cop instead of a firefighter and never heard the end of it.

His brothers Frankie and Finian would have fallen at the clerk's feet. Not him—especially not if Ruggiero and Gallo were the ones saying she was hot for him. They'd pulled so many pranks at the station that the captain had dragged them into his office and reamed their asses more than once for it.

"Like I'm gonna believe you two," Ford said, looking around the lobby for Kapowski, who'd promised he'd be here if he could.

Gallo held up three fingers. "Scout's honor."

Ignoring the obvious setup, Ford brought it back to business. Trying to shame these two into good behavior worked about as well as it did on a dog—momentary remorse followed five minutes later with Rover being snout-deep in the kitchen garbage. Again. "Has Kapowski showed up with the files about the latest Esposito surveillance yet?"

Gallo shook his head. "That would be a negative."

"And you two are out here waiting on him so you can review it in a timely manner?"

"Fuck no." Ruggiero held up his glass, clinking the ice cubes in the international sign for another drink. "That's what we have you here for, son."

"You're a real piece of work, Ruggiero."

"I know." He flashed a grin, obviously unperturbed by the dig. "It's why all the ladies love me."

Gallo laughed loudly. "There is no one who believes that."

"Tell that to my wife," he groused. "She's convinced I'm banging half the nurses at St. Vincent's."

Ford didn't want to touch that, not even with Gallo's probably radioactive dick. "I'm heading up. If Kapowski ever gets here, you can just have him deliver the info to room two-oh-five."

Why was he so ready to spend a night working instead

of following up with the wedding planner, no matter what Ruggiero and Gallo said about her? Because there was nothing in the world Ford wanted more than nailing the Esposito crime family.

He'd been close, *so close*, to making a case against the organization. But as his grandpa had always said, close only counts in horseshoes and the backseat of a car. It definitely didn't count in police investigations, and *that's* why he was stuck getting brain rot as the task force's low man on the totem pole for the foreseeable future. But he wouldn't be there forever.

Growing up as the odd man out of the seven Hartigan kids, he'd learned early on that it wasn't about winning the battle, it was about winning the war. Eventually, if he played it smart—which he always did—he'd move up to running the task force. Then, give him two decades and, at fifty, he'd be the youngest police commissioner in Waterbury's history.

Gallo gave him a questioning look. "You're staying here?"

"I've had two beers," Ford said, stopping before he sang them song and verse on department policy and the law.

"Jesus, Joseph, and Mary," Ruggiero said and took a drink from the red cocktail straw of the new amaretto sour the bartender had handed him. "Even my grandmother can drive home after two beers."

"It's against department policy." Section forty-two point eight point three, to be precise.

"Fucking rule follower." Gallo rolled his eyes and turned his barstool back around to face the bar and the giant TV screen showing the Harbor City Ice Knights losing. Again.

"We *are* law enforcement officers." Which meant they needed to hold themselves to a higher standard, to put law and order above everything else.

Ruggiero snorted. "That doesn't mean we have to be

know-it-all assholes."

Ford clamped his mouth shut and hammered the tip of his middle finger against his thumb, counting down from twenty-five because ten wasn't going to do it with these two.

Once he tapped to twenty-five, he let out a breath. "Just have Kapowski bring up the files if he stops by. We need his detail tonight to pay off. If the tip about the massive drug deal we got was right, the Espositos will be flooding Waterbury with heroin."

Even Ruggiero and Gallo grimaced at his words.

Despite their general assholery, they knew a lot of people would suffer if they didn't stop this deal—and right now they didn't have jack shit on it.

Ford grabbed his key out of his inside jacket pocket and handed it to Ruggiero. "Room two-oh-five. He can leave the files and the key on the desk in my room. I need a shower."

Ruggiero shrugged, his grimace replaced with a shit-eating grin. "Maybe I'll have that hot receptionist bring them up instead."

"You're hilarious," Ford said and marched toward the elevators so he could get out of this monkey suit.

If Ford had been one of his brothers, he would have been able to cajole the other men into not being such giant assholes. However, Ford had long ago accepted that he wasn't like the rest of his family. Brusque. By the rules. No-nonsense. That was him, the boring, dark-haired, odd man out of the wild, fun-loving, rough-and-tumble Hartigans—the guy who had women sprinting away from him after a single kiss. Yeah. He was a real catch.

Chapter Two

Gina's stomach was still going all woozy whenever she thought back to that kiss, but the wedding reception had finally wound down and the happily-wedded and sloshed couple had disappeared into their honeymoon suite. That meant Gina's time in hell was done. Thank you, baby Jesus.

She loved her job as a wedding and event planner—really, she did—but nothing was ever as sweet as the moment she walked away from a job well done. In T-minus twenty minutes, she'd be out of these heels and cute-but-not-revealing green dress and back in her own home, with nothing but the creaky silence of the old Victorian for company. She couldn't wait.

It wasn't the most exciting life—she owned that—but it was hers, and she was determined to make the most of it. No sitting around waiting on Prince Charming, who only existed in storybooks. Forget that pampered dweeb. What she needed was a handyman who wouldn't run screaming from her home renovation to-do list. Well, that and more clients for her start-up business. Orgasms would be nice, too, but she'd found her vibrator was a hell of a lot more reliable for that than the few men who'd been in her bed.

Purse in hand and gaze locked on the hotel's front door so she couldn't get flagged down by any drunk guests, Gina almost slammed right into one of the cops who'd been the source of the newly married couple's tequila supply. *Way to go, Regina.*

The guy—what was his name, it was something with a G, Gerry? Gionni? No. Johnnie—had stepped away from the hotel's reception desk and directly into her path. How she managed to stop in time, she had no clue.

"How you doin' tonight, Miss Wedding Planner?" Johnnie asked, trouble brewing in his slightly unfocused eyes.

Great. This was the last thing she needed right now.

Okay, the real last thing was getting called back to duty by a more-than-tipsy bride, but a run-in with a drunk guest was a close second. Blowing him off wasn't an option, though.

She had her reputation to consider, and her fledgling company didn't need the bad word of mouth because he perceived her as being rude. Add to that the fact that her brothers, Paul and Rocco, were known to have had multiple run-ins with the cops, so giving the detective a reason to give her—or her family—a hard time wasn't a smart move. Sure, it wasn't like her brothers were top-level guys in the Esposito organization, but they had plans—the stupid kind of ideas she'd spent her entire adult life trying to talk them out of.

The only good part of them being the neighborhood loan sharks was the fact that they actually helped a lot of people who were struggling, much to the detriment of their bottom line. They were the softest loan sharks that ever existed. Her brothers would help anyone with a sob story and give terms that didn't involve broken legs for late payments. It wasn't the usual route for loan sharks and that meant their profit margin sucked. They hadn't told her directly, but she'd heard they were trying to get a better position with the Espositos so they could get someone else to do the debt collecting. Her brothers were softies, but they also wanted to make a buck.

So while she didn't have anything, even peripherally, to do with the family business, pissing off the cops and making her brothers targets was not an option. Damn. Some days there really was no winning.

"I'm doing fine, thanks," she said, using her I'm-here-to-help work voice. "Did you need help with something?"

"I'm good." He paused, seemingly for effect. "However, there is something that *I* could do for *you*."

There was an awkward pause as he continued to stare at her, and her brain went on the fritz when it came to coming up with inane conversation—because she highly doubted there was anything this guy could do for her. And in her experience, when someone told her they wanted to do her a favor or gave her an I'm-interested look, there were ulterior motives at play. That lovely reminder of how her life worked brought back the old familiar clammy hands and tight chest feeling that hit her hard.

It took a couple of deep breaths, but she got the anxiety under control so much faster than she had in the past. Three cheers for growing up.

"As fascinating as I'm sure the offer is, I'm gonna have to pass." She tilted her chin back toward the closed ballroom doors, where the pumping bass for the stragglers going late after the newly married couple retired was still going strong. "That wedding tuckered me out."

"Sure, sure," Johnnie said, tapping a hotel key against his meaty palm. "It's just that Ford Hartigan asked me to keep a watch out for you. You know our boy Ford, right? He was the guy you kissed tonight."

Her cheeks flamed. "Why would he want someone to be on the lookout for me?"

"I couldn't say for sure," Johnnie said and then looked

over both shoulders before taking a step closer and dropping his voice to a low whisper. "But he asked me to watch out for the hot chick from the Kiss Cam. I think he's interested, if you know what I mean."

Gina stiffened. In her entire life, no one had called her "the hot chick." Absolutely no one. She wasn't pretty, let alone hot, and denying that fact wasn't ever going to do her any favors.

Keeping her chin high and her breathing steady—thank you, hours of yoga training—she put on her neutral smile and took a step toward the door. "I gotta go."

He held up the hotel key card. "Room two-oh-five."

That stopped her. "What are you talking about?"

"It's his room number," he said. "Ford wanted to see you, but he's stuck in his room waiting for a report to get delivered."

"Why does he want to see me?" Her natural cynicism warred with the hope for something different this time. He had offered to buy her a drink. She'd been the one to spurn him. And that kiss... Maybe he was hoping for another chance? Could that be possible?

The detective continued, "Look, you're a smart woman. You know the Kiss Cam was a setup. Ford had been watching you all night, and you may not believe it, but he's kinda shy and didn't know how to approach you. The guy's married to his job. I mean he *never* dates. I was just trying to do a friend a solid."

"Really?" She didn't bother to keep the yeah-sure look off her face even as the quiet voices urging her to believe got louder and louder.

"I know, he's not the most, shall we say, emotive guy out there, but he's interested in you, ya know?" Johnnie shrugged. "But if you don't feel the same, I can pass that message along. He'd just hoped..."

The cop shrugged and let the rest of what he was going to say fade away.

None of this sounded right, but a helium balloon of hope filled her chest anyway. "No offense," she said. "But why should I believe any of this from you?"

He smacked his hand against his chest over his heart. "Right in the ticker." Then he held out the key. "Look, you don't know me from Adam, but I swear I have my buddy's best interests at heart here, and you seem like a nice lady." He held up his free hand to stop her from interrupting. "I hate that I put you on the spot with that Kiss Cam thing. Ford feels like shit about it, even though he had no idea what I was up to. He wants to make it up to you. Wanted to at least apologize in person. No one's forcing an independent, smart woman like you to do anything. Take the key and go talk to Ford or don't, it's your choice."

Gina stared at that key card. Maybe this was a sign that life for her was about to change. That's what her grandfather would have said.

He would have told her to take this opportunity and seize adventure whenever she could. Spending the night—because they were all grown-ups here, and even though no one was saying it, they all knew that's what they were talking about— in an overpriced hotel room with a seriously sexy man? That wasn't something offered to someone like her every day, not even every five years. Who knew if the opportunity would ever come again? And what kind of giant chicken would she be if she walked away from this chance—especially when she wanted him as much as he seemed to want her?

"Fine. I'll at least let him apologize in person." She plucked the key from his fingers, pivoted direction, and headed toward the elevators, ready to give opportunity, adventure, and a night of steamy sex with a hot cop a shot.

...

Hot beads of water pounded down on Ford's shoulders, taking away the tension that had been building there since the disastrous kiss with Gina. *Gina.* He liked the sound of her name. It rolled off his tongue like a mix between a groan and a wish—especially while his eyes were closed and his hand was wrapped around his cock, giving it a slow, tight stroke.

He hadn't been lying downstairs. She may not be what anyone would call a beauty queen, but there was something about her, something tempting and challenging, that had caught his attention and made him wonder about… everything. Just how soft was her skin at the dip in her waist? Was her laugh low and dirty or a warm soprano? Would she moan when he unzipped that green dress that had clung to her every curve? What would make her call out his name?

What could he say, he was a cop down to his core.

Finding the answers to all of life's questions turned him on—especially if they were about Gina. She made him so fucking curious. He slid his palm up and down his length, his other hand planted, fingers spread wide against the hard wall tile, and let the fantasy take him. One stroke. Two. Then the unmistakeable sound of his hotel room door opening caught him halfway down the shaft. His eyes snapped open as reality slammed into him.

Shit.

Kapowski.

The stakeout report.

Grateful that he'd mostly shut the bathroom door, so at least the patrolman snagged for the special detail wouldn't get an eyeful of Ford jerking off, he turned in the shower right in time to see a flash of a green dress and wavy brown hair pass by the door. Then it was gone. Kapowski was blond and stuck to all black. So who in the hell… His fast-thickening dick figured it out quicker than his brain. Gina the wedding planner was in his room.

What was happening?

How did she get in?

Why was she here?

That's when he heard a voice shouting in his head, *Who fuckin' cares? She's here and she wouldn't be if she didn't want you.*

Maybe refusing his drink offer had been because she was still on the clock and not because of him?

Stop asking yourself questions while your hand's around your cock and talk to the woman in your hotel room, the voice yelled.

"I'm in the shower," he called out, which was fucking brilliant repartee in its obviousness.

The lights in the bedroom clicked off right as she said, "I picked up on that."

Figuring that if he thunked his head against the tile it would be loud enough for her to hear in the other room, he clamped his eyes closed and counted to ten instead. Then, he turned the shower knob all the way to the left, letting it linger at the apex of cold for a minute to try to clear his head and deflate his hard-on so he wouldn't walk out like a fucking loser who'd been jerking off in the hotel bathroom by himself.

Which he was.

But she didn't need to know that.

By the time he turned the water all the way off, music was playing in the other room. It wasn't gonna-bang-you-against-the-wall or make-love-to-you-all-night long stuff, it sounded like what his sister Fallon listened to when she did yoga. *Oh God.* Thinking about his sister right now was *not* what he wanted to do. His dick shriveled up. Fuck. Going out there as Danny Dinky Dick was not what he wanted, either. Could he catch a fucking break?

Beyond the fact that a chick you were just thinking about while your hand was around your cock is in your hotel room, chucklehead?

He snatched the towel off the stack on the shelf and dried off. "I'll be right out."

"Take your time," she said, her words coming out in a breathy rush.

That made him pause. Something was off about this. However, the blood rushing back south as soon as he heard her voice was louder than that quiet thought. Still, he was a man who always followed the letter and spirit of the law. Consent wasn't something he took lightly.

"Is everything okay?" he asked. "You don't have to be here if you don't want to."

There was a short silence that lasted four hundred and eighty-two years while he stared into the dark beyond the partially closed bathroom door and felt like an idiot.

Finally, she asked in a soft voice, "Do you want me to leave?"

"Hell no." Like he had to think about that.

She laughed. It was a smoky alto—one question answered—that went straight to his dick. "Then what's there to talk about?"

Not a damn thing. He wrapped the towel around his hips and reached for the door.

Chapter Three

With the music from her phone filling up the dim space of the hotel room, Gina pushed past the adrenaline and anticipation pumping through her veins with enough force that she could practically hear it and reached her hands behind her back, making a desperate grab for her dress's zipper tab. Maybe it was the pressure of the moment, maybe it was the fact that Satan had designed her dress, but she had to use all of her yoga stretching skills to reach the damn thing. Then, she had to not have an anxiety attack while in the process of inching the zipper down using only the very tips of her fingers.

She kept an eye on the bathroom to make sure Ford didn't walk out and catch her looking like a twisted-up Cirque du Soliel reject.

Stress-induced perspiration curled the hair near her temples into frizzy ringlets. Okay, she couldn't see they were frizzy because she'd turned off the lights, but she *knew* that's what had happened.

Finally, she got the damn zipper down far enough to slide the dress over her hips right as the bathroom door started to open. Shit. She wasn't prepared. She needed five more minutes. Didn't he still need to condition his hair? Did guys even do that?

Shut it, Regina, this isn't the time for stupid questions.

Right. She was right. A nervous giggle escaped. God, she was not only talking to herself, she was confirming her answers.

From her spot near the end of the bed, she could just see into the bathroom. That gave her a perfect view of Ford as he completely opened the opaque glass bathroom door. Or it would have, if total and complete panic hadn't sent her flying onto the foot of the bed, where she scrambled on her hands and knees like a deranged gazelle on speed to the top of the bed and slid under the covers. Of course, her underwear went up her butt in the process.

She groaned out loud and squeezed her eyes shut. She'd worn her evil granny panty stomach minimizers. She hadn't been planning on getting laid. Didn't men know a woman had to *plan* for these types of things? Like, what if she hadn't shaved in a week or was on her period? Didn't they even consider the possibilities?

"Hey there," Ford said, the pitch of his voice giving it a sexy gruffness.

Her belly fluttered, and her nerves melted away in the onslaught of hot desire that flooded her limbs.

"Hey yourself," she answered as she hooked her thumbs in the waistband of her panties and used the kind of strength they talk about mothers having when they lift cars off their children to shove them down and then fling them over to where her dress lay in a puddle on the floor. Palms sweaty, she ripped off her bra before Ford stepped out of the bathroom, pausing in the pool of light coming out of the open door.

Thanks to her brief moment of sanity when she'd walked into the room and killed the lights, she had a better view of him than he did of her. Outlined by the light behind him, he stood silhouetted in the door. Broad shoulders, defined arms, and narrow hips that had a towel slung low around them. Wow. Ford was the exception to the looks-better-with-clothes-than-without rule, even when she could only see him in outlined form. She tried to think of something flirty to say, but her brain had checked out—right up until the moment when he reached for the light switch outside the bathroom door that would turn on the bedroom lights.

"No," she said, slinking farther down under the covers. "Leave it off."

Hello, this is your subconscious calling, and I know why you'll only do this in the dark.

Yeah, because it was harder to notice her face this way. *Oooff.* That hit like a solid punch to the gut. However, before self-doubt could grab hold, Ford turned off the bathroom light and the room plunged into near darkness, thanks to the hotel's mostly closed blackout curtains. Thank God enough light from the streetlamps snuck through the space between the curtains that she could watch as he walked toward her, unwrapping the towel as he did.

Thank you whoever is up there for letting me see this. I promise to be a much better person from now on.

And that was the last thought she had, because that's when his towel hit the floor.

The bed dipped a little as he got in, and her nerves came rushing back. Saying it had been a while since she'd been naked in bed with a man was an understatement. Then, he reached over and cupped her cheek in his warm hand, and his lips came down on hers, and her nerves disappeared like free drinks at a wedding reception.

Strong, firm lips pressed against hers, and his tongue slid against the seam of her mouth, not demanding entry but not begging, either. He was...tempting her, and her body was responding like she'd been waiting her whole life to take him up on that offer. That realization of the rightness of the moment and the man—okay, and probably a metric ton of her pheromones crushing on his pheromones—made something click inside her, and all the doubt and insecurity disappeared.

In the next heartbeat, they were laying facing each other in the dark—but it didn't matter because her hands were everywhere, the darkness heightening every touch as her fingers followed the muscular plane of his abs, glided over the high round curve of his ass, and slid down the outside of his hard thighs.

Could she get high from touching someone? Because that's what it felt like. Her whole body had turned electric, and just when she thought it couldn't get any better, he stopped cupping her face and his hand moved down to her hip, his fingers pressing into her flesh with just the right amount of pressure as he tugged her close and his hard, thick cock brushed against her tight curls. For once, she didn't overthink. She brought her leg over his and tilted her hips so she could rock her wet, swollen core against him.

His low rumble of a groan brushed against the sensitive skin of her neck. "Fuck, I'm so glad you found a way to get in here."

Gina froze, nothing but white noise filling her brain. "You left me a key."

"What key?" he asked, swinging his arm back and hitting the button on the bedside table lamp.

For a second, she couldn't see as bright light filled the hotel room. Blinking, she cleared her vision and— "Oh my God, *you* didn't leave me a key, did you?" She planted both hands on his chest and shoved Ford away from her, panic buzzing through her body with the sting of a thousand bees.

He shook his head, then his eyes narrowed. "Who gave you the key?"

"The key," she asked, repeating him because her brain couldn't keep up. Then, the words poured out of her in a freaked-out rush. "You left me the room key with your friends, Johnnie—"

Understanding punched her right between the eyes, and the rest of her explanation turned to poisonous ash in her mouth. She wanted to throw up. It was a setup. The whole thing had been a setup. If not by him, then by his asshole friends.

It wasn't the first time she'd been made a fool of just for laughs. God knows, she'd lived through it enough growing up. And Johnnie's story hadn't sounded *that* crazy. A little off, but still reasonable. Why? Because that's what a liar did. He stayed as close to the truth as possible to make the lie believable. She *knew* and still had totally fallen for it.

Nice going, Regina.

Clamping her teeth together to keep from crying, she clambered over Ford and got to the edge of the bed with lighting speed.

"You didn't want to be here?" he asked, curling his fingers around her wrist as he sat up.

She jerked her arm away. "Does it matter?"

The question came out in a half croak as her feet touched down on the towel he'd let fall to the floor before getting in bed. How in the world had she let this happen? Why had she thought this time would be different?

Panic made her jittery so she had a hard time seeing her stuff scattered on the floor, but there was no missing the man in the bed. He was imprinted on her brain. Dark hair with the slightest wave, dark green eyes without any laugh lines around them, and a mouth—that mouth—that he may have used to kiss her senseless but didn't look like he ever used it to smile. He was hot. Too hot for most of the population, let alone someone like her. Fiery tears of humiliation burned at the back of her eyes.

She needed to get out of here. Now.

She rushed forward. Her foot caught in a twist of the towel, and she went down. Her ass hit the carpet with a hard thunk that did more harm to her pride than her tailbone, but her pride was already pretty dinged up and didn't need the extra scuffs. Closing her eyes, she hung her head so her hair fell in front of her face to form a frizzy curtain while she took a deep breath. Of course, it wasn't like her humiliation would be complete with only one massive, sixty-story-skyscraper-sized gut punch to the ego. No, she had to be a total klutz, too.

"Are you okay?" Ford asked.

Huffing out a breath, she sent her hair flying out of her face, determined not to let this man know how embarrassed she was. So she looked up—way up—at him, and her brain stuttered to a stop as soon as her mutinous gaze landed on his thick, muscular body, hard dick poking against the sheet, and handsome face. Good Lord, did the fates have no mercy? Before she could reach out and touch him to make sure he was real and not another hoax, some last vestige of self-preservation kicked into gear and she averted her gaze and kept her hands to herself.

"Just peachy," she said as she got up, her right ass cheek protesting after that tumble, and hustled over to the small piles of her discarded clothes.

Ignoring the granny panties in her hurry to get the hell out of there, she pulled on her dress and reached around in an awkward move for the zipper.

Ford stood up and reached out toward her.

Her heart leapt into her throat, and she jumped back. "Don't touch me."

His hand fell to his side, and his shoulders sank. "I was just going to help with the zipper."

Okay, that would be nice since she was tugging for all she

was worth and still only had the damn thing halfway up, but it wasn't going to happen. She'd had all the embarrassment she could take, without adding being dressed by a man who'd never left her his hotel room key to the list. How pathetic must she have seemed, just showing up and sneaking into his room? It probably happened all the time to someone like him. That thought pissed her off, too.

She glared up at Ford. "How about you just pull the sheet around you instead?"

He swiped it off the bed and wrapped the thousand-count material around his waist. "I'm gonna get Gallo and Ruggiero to apologize to you. This was beyond going too far."

The guy seemed genuinely pissed, as if this sort of thing didn't happen in his world. In fairness, it probably didn't to someone like him.

Tall, good-looking—her gaze landed on the police badge on the bedside table—and a cop, everything probably went his way. That last detail registered in her brain. Cop. *Oh my God.* Just when she thought the whole situation couldn't get any worse, she'd forgotten that Ford was a cop, just like almost everyone else at the wedding. Shit. If her brothers knew, they'd kill her, or maybe him. Probably him. They may have been loan sharks but they were overprotective brothers right down to the cellular level. They'd lose their minds if they ever found out. Some things—some people—just weren't done.

Giving up on getting her zipper any higher than her shoulder blades in her desperation to get away from the scene of the crime, she shoved her foot in a shoe. "I'm leaving."

Ford's face darkened, and his square jaw tightened. "Maybe we can figure something—"

"Let's not, okay?" she interrupted him as she jammed her foot into her other shoe. A pity fuck? Yeah, she wasn't going there. She counted to twenty in her head to distract herself from the tears making her eyes hurt and the sinking, fatalistic feeling of this-is-as-good-as-she-can-ever-expect that sucked the air out of her lungs. "Your friends are real pieces of work."

What else could she say? Nothing. And to top it all off, those jerk friends of his were probably still at the bar, waiting to watch her walk of shame out of the hotel. They were probably laughing their asses off about the whole thing right now. And she'd have to fake being all right until she could get home and finally let her real emotions show.

Twenty minutes. That's all you have to get through, Regina. You can do this.

Pep talk completed, she pivoted and headed for the door without giving Ford another look—she just couldn't. Even with her high humiliation tolerance, this was right on the edge of what she could take. Her hand was on the doorknob when his voice stopped her.

"I'm sorry," he said, his voice soft, apologetic.

She squeezed her eyes shut for a moment to block out the kindness in his tone, because that was the last thing she needed if she was going to make it out of here without falling apart.

Steadier after a breath, Gina opened her eyes and pulled open the door. "Yeah. Me too."

Then, her throat tight, she walked out the door.

If there was a silver lining to this shit cloud, it was that she'd never see Ford again.

The door felt like it weighed a million pounds as she started to pull it closed behind her. And saw the shocked faces of her brothers. She was too startled to even wonder why these two were at the same hotel as a cop's wedding.

Rocco and Paul gaped at her. Both had their arms slung around women she'd never met before and wasn't supposed to, guessing by the scarlet flush eating its way up Paul's throat as he moved to stand in front of the bottle-blonde in the micro mini-skirt swaying just a bit in her four-inch heels.

"What in the hell are you doing here, Gina?" Rocco asked, his tone calm, not that that fooled her.

Older than her by four years, he'd assigned himself the role of guardian-in-chief when their parents moved down to Florida. The fact that she was a grown woman or that he wasn't exactly on the legal up-and-up didn't seem to make any difference.

Stuffing her granny panties farther down in her small clutch before reaching behind her for the door handle to steady her, she glared at her brothers. "I had a wedding."

"In a hotel room?" This from Paul, who was recovering his equilibrium, no doubt as his suspicions grew about why she was walking out of a guest room.

"Not exactly," she said, attempting to finish shutting the door behind her as subtly as possible. Too bad something hard blocked the way. If she had to guess, she'd peg the obstruction as one that belonged to the man she'd been in bed with moments before.

Some of her annoyance must have shown on her face, because Rocco dropped the hand of the tall redheaded woman he was with and took a step closer, peering over her head into the sliver of darkness slipping through the not-quite-closed door.

"Who's in there with you?" he asked.

She yanked harder, but Ford didn't take the hint. The obstruction remained. "No one."

One of Paul's bushy eyebrows shot up. "If our mother heard you lie like that, she'd be lighting candles at church."

Their mother had been doing that for all of them since they'd been born—not that it had helped. Gina was still single, and her brothers were still involved with the wrong people. The blonde behind Paul took a weaving couple of steps forward and flashed a friendly smile at Gina. The woman may not be the smartest for getting involved with Gina's brothers—definitely love-em-and-leave-em types, but that wasn't Gina's call to make, just like it wasn't theirs to get all judgy on her. Of course, that didn't mean she wanted them to know anything about the guy lurking behind the door, and he *was* lurking. She knew that because she'd tried to yank the door closed twice now and he hadn't moved his stupid foot. Time to get her brothers out of here. Now.

Gina gave her brothers her most innocent wide-eyed look. "You two look busy, why don't you just go—"

Rocco interrupted, "Who are you with, Regina Marie?"

Her middle name? Really? Like she wasn't thirty-one years old with a mortgage, job, and brain of her own?

"You're not Mom or Dad, so don't use that tone with me." She let go of the doorknob so she could cross her arms and give her oldest brother the death glare he deserved, with a popped-out hip and everything. "And for the last time, I'm—"

The hotel room door swung open.

"With me," Ford said from behind her.

And totally not shockingly at all, the floor did not open up and swallow her like she so wanted in that moment. Instead, she got an up close and personal look at her brothers' faces as they turned blotchy with anger way out of proportion for even her overprotective, we-wish-we-lived-in-the-caveman-times brothers. Instinctively, she took a step back so she blocked a direct line of attack against Ford and, hopefully, made it harder for her brothers to notice that the other man was wearing only a sheet.

"Hartigan?" Rocco practically spit out.

Oh. Shit. "You know each other?"

The men ignored her while the women just watched with wide, unblinking eyes.

"Is this what your little task force has sunk to?" Paul

asked, taking a step closer to where she stood in front of Ford. "Pillow talk with our sister?"

Crap on a gluten-free cracker. Ford worked on a task force. And her brothers knew him. That meant only one thing. He worked organized crime, and that meant he was all up in her brothers' business. Judging by the way Rocco's hands were fisted at his sides and Paul's not-very-subtle move toward the inside of his suit jacket, things were about to escalate quickly. *That* she would not have.

Her brothers might be idiots sometimes, but they were her brothers, and she wasn't going to have them going to jail for assaulting an officer just because she'd been dumb enough to believe that Ford had actually wanted to sleep with her.

"Stop all of this now," she said, standing as tall as she could. No one paid attention. "He's not after information about you," she tried again, her voice rising as panic made her nerves jangly. Desperate to stop this before she couldn't, she blurted out, "He's my boyfriend."

"What?" Rocco bellowed.

Ford stiffened behind her. She couldn't risk a look back at him to let him know she wasn't stupid enough to believe what she was saying. If she did, she'd blow everything. She could fix the lie. She couldn't fix her brothers going to jail, and she'd promised their mom that she'd watch out for them.

"Yeah," she said in a voice that shook even on that one-syllable word. "We've been seeing each other for months."

"And you've known the whole time that he was a cop?" Paul asked, his hand still resting inside his jacket.

Ford made a growl of a sound, and she reached behind her back without looking and grabbed his hand, squeezing it tight enough that even a completely clueless person would know it was code for "shut the fuck up."

"Ever since I met him." Okay, not a lie. Not the whole truth, but not a lie.

"I don't like it," Paul said, but he moved his hand from being half hidden beneath his jacket to totally in view at his side. "Just imagine a cop at Grandma's ninetieth birthday party next week."

"You don't have to imagine, because he'll be there." She could brazen this out. She could. *Oh my God, let the earth swallow me up at any moment, please.* "I'm a grown woman, and I don't need your permission when it comes to who I date."

Rocco's vein pulsed near his temple. "I don't approve."

"I don't care." She shrugged, hoping like hell that it looked natural instead of like a jerky movement brought on more by nerves than actual confidence. "Look, I've watched out for you two for years since Mom and Dad moved to Florida. Now it's my turn to have a little fun."

What she didn't say—and her brothers didn't call her on, because despite all the posturing, they did love her—was that she wasn't normally the kind of person who *got* to have that kind of fun.

She stared at her brothers, daring them to try to argue. Making the smart choice, for once, they kept their mouths shut.

"Just be careful," Rocco said as he took his date's hand and led her down the hallway.

Paul and his date followed suit, with the leggy blonde giving Gina a chipper wave goodbye as they did so. Once the foursome got far enough down the hallway that they hit the end and had to turn left, disappearing from view, Gina let out a sigh of relief. She would have sank back against the wall, but the one behind her wasn't made of sheetrock, but muscle.

"We need to talk," Ford said.

She turned and faced her make-believe, not-even-for-a-whole-night boyfriend and shook her head. "I don't have anything to say to you."

Really, what could she say? Sorry I totally lied about you, but it's because I didn't want my idiot brothers sent up the river for punching a cop in the face because of their misguided sense of honor? Yeah, it was time to slink on home like she should have done in the first place.

"Too bad, because I do." He pressed the hotel room door open wide, the move highlighting his ropy forearm and just how big his hands were. "And I think you do, too."

Her dress was still partially askew, her panties were in her purse, and her nerves were all twangy, and he wanted to *talk*? He had to be joking. But then she looked up—way up—at his face and realized he was deadly serious. Either that or he had a resting scowl face. Her gut sank down to her toes. What in the hell had she done when she'd taken that hotel key?

• • •

Ford flipped the deadbolt on the hotel room door and stayed there with his back up against the wall and watched Gina take a weaving path as she paced in front of the bed. The woman should never play poker—especially not at the Hartigans' weekly game. She was nothing but a jumbled set of tells. The way she fiddled with the handle of her purse. The way her gaze flicked from one part of the room to another, studiously avoiding him. The way her steps seemed both hesitant and speedy. The Hartigan siblings would empty her kitty of pennies before the fourth hand.

Of course, that wasn't the only reason why he couldn't bring her to play poker. The wedding planner, with her cute blushes and awkward nervousness, was Gina fucking Luca. Sister to Rocco and Paul Luca, two neighborhood loan sharks with delusions of grandeur. That her name had never come up in the task force's briefings wasn't a surprise. The Lucas were bottom feeders, no matter how well-informed they were about the Esposito organization.

So why had he brought her back into his room? It sure wasn't because it gelled with standard operating procedure to invite a relative of known crime associates into his hotel room while he was wearing only a sheet. If internal affairs knew, his ass would be missing several bite-sized chunks out of it.

Finally, she stopped, crossed her arms in front of her stomach, and lifted her chin a few inches before her gaze dropped from his. "Well, what did you want?"

"You're Gina Luca." The words came out because he had no idea what else to say.

She shrugged. "And?"

"Your brothers are Paul and Rocco Luca."

The tip of her nose turned red, and a splotch of color appeared at the base of her throat. "This is what you wanted to talk about? My family tree?" She tightened her arms around her midsection. "Well, my mom's Barbara, my dad's Sal, and my grandfather is Big Nose Tommy, well, *was* is probably a more accurate description. He disappeared twenty years ago."

Disappeared. Yeah, that was one way to put probably wearing cement shoes at the bottom of the harbor.

"You need a date to Grandma's birthday party, and you just told your brothers that I'm your boyfriend." Okay, not the smoothest of lines or a smart move according to regulations, but he'd never claimed to be the suavest Hartigan in Waterbury.

She snorted. "That was because I didn't want to have to bail my brothers out of jail because they figured knocking you out cold was the honorable thing to do. Now if that's all, I've got to go."

So she had idiot brothers, too. He could identify. He needed to step to the side, open the door, and let her go back to whatever life she led. Instead, he stood there like a stump—useless and in the way.

"I've been where you're at," he said out of fucking nowhere.

One side of her mouth kicked up into an almost smile. "Standing in a hotel room with your panties in your purse?"

He chuckled unexpectedly. "Not quite." He shoved his hand through his hair. Where in the hell was this coming from? He didn't talk about this shit. What was next? A look into his feelings about fighting for every case that came his way because everyone on the force seemed to live under the same misconception as his brothers that he should have been a firefighter, like every other Hartigan male since his great-great-whatever got off the boat? Even the idea of doing that made him want to hurl. "I've been the one who didn't quite fit in with my family."

She rolled her eyes and got some of the same attitude she'd had when she was telling her brothers to take a flying leap. "I have a hard time believing that."

"Trust me, it's true." If she only knew.

Gina just gave him a look that screamed *whatever* and started toward the door. "Look, I'm sure you're Poor Mr. Misunderstood, but I've got two overprotective brothers who are going to be watching me like hawks after this disaster, a business I'm fighting to get off the ground, and a Victorian that I thought would be a simple renovation, which it would be, if I could keep a damn handyman for longer than a week. I don't have the time or emotional energy to take a fake date to my grandmother's party. Thank you but no."

She stopped in front of him, just outside of arm's reach, her gaze direct. Her look was the equivalent of a shy-but-still-doing-it-anyway fuck you, and he couldn't help but grin at her. What could he say, he was an asshole, and her unconscious comfort level with her own vulnerability was endearing.

In his own family, bluster and bravado came in equal, mega-sized servings. To acknowledge weakness was to admit defeat. But with Gina, it didn't come off that way. She was, as his mom would say, plucky. Sure, she was totally in over her head, but she was plucky—and that turned him on.

"So, this is it?" he asked, his gaze dropping to her mouth.

Her full lips disappeared, pressed into a thin line before she said, "Yeah, I'm sure you're not used to hearing that."

"Only because I don't give up easily." Still, he turned the doorknob and held the hotel room door for her.

"Goodbye, Detective Hartigan," she said, her voice breathy.

Nope. He didn't like the finality of that.

"Good night, Gina Luca."

That telltale splotch of blush of hers bloomed even brighter at the base of her throat, and she hustled down the hall to the elevators. Unlucky for him, the doors opened as soon as she hit the down button. He watched until the doors closed and then went back inside before someone reported a perv in the hall wearing only a sheet.

The door clicked shut behind him, leaving him alone, surrounded by the scent of Gina's perfume. Too bad that's all of her he'd ever get. A Luca and a detective on the organized crime task force went together like bulletproof vests and yoga.

After tonight, he wouldn't be seeing her again. And he refused to examine the tightness growing in his chest at that thought.

Chapter Four

One Week Later...

Gina had a sledgehammer, and she knew what to do with it. Okay, she didn't *really* know what to do with it, but she'd watched enough home renovation shows to look like it as she hefted the damn thing up and took aim at the half wall dividing the attic of her historical—fine, desperately in need of serious love—Victorian home into two rooms and cutting the flow of the space. The metal head of the sledgehammer made a satisfying thunk as it bashed through the poorly-constructed half wall for what felt like the millionth time that morning.

Arms aching from the effort of swinging the fifteen-pound hammer, she took a step back and set it down to admire her work. The half wall was toast.

Sure, there were still odds and ends she'd have to yank out of the floorboards, but the sun pouring in from the stained glass window on the east wall into the large open space left dots of color across the dusty hardwood floor that made her smile despite the mess.

The attic would be perfect for the new headquarters of Consider It Done Wedding Planning. She'd meet clients downstairs in the salon with its own door to the wide front porch, but this is where the magic would happen. The planning, the plotting, the everything coming together—that would be done here. If only she could take care of her other problems so easily.

Yeah, so she was doing a little home renovation therapy. Who would blame her? It had been seven days since she'd hightailed it through that hotel lobby, and she could still hear the cackling laughter from those asshole cops at the bar chasing after her.

Instead of thinking about it, though, she'd taken the DIY approach and pictured the cops' faces on every piece of drywall she'd smashed through. Okay, she might have a little of her brothers' Sicilian temper and lust for blood herself, she'd just figured out how to channel it better.

Now she no longer saw the jerks' jeering faces in her dreams. Instead, she only saw Ford's—and that was kind of worse, because she also heard his clit-whistle of a throaty groan every damn time she collapsed in bed at night. That was just unfair.

Had he been in on the whole humiliating charade and just played it off as being a total surprise to him? Possible, but she couldn't get herself to believe it.

Anyway, it was nicer to pretend he hadn't been. A girl like her needed the fantasy of a good man who didn't lie or use people, who wanted her just because he did. All she had to do to make that happen was to bring her late-night fantasies to a grinding halt the moment before he told her he hadn't left his hotel room key for her.

Kinda depressing thinking there, Regina.

Her inner voice wasn't wrong. She swiped her water bottle off the floor and took a long drink. Time to keep moving forward and fixing up the home she'd inherited from her grandfather. The courts had declared a few months ago that the man she'd adored growing up and had been missing for twenty years was now officially deceased. And thinking about that was just going further down the rabbit hole that only led to sniffles and tubs of Rocky Road, which she wasn't going to do because her life had been sad enough up until now. Things were finally going to change for her. She refused to let her looks or her family or her perpetual spinsterhood—*hello, too much Austen on the bookshelf*—stop her from doing what she wanted any longer.

It was time to make a new life for herself, and it started with renovating her grandfather's home that had been sitting vacant for umpteen years by getting rid of the random boards still left standing after her spin with the sledgehammer. Her grandfather would have been proud of his girl finishing the renovations that he'd started so long ago. It may not be the usual tribute to a grandparent, but it was one he would have appreciated.

"Alexa," she called out to the electronic hockey puck plugged into the wall near the stairs. "Play my renovation playlist."

Instead of her normal happy, female singer-songwriter tunes, the alto growl of chicks done wrong who weren't gonna take it anymore boomed through the speakers. Now *this* she could get her hammer swinging to.

Chin high, shoulders back—and gait lopsided because the sledgehammer was heavy—she marched back over to the half wall. In the movies, this is where she would have gone to town on what was left of that wall, smashing it to smithereens and turning in a circle triumphantly to view her accomplishment. Her life was a different kind of movie, though, because instead of the hammer coming down and taking out the two-by-four, it went flying out of her hands—thanks to a mixture of palm sweat and condensation from the water bottle—and sailed across the room, landing with a thud on the floor on the unfinished side of the attic.

"And you wonder why you don't have your own home reno show," she muttered to herself as she crossed the room to see the damage she'd inflicted.

Stepping carefully because there weren't any floorboards laid across the insulation on this side of the attic, she held her arms out for balance and tiptoed across the crossbeams to the east wall where the sledgehammer lay in a puff of pink-wrapped insulation. The light coming in through the stained glass window danced across the insulation like mini-rainbows on a pink sky. It would have been pretty if it hadn't been another reminder of the amount of work she still had to do on the house.

As she was reaching for the hammer, a glimmer caught her eye. It was different than the other colored spots from the window, more solid and golden. She leaned forward. The sparkle was coming from a spot under the bent corner of the insulation. A tool dropped into the space between the beams?

She moved the hammer over and pulled back the insulation, careful not to tear the wrapping so she wouldn't inhale the probably poisonous strands inside, and revealed a narrow strip of open space that, though dark, seemed to go on down to the basement, judging by the cool, still air wafting up from it. The space had to be the top of one of the walls, which were built with tight crawl spaces inside them. She'd learned about that the smelly way, when a squirrel who'd been squatting in the attic found its way into one and couldn't get back out. The exterminator had given her all the gory details.

Did squirrels collect shiny objects? Maybe it had left behind some doodads? She grabbed her phone from her back pocket, slid her thumb across the screen to turn on its flashlight, and shined the piercing beam into the darkness.

Four spindly sticks lay in a line, one with a gold ring around one of them. *That's weird—*

Realization slammed into her, knocking her back onto her ass. She didn't care, she just did the crab walk on her hands and feet in her rush to get away from the crevice between the walls, because it hadn't been four sticks. They'd been bones. Finger bones. And the ring? It had been her grandfather's.

...

"Hartigan," Captain Grant hollered across the Waterbury detectives' bullpen as he stood in the door of his office. "In here. Now."

Ford's shoulders jerked closer to his ears before he could stop the reflexive reaction. This wasn't good. Not being called into the captain's office, but that bark of an order usually meant a shit assignment was incoming.

The last time he'd gotten that, it was after the deputy chief's son had gotten picked up on a pot bust. That case had been radioactive. They'd given it to Ford because he wasn't the kind of cop who gave a rat's ass about whose kid a perp was. Rules were rules, and they were meant to be followed.

He got up from his desk, shoving aside a box of Chapstick with the word *bleach* scrawled in Sharpie across the label. No doubt they were from Ruggiero and Gallo. The way they were describing what happened at the wedding to the rest of the squad was that they'd set him up with a life-sized Troll Doll who happened to have mob connections for that Kiss Cam stunt. Everyone had gotten a good laugh about that. Assholes.

At least the idiot duo hadn't gone on to tell everyone about them giving Gina his hotel room key. That meant either the two of them finally discovered they didn't have to be dicks all the time, or they were just holding onto that little tidbit until the worst possible moment—like when he got called into the captain's office, so they could watch as the captain dialed up internal affairs and informed them of a possible compromised detective on the task force.

Ford strode into the captain's office in the corner and stopped inside the door. "You wanted to see me?"

The captain didn't look up from his computer screen. "Shut the door and sit down."

The hairs on the back of Ford's neck did the conga, but he did what he was ordered, just like he always did. Anyway, if this was going to turn into an internal affairs colonoscopy, he'd rather get the bad news without the entire squad listening in.

"I understand you had an incident this weekend with Gina Luca." The captain turned in his chair, slid his glasses down low on his nose, and watched Ford over the rims of his bifocals. "Something about a Kiss Cam?"

Ford let out a breath. That had been embarrassing, but not something that internal affairs would want to talk to him about. "Yes."

The captain took off his glasses and cleaned them with a small cloth beside his keyboard in total and complete silence. First the right lens, then the left, then flip the glasses and do it all over again. Slow. Deliberate. Total power move. The captain loved to make subordinates wait on his next words, and it drove some guys nuts. Ford wasn't one of them. He just took the opportunity to let his brain spin out the possibilities of what could come next and options for dealing with them.

Finally, the captain replaced his glasses, then folded the cloth in half and then half again before placing it on his desk at a perfect parallel line to his keyboard.

"Is there any reason why you couldn't interact with Ms. Luca in a professional manner?" the captain asked once he finally looked up at Ford.

"No sir." He could get past having seen her naked—having trailed his fingers down her smooth skin—even if he couldn't seem to stop thinking about it.

"Good, because we need to use that perceived connection on her part to our advantage."

Of the forty-eight possibilities he'd worked out, that wasn't one he'd been expecting. "Sir?"

"She just called in a deceased person in her attic." The captain templed his fingers and tapped them to his chin, silent and waiting for Ford to pounce. When he didn't, the captain went on. "The body's been there a while, decades, probably. Cold cases should take it but, as you know, her brothers have been making moves." Another dramatic pause. The captain was a main player in the Waterbury Community Playhouse, and it showed. "We need someone who can give us intel on how much progress they're making and if it's tied to the heroin shipment that informant mentioned this week."

"And you think she knows this?" Gina was close to her brothers, he could tell from the way they'd interacted at the hotel, but according to mob organization rules it would be beyond unusual for Rocco and Paul to share inside information with her. And on the off chance that they did, she wouldn't be the kind to rat out her brothers. Her sense of loyalty might be misguided, but—after watching her with her brothers—it had been as obvious as the raspberry jelly on Gallo's tie this morning. Still, there was something to be said for being in the right place at the right time, and since Kapowski's stakeout the other night had turned up exactly nothing new, the task force couldn't afford to turn down any opportunity as the date for the shipment got closer and closer. Fuck. He hated to admit it, but the plan to use Gina had merit.

"No," the captain said. "All indications are that she's clean. *However*, a good investigator can pick up all sorts of information—especially about something as big as that Esposito heroin deal is rumored to be." Off came the glasses again. He picked up the cloth and unfolded it. Wipe. Wipe. Flip. Wipe. Wipe. Fold. Fold. Cloth down. Glasses on. "Are you a good investigator?"

"Yes sir." It wasn't ego. It was the truth. And he was beyond ready to prove it. "So, the plan is to get close to Miss Luca to gather intel about the workings of the Esposito family and the upcoming deal?"

All he had to do was get Gina, an innocent bystander, to trust him so that her brothers would as well. People said a lot without ever opening their mouths, every detective knew that. Still, guilt coated his tongue like he'd just taken a swig of rotten milk. That Kiss Cam kiss and the silk of her skin had been on almost constant replay in his mind since the wedding.

She may have thought he'd been joking about him going to her grandmother's party with her, but he hadn't been. There was something about Gina that got to him, and that's why this whole situation pissed him off.

If her brothers cared for her as much as she claimed they did, why weren't they protecting her from their business better? The whole reason he'd dodged the family business and become a cop was because he believed in fairness, in the importance of looking out for those who couldn't look out for themselves. Moving in on Gina on false pretenses was an asshole move—he fully admitted that—but that didn't make it the wrong move, and it was for her own good.

He could do this without hurting Gina, while still getting the kind of information that could put bad guys behind bars and save lives by keeping that heroin from hitting the street. She never had to know her part in this. Correction. She never *would* know her part in this. He'd do whatever it took to make sure of that.

The captain nodded. "You'll go in and take a look at the body that, according to the description from the first reporting officer on the scene, looks like what remains of Big Nose Tommy Luca. Then, you'll find a way to gain her trust and entry into her environment to deduce what the brothers are up to. We know the date of the heroin deal, but not the location or time. From their briefing files, it's clear she's close with her brothers. You stay close to her, see what you hear."

Ford tapped his thumb against the tip of his middle finger too fast to count the beats. "Don't you think this is a long shot?" Like the Ice Knights with their losing record getting into the hockey championship playoffs long.

"I realize this assignment doesn't gel perfectly with your sense of cut-and-dried, by-the-regulations way of living, so if it's too much for your delicate sensibilities, just say the word and I'll assign someone else. Gallo has time available."

The station coffee swirled in his stomach. There was no way that Gallo should be within a mile of Gina. It wasn't that the guy would make the same dumbass comments he'd been making around the bullpen to her, but the idea of him being close to her made Ford want to chew the bark off a tree. He couldn't explain the visceral reaction to the idea, but it was there, and as a cop he'd learned to trust his gut.

"No need for Gallo," he said as he stood. "I'll take the case."

"How will you gain entry?"

"I'll find a way." He always did.

"Excellent. Then you have somewhere else to be right now," the captain said. "Dismissed, detective."

Ignoring the questioning looks from the rest of the task force squad, he grabbed his coat and his umbrella—fifty percent chance today—and headed out the door to go lie to a woman to save her from having Gallo on her doorstep. What could possibly go wrong?

Chapter Five

Gina was three seconds away from losing her shit completely. Everything was going so wrong that the people at Merriam-Webster or Urban Dictionary needed to come up with a new word for it.

Ford Hartigan was in her house. Her brothers were in her house. A dead body that was probably her long-assumed-dead grandpa was in her house. And all she could think about was the fact that she was in holey leggings and a paint-splattered T-shirt with a drawing of a dog humping a houseplant on it.

The shirt had been a gag gift from one of her besties, Lucy, who lived to buy totally inappropriate things just to watch Gina turn sixty shades of red. In return, Gina left the radio on full blast whenever she borrowed Lucy's car.

If they hadn't been friends since they'd discovered their shared love for extra-sour candy in college, they probably would have killed each other years ago. As it was, they were the best of friends.

What she wouldn't give to have Lucy here now—or Tess, the quiet third of their undateable crew. Although, they liked to refer to themselves as Single and Slaying It. Definitely had a more empowering vibe, she'd agreed. Instead, it felt like her girls were the only ones in all of Waterbury not stuffed into Gina's kitchen, which was packed with DIY supplies and boxes, staring at her like she had any answers at all.

"So, walk me through this again," Ford said, looking way too sexy for a guy wearing a rumpled sport coat that looked like he only put it on in the first place because he was forced to due to some detectives' dress code regulations. "You were throwing your sledgehammer—"

Rocco turned to her and cut Ford off. "What were you even doing with a thing like that? You coulda killed yourself."

Really? Her blood pressure spiked. That's where her brother wanted to go with this conversation? "Grandpa's body has been trapped between the walls in the attic for years, and you're worried I'll brain myself with a sledgehammer?"

He shrugged, obviously unimpressed by her outburst. "Excuse me for caring about my only sister."

"And how do we even know that was Grandpa?" Paul broke in, his wavy hair sticking up in every direction because no amount of gel could stand up to the constant assault of his fingers plowing through the thick mass since he'd walked in the door. "It could be the bones of some perv who likes to live in the attics of single women."

God bless him. He was holding out hope that someday Grandpa would come back. She hadn't. Somewhere deep down, she'd known for years that the man who brought her Twizzlers and packs of glitter pens was gone. She'd done her mourning a decade ago. Her brothers hadn't. They might be criminally minded, but family meant a lot to them. To her, too. She walked over to him and gave him a quick hug.

"I saw the gold ring, the one he always wore," she said, her voice quiet. "It was him. I know it."

Ford cleared his throat. "The medical examiner will

confirm the identity and try to determine cause of death."

"Yeah?" Rocco said with a sneer. "And will that same fine medical examiner also be able to explain how our grandpa has been rotting away for two decades and no one ever noticed? You're telling me none of the renters who came in over the past ten years noticed?"

Ford narrowed his green eyes and slid the small notebook he'd been using into the inside pocket of his sport coat. "I don't like to speculate."

"Do it anyway," Paul said.

"Please," Gina added.

For a minute, Ford just stared at her brothers as they stood on the opposite side of the kitchen. Rocco had his back against the fridge, arms crossed, gaze hard. Paul was pacing in the area in front of the bay window with a built-in seat covered by a single long, threadbare cushion. Stillness and motion, that was her brothers. And her? Per usual, she was somewhere in the middle, standing between the two factions and fidgeting with the knob on the junk drawer that always seemed to be loose. Her gaze locked with Ford's, and her fingers stopped turning the knob. Some expression she couldn't read passed across his face, and then he began to speak.

"*If* it is your grandpa, he's been missing for twenty years," he said. "*If* this was due to natural causes, he could have been in the attic, taken a wrong step on the joists since there isn't a floor up there, and slipped into the small space between the walls. At that point, as no one else lived in the home and your grandpa had questionable ties, shall we say, everyone assumed he'd either skipped town of his own accord or was taken care of in other ways. So, the house stays empty for a number of years. How many was it again?"

"Ten," Gina said. "My mom really held out hope that he'd come back."

Ford gave her a small smile, then turned his attention to Rocco. "So, by then the natural decomposition—or at least the bulk of it—would have been completed. It usually takes six to twelve years. After that, no decomposition, no smell. Of course, we won't know any of that until the medical examiner finishes her report and until then, this is considered suspicious and will be treated as such."

"You'd say all of this in front of our sister, *your girlfriend*, without even a twitch of revulsion?" Paul asked, shoving his fingers through his hair again. "She's fucking delicate."

Gina couldn't decide whether to strangle her brother or hug him.

"I'm not delicate," she said, ignoring the other part of what he'd said. "I'm a grown woman."

"And we're here to protect you," Rocco said. "Because you can't trust the cops."

Ford's jaw clenched.

"I can trust *him*." The words came out before she could consider the truth of them, but as they hung in the air, she realized it was true. There was just something about him that settled the frazzled worry that always seemed to be buzzing in the background of her head.

Rocco let out a humorless chuckle and strode to the table, planted his hands on the back of one chair, and leaned forward. "Yeah, we'll see. He's sure not acting like a boyfriend."

This time, it was Ford's turn to shrug. "She didn't tell you I was moving in?"

"What?" she said at the same time as her brothers, no doubt all with different reasons for the look of horror on their faces.

Ford crossed over to her and slid his arm around her waist, drawing her in close. "It seemed prudent. If your grandfather was murdered, then whoever did it might come back to make sure there wasn't any evidence, since there isn't a statute of limitations on murder."

The scent of his cologne teased her senses while the touch of his fingertips on her hip, over the yoga pants and under the hem of her hideous T-shirt, made her lungs tighten. Ford? Here? No. It wasn't true. She repeated it in her head. He was just trying to be nice. A pity kindness to get her brothers to chill the fuck out. He didn't mean it.

Rocco looked from her to Ford and back again. "I don't like it."

"You don't have to," she said, concentrating on the words instead of the butterflies doing the Cha-Cha Slide in her stomach—because Ford being this close and touching her was doing a helluva number on her ability to remember to breathe. "But as you can see, everything is being handled. Why don't you guys go home? I'll let you know any updates as soon as I get them."

Her brothers looked at each other and had one of those silent conversations they'd had her entire life, where things got decided without a single syllable being uttered. Finally, Paul turned to her.

"Okay," he said. "But call us as soon as you know anything."

A few minutes of hugs for her and dirty looks for Ford, and her brothers were gone, leaving her alone in the kitchen with Ford while a small army of cops clomped up the stairs to the attic to do all of that crime scene stuff that turned her stomach whenever she accidentally stopped on one of the true-crime shows on TV. Needing something to keep her hands busy, she turned on the burner under the kettle and grabbed two mugs from the cabinet and set them down on the counter. Just because she was about to kick Ford out of her house didn't mean she was going to be rude.

"You are not staying here." There. Firm and assertive,

but not rude because she said it while handing him a tea caddy with seventeen varieties of green tea. As her mom always said, the little things mattered.

He picked out an orange jasmine without even looking at the labels and handed it to her. "If I don't, then you can't, either. Your entire house is a crime scene."

Everything stopped for a second. None of that sentence sounded right. She wasn't the kind of person who had threats leveled against her. Well, unless she counted the bridezillas on the warpath, but even that was usually fixed with chocolate or champagne.

"What are you talking about? You said it's probably natural causes," she said.

Ford held her gaze. "We won't know that until the ME's report, so this is going to be treated as a homicide until we know different."

"Bullshit." The kettle's ear-splitting whistle sounded at that moment as if the universe was putting an exclamation on her statement.

"Look, we have to treat the threat with a higher level of concern than we would if it had been called in about a normal citizen."

She dropped the tea bags into each mug and poured the steaming water over the top. "You mean one without ties to organized crime."

"Exactly." As if he owned the place, Ford reached over and set the timer on the oven display for three minutes, the exact amount of steeping time recommended on the back of the tea packets.

He had just told her that her house was a crime scene and because her brothers were idiots involved with the mob the cops were taking it seriously, and yet he still thought it was important to steep his tea properly? What the hell? It was just one more thing to annoy the shit out of her about this entire situation. Why was it that the men in her life felt the need to run roughshod over her?

"So, I'll just be staying on your couch for a few days until the medical examiner confirms her initial theory that your grandfather died of natural causes after slipping between the walls, and we can make sure that no threats are made against you."

"Are you deranged?" She yanked the tea bag out of his mug even though there was a full minute and a half left on the timer and tossed it into the trash. "You think I'm just going to agree to that because we told my brothers that you were my boyfriend—as if anyone would believe that. What, do you think people believe this is some lame romantic comedy where the hot guy falls for the ugly chick? Newsflash, I don't wear glasses, so there's no taking them off and then suddenly I'm a total babe and believably your girlfriend."

The words came out in a rush, and by the time she was done her breath was coming out fast and hard. Her cheeks hurt from the heat of embarrassment. God. She thought she'd gotten past all this hurt from being the ugliest girl in the class, but one wedding night prank had raked it all up to the surface, and all of a sudden she was sixteen again and hearing the giggling whispers of Butterface as she walked down the hall.

Clenching her jaw tight so her chin couldn't tremble, she focused all of her attention on her own mug. She put way more effort into carefully removing her tea bag and putting it into the trash than she had with Ford's, all so she could have a few precious seconds to take a breath and pull herself back from the edge. Once she could trust her voice, she turned back to the man who kept bearing witness to her most humiliating moments this decade.

Keeping her gaze on his chin with its dimple in the middle, because looking him in the eyes was so not going to happen right now, she said, "This isn't just my house. It's my place of business."

"We can arrange it so that only the attic is off-limits," he said, his thumb tapping against the mug's handle.

Her confidence coming back with each inhale, she raised her chin and her gaze. "If someone did kill my grandfather, then they're long gone."

His thumb sped up its rat-a-tat-tat beat. "Are you so sure of that?"

"I could just tell my brothers that I need them to help out." Ugh. Saying it out loud sounded like a worse idea than just thinking it in her head. Still, it was better than the alternative. Ford? In her house? Nopity nope nope. "They'll stay here."

"Is that what you want?" Ford raised an eyebrow and took a sip of his tea. "The chance of your brothers going off half-cocked when the mail carrier rings the doorbell to drop off a package? And anyway, the only choice you have is me staying here or you at a hotel."

The tea burned her tongue, but she didn't care. She needed something in her mouth to stop herself from screaming NO! Because he wasn't wrong. Rocco and Paul were beyond annoying in their attitude toward keeping her safe. They'd been like that since the first time some jerk on the block had started making fun of her. They were good brothers. They were also total idiots who would punch first and think later, which was very not good if the person who ended up with a broken nose—or, she had to face it, worse—wasn't someone threatening her.

She put the cup down and looked around her kitchen, taking stock of the boxes of tiles, the PVC pipe and paint brushes—really anywhere but at the man in her kitchen who discombobulated her thinking.

Her brothers were the last ones she needed at her house. And while Tess was supportive in her own super-quiet way and Lucy as enthusiastic as she was impulsive, on the off chance her grandfather *hadn't* just slipped into the space between the walls on his own, she didn't want to put either of her friends in danger by having them stay here.

Finally, her gaze landed on Ford. More specifically, she zeroed in on his hands as they practically dwarfed his tea mug. They were strong hands. Capable hands. The kind that had felt so good on her skin as he—

Girl! You're in danger!

Gina stopped that line of thought before it could go any further. "Are you any good with your hands?"

Ford set down the mug on her counter and smiled. "I'd like to think so."

She couldn't swallow the tea in her mouth as she stared at him and the cocky upward curl of his lips. It just sat there like hot judgment on her tongue while her body forgot how to do basic tasks.

Oh, she remembered how good he was with his hands. She'd only been remembering in vivid detail what he'd done in the hotel room every night in her own lumpy bed. Where was the hole in the floor, because she really wanted to slide down into it. No, really. There was a hole in the floor of her kitchen. Owning a Victorian in need of so many repairs really did have its privileges. Too bad she'd moved the kitchen table over it so no one would accidentally fall.

Nice move being all safety first, Regina.

At the realization that once again the embarrassing truth of the matter was written in red all over her face and that there was no escaping it, her body suddenly remembered how to move. She swallowed the tea, set down the mug on the counter, and gave Ford what she prayed was a snotty glare.

"I think this whole thing is crap, but if you're going to stay, you're going to have to help with renovations."

There. That should send him running.

It should have. But he didn't disappear.

"I worked my way through college on a construction crew." He picked up his mug and took a drink, never looking away from her. "Home renovation is in my wheelhouse."

Of course it was.

...

It was hours later, after the crime scene techs had left, leaving a trail of black fingerprint dust behind them and a big *X* of police tape across the door leading to the attic stairs, before Ford got a chance to call his captain.

He'd basically blackmailed Gina into letting him stay. He could claim it was for his job all he wanted, but it wasn't.

Initially, it may have been to save Gina from having to deal with Gallo, but the captain was going to try to tap her for information one way or another. If Ford had said no and Gallo wasn't an option, the captain would have gone with someone else. That didn't make lying to her any better. It made it worse. Why? Because there were other ways to get the information they needed.

But in the kitchen, with her brothers hovering and crowding her space, she'd looked like she'd needed his help. And he wanted to keep her safe. He hadn't lied about that. If someone *had* killed her grandpa, odds were they'd come back to check that they'd not left anything at the scene. And the idea had just come to him. Stay with Gina and keep her safe, keep the captain from getting anyone else to stake her out, and keep her close enough that *if* her bonehead brothers were getting more involved in the Esposito organization, he might be able to protect her.

He glanced around the house he'd just agreed to help renovate for a few days.

The setting sun coming in through the big bay window

bathed the living room—a salon, as Gina had called it—in a warm, golden glow. The house had good bones, but there was obvious neglect everywhere the light hit.

The fact that Gina was even willing to tackle it was impressive. He wasn't surprised she'd had trouble finding contractors and others willing to take on the specialized work to get it not only up to code but keep it true to who she was.

He dialed the captain's office and pulled gently on the torn wallpaper hanging on one wall, so he could get a peek at what was underneath while the phone rang.

"Tell me you have good news," Captain Grant said in greeting.

"I've made up the couch, if that tells you anything." Gina had given him a pillow, a sheet, and a thick Go Ice Knights Hockey blanket before disappearing into another part of the creaky house.

"I don't need to go over the rules with you, do I?"

"No sir."

"Let's just summarize it into two, then," the captain said. "One, get the information from the Luca brothers we're after. Two, Ms. Luca is not a target, but she is off-limits—not that there's really any reason to worry about that, considering what Gallo and Ruggiero are telling the squad about her." The captain paused. "So how bad is she?"

Well, there was no missing the family resemblance with Big Nose Tommy, and her eyes didn't quite fit her face, but it wasn't like she was some kind of snaggletooth troll with poisonous drool. She definitely didn't look like the women he normally dated, which made the fact that he'd gotten hard almost every time he'd thought about her during the past week more than a little interesting. So how bad was she? He heard her voice in his head talking about the fact she didn't wear glasses and therefore couldn't take them off and be suddenly beautiful like in the movies. His gut flopped.

"It's not pertinent to this investigation," he said without inflection.

"That's what I like about you, Hartigan." The captain chuckled. "You're always by the book. I don't have to worry about you going off the deep end."

"No, sir." He was the guy who double tied his shoes, kept his receipts, and waited for the walk signal before crossing the street—at the fully-marked crosswalk.

"Any word from the ME?" the captain asked.

"Confirming Big Nose Tommy's identity is a formality." Okay, Dr. Dev had told him she'd need to get dental records, but considering the circumstantial evidence of where the body was found, the ring, and the body's physical stature, she was putting a positive ID at 96.8 percent. That was the kind of specificity that he could appreciate. After that it was just confirming cause of death.

"Foul play?"

"The good doc says not according to initial indications." She'd gone into detail about the whys and the hows of that, but he wasn't even going to try to repeat it to the captain.

"Where's the lady now?"

Ford turned toward the closed pocket doors that blocked off the room he was in from the large foyer and staircase that led up to the next floor. "Her room for the night."

"And she bought your story about why you need to be in the house?"

He pictured her as she handed him the blankets. She hadn't said anything, but there was no missing the suspicion written all over her face. The woman really should never consider a job as a spy.

"For a limited time."

"Then you should consider the clock ticking, Hartigan. Act accordingly."

His grip tightened on his phone. "I'll do my best."

"I'm counting on it, because the chief talked to me about shaking up the task force. This is a great opportunity to either prove you've got what it takes or that everyone who says you should have joined the fire department like the rest of your family was right."

So, minor stakes, then, for a shot in the dark assignment. Great.

Chapter Six

Ford woke up the next morning on the couch and felt like shit. No. He felt old. And achy. And like someone had grabbed a pair of putters and taken a few whacks to his neck. The pleather couch might be good for watching a game—if the room had a TV—but it sucked to sleep on.

Blanket around his hips, he searched for the T-shirt he'd tossed off in the middle of the night, and a sharp pain shot from right behind his ear down his shoulder.

Fucking A.

He reached up and rubbed the aching spot between his neck and shoulder blade. The knot was just starting to ease when a woman's squawk of a scream echoed through the drafty house, coming from the direction of the kitchen. Ford grabbed his gun and sprinted toward the sound, sliding to a stop in his bare feet in the doorway of the kitchen.

Gina stood in front of the sink with part of the faucet in one hand and her other hand pressed to where the water came out. What must have been one helluva water spray had plastered her brown hair to her head, and one long wet strand was stuck to her nose, running down the length of it, coming to a stop at the tip. As she looked at him, her eyes wide with surprise, a big drop of water hanging from the end of her nose fell. Of course, that just took his attention south over her chest—her nearly see-through tank top was so wet that it must have been in the direct line of the spray zone—and then farther down to the soft pink cotton sleep shorts that ended just below the round curve of her ass. His morning wood woke up again.

"Having a little bit of a problem?" he asked, letting his gun arm relax.

She huffed out a breath, no doubt aimed at the wet hair glued to her nose, and gave him a death stare. "Please tell me you weren't lying about knowing home renovation stuff and that you can actually turn off the water."

"That I most definitely can do." He walked into the kitchen and put his gun down on the table before crossing over to her in front of the sink. "If you can just move over, I can open the cabinet doors and get to the valve."

"If I could move, don't you think I would have? One inch and the water cannon goes off again. My seal on this thing is tenuous."

Great. She stood, feet planted shoulder-width apart, directly in front of the cabinet. "Can you pivot the lower half of your body?"

She turned in toward the cabinet.

"No." He squatted down beside her, grabbed her hips, and rotated her the other way. "Like that."

Except *like that* was bad. Very bad. Her sleep shorts were as thin as they looked, meaning not only could he feel the heat from her body where his palms cupped her hips, he could see the dark outline of the panties she wore under the shorts. His thumb started tapping a beat against her hip, and she inhaled a sharp breath. He looked up, took in how her nipples had pebbled against her tank top, and the desire turning her brown eyes to a dark walnut.

All of the air in his lungs came out in a rush. It wasn't a frustrated groan, it was an exhale. So what if that was a Pyrrhic victory, he'd take any victory at all at this moment.

"Sorry about that," he mumbled and opened the cabinet.

"No problem," she said, her voice breathy.

Trying his best to ignore the woman with the mile-long legs next to him, he peered under the sink and located the valve. Finally, something going right this morning. He grasped the knob and turned his wrist. The knob didn't move, though. Lucky him, he had some built-up frustration that he could pour into it like WD-40. He gripped the valve tight and tried again. This time the damn thing, which probably hadn't been touched in fifty years, gave way.

"Try now," he said.

A half second later, cold water was everywhere and Gina was screaming curses again. By the time he'd stood up, though, she had her hand pressed against the half of the faucet that had been gushing water. A fresh river was dripping off her nose, and now her shirt was just wet and clinging to her tits in a way that made his mouth go dry.

Off-limits, Hartigan. She's very off-limits.

That reminder was enough to move his gaze up to see the very-not-amused expression on her face. "Let me go check the main valve."

"Good plan," she said through clenched teeth.

"You know where it is?"

She closed her eyes and let out a sigh that would translate in any language to *idiot*. "Basement."

He'd never been so glad to get out of a kitchen in his life. Not even when he was growing up at home and the rule was last one in the kitchen with Mom after Sunday family dinner had to do the dishes. He had six siblings, and at six foot two he was considered one of the short ones, so there were a lot of dishes after feeding a lot of big people.

The basement was at the end of rickety stairs in a dark room that had a single lightbulb with a pull string hanging from the ceiling. In other words, it was a basement he would have fully expected to get called to for work. Despite the atmosphere and the fact that the basement used to belong to Big Nose Tommy Luca, he didn't find a body—at least not another one—but did find the main water valve behind a stack of boxes that looked like they'd been in the basement for the past century. He turned the main water valve off and hustled upstairs to the kitchen, where he almost had a heart attack.

Gina was sitting at the kitchen table—still more wet than dry—breaking down his service weapon like a pro.

"What in the hell are you doing?"

"I don't allow guns in my house."

She grabbed a flat-head screwdriver and pushed down on the black collar around the exposed portion of the firing pin while simultaneously sliding the back plate back. A rookie would have let go of the firing pin and the big steel safety pin and sent them flying across the room, but not Gina. She kept ahold of both and then removed them and sat them on the table beside his nine millimeter's magazine.

He'd never gotten turned on by a woman who knew her way around a gun before. Watching her changed that.

What in the hell was wrong with him? Forbidden fruit really wasn't normally his kink. He went for the future soccer mom type who followed the rules and kept to a schedule. This detail was just messing with his head—both of them.

"You do remember I'm here on official business?" he said, striding into the kitchen and stopping on the opposite side of the table, leaning forward for emphasis. "There may be someone waiting for the perfect moment to clean up any details they'd overlooked before with your grandfather."

She kept on with what she was doing, not even bothering to look up. "You do remember I pay the mortgage, so you have to follow my rules and I don't allow firearms in my house."

"This is ridiculous."

She shrugged. "Then leave."

"That's not gonna happen." Not with her other option being Gallo at her kitchen table to find out what he could from the Luca brothers' totally off-limits—*remember that part, Hartigan*—sister. "And neither is me giving up my gun."

• • •

Gina tried her hardest to ignore the way Ford's forearms looked when he pressed his palms to the kitchen table and leaned forward. She totally failed.

Before, she'd never really gotten why some women raved about arm porn. Now she did. She shifted in her seat and sat the flat-head screwdriver down next to the nine millimeter's slide and spring.

"If you're in this house, it's without your gun." That was her line in the sand, and no one got to cross it.

She didn't believe this cock-and-bull story about someone out there lurking to clean up a mess left behind after they'd offed her grandfather twenty years ago. That meant only one thing. Her brothers were up to something more poorly thought out than usual and it had gotten the attention of Waterbury's finest. Playing along with this nonsense was her best option to find out what Paul and Rocco were doing, which was the only reason she'd agreed to let Ford stay. Really. That was it.

"No gun?" He stood straight and crossed his arms over his bare chest. "That's total nonsense."

"I don't like guns." *Brilliant comeback, Regina.*

She could have come up with something better if she had gotten to make the pot of coffee she'd been starting when the damn faucet she was trying to tighten at the base came off and sent water everywhere. That's all it was. It sure wasn't because she was distracted by his biceps or his washboard abs or the dark happy trail that started right below his belly button and disappeared beneath the waistband of his low-slung jeans.

"Well you sure are comfortable with them." He jerked his chin at the separated pieces that made up his nine millimeter that were spread out over her kitchen table.

He wasn't wrong. The Lucas could trace their connections back to the old country, but her dad had been the odd duck of the family who walked away from the family business. There weren't any guns in her house growing up, but here in this one? Yeah, that had been different when her grandfather had been alive.

"It was my grandfather who taught me how to do this." It hadn't been the usual grandpa and granddaughter bonding experience, she guessed, but it was theirs.

For the most part, her parents kept her, Rocco, and Paul away from their grandfather's bad influence, but they still managed to sneak in time with him. The man was far from perfect, but they were kids and that hadn't mattered to them.

Ford pulled out a kitchen chair and sat down, his posture relaxed but the look in his eyes sharp. "And your brothers followed in Big Nose Tommy's shoes?"

A person didn't have to have connections to organized crime to see the trap he was laying there. "I'm not talking to you about that. Look, they might be assholes, but they're *my* assholes."

His lips twitched. "Your assholes?" he asked, emphasizing the plural ending.

It took her a second and then she realized what she'd just

said. "You know what I mean."

They made it four seconds in silence before both of them started giggling like twelve-year-old boys. Immature? Very. Needed to break the tension making her gut clench? Absolutely. She let out a breath, and her shoulders relaxed a few inches.

"Okay, so coffee is out of the question, but I've got cereal and milk."

He did that half-smile thing that made her stomach flutter. "Sounds like a plan."

A few minutes later, after she'd changed into a dry T-shirt and yoga pants and he'd gotten a shirt on, they were sitting on opposite sides of the small kitchen table finishing up their bowls of Peanut Butter Crunchies. While she'd changed and called the emergency plumber, he'd dried the puddles on her kitchen floor and had wiped down the counters. However, he'd left his gun where she'd put it. Smart man. The broken-down nine millimeter took up a good chunk of the middle of the table between them. Gina glanced down at it and back up at Ford.

"I have to have my gun," he said. "It's my job."

"Your job sucks," she said as she stood up and then took her empty bowl and spoon over to the sink that was no longer trying to drown her.

"That's a negative." Ford followed her to the sink, bowl and spoon in hand, and left his dishes in the corner of the sink with hers.

"What is it that you like so much about it?" Because, for the life of her, she didn't get it. It was all black and white, and the world had so much more color than that.

Ford turned to face her. The morning sun coming in through the window above the sink highlighted his strong chin and the lighter brown strands in his dark brown hair. The urge to let her imagination go lower to wonder if his chest hair poking out of the shirt had the same variation in color was so frickin' tempting, but she held strong. Okay, she didn't. She pictured it in her head. The hair dusting his pecs would totally do the same thing. What could she say, she was human and he was a very good-looking man standing in her kitchen. What kind of underwear was under those jeans of his? Boxers? Briefs? Questions to ponder another time, not when Ford was looking at her with a serious expression that made her insides a little fluttery.

"I like to figure things out. I like order. I like to know that someone is out there making sure people follow the rules. I like the idea that those rules are keeping people safe."

Now, Gina was a woman who liked her spreadsheets, and walking into The Container Store gave her the happy sighs, but getting locked into following a set of rules devised by someone else? Yeah, totally not her game. It's why she liked yoga. There were set steps and guides, but it was all about listening to her body and knowing what it needed. Some days, she could do the shoulder-pressing pose where she balanced her entire body on the palms of her hands while her legs were wrapped around her arms. Other days, it was all she could do to make her warrior fierce.

"Life is too crazy to *always* follow the rules," she said. "Sometimes you have to adapt and be flexible."

"Flexible," he scoffed.

Fine, Mr. Rule Follower, time for a demonstration.

"Yeah, you know…" She took a few steps back, inhaled, and as she exhaled let herself stretch into a standing split, with her nose nearly touching one kneecap and her other leg pointed up toward the ceiling. "Flexible."

Oh, she was definitely going to regret going straight into that pose without a warm-up first, but it was totally worth it for the stunned look on Ford's face when she put both feet back on the ground. She had a feeling it wasn't very often that he got that fish-out-on-dry-land gobsmacked look. *Victory is mine.*

"There's no way in hell my body is ever going to do that," he said, his voice raspier than it had been moments before.

"You never know." She shrugged. "Come to a few yoga classes and you might surprise yourself."

The doorbell bonged. The plumber. She was going to owe Huey his weight in cannoli for getting out here so quick. She started toward the foyer, but Ford's voice stopped her.

"I'm gonna have my gun, Gina. It's part of my job, but you won't see it."

She stood in the doorway but didn't turn around. She didn't like guns. Hated them. But he had a point. The story about someone coming back to clean up after Grandpa was suspicious, but if it was on the level…

"Fine," she managed to get out through clenched teeth. "But I don't see it. Ever."

"Not unless you're in danger."

Now she did turn around. Ford was standing by the sink looking like a model but in well-fitting jeans instead of… briefs. Yep, he was totally a briefs guy. They were probably white and saggy tighty whiteys and OMG she couldn't even lie to herself about it, judging by just how low his jeans were riding this morning, making her imagine those V lines that made smart people do very dumb things, she liked to think that he didn't have any underwear on.

Focus, Regina! You're about to tell him off. Remember?

Oh yeah. That. Questionable threat story. Cop sniffing around. All thoughts of Ford's undies—or lack of them—faded to the background.

She crossed her arms and gave him what she hoped was a snarky smile. "And we don't really expect me to be in any real danger, now do we?"

One eyebrow went up before he mirrored her posture.

"Like you said, you never know. That's why it's important to be flexible."

The doorbell rang again. Huey was a good guy, but he wasn't going to wait forever on her front porch with its creaky boards that dipped and shimmied even when a squirrel ran across them. Letting Ford have the last word grated, especially when they were her words, but she wanted to take a shower today and that wasn't happening until Huey worked his magic. After shooting her uninvited if totally hot guest one last dirty look, she strode out of the kitchen and answered the front door.

They would pick this conversation up later, though. She hadn't missed the way his gaze had shifted away from hers in that last second.

Ford was definitely hiding something.

Chapter Seven

Donna Taylor and Scott Drake were the sweetest couple, but Gina was going to kill them, and considering that there was a cop just outside her door, that would be equally bad for her business and her determination not to be a Luca that ended up behind bars.

"I don't know. The pink is so pretty but I love yellow." Donna looked up, her big blue eyes filled with a silent plea for help. "I just can't make up my mind. Scott, honey, what do you think?"

Scott glanced down at the envelopes—not the actual invitations, just the envelopes they'd come in, and got a deer in the headlights look.

It had been like this with every decision—*every* decision—these two had to make as part of the wedding planning. Oh sure, Gina had dealt with brides who changed their minds, control freak mothers, and soon-to-be grooms who showed up drunk, but nothing like Donna and Scott, who wanted to make every decision themselves but spent hours analyzing each and every choice. How these two had actually managed to make up their minds enough to get engaged was a mystery to Gina.

Luckily, after five years of dealing with the chaos of wedding planning, she knew exactly how to steer the happy couple so they made forward progress. Gina let out a breath and framed herself in the big bay window that looked out over the Victorian's backyard—the one that someday would be the perfect location for intimate weddings—and turned her attention to Donna and Scott as they looked between the envelope samples as if the fate of the free world was at stake.

She had no more than opened her mouth, though, when the door between the front room and the foyer opened up, revealing her not-exactly-invited house guest in all of his tight-fitting-jeans glory.

"I don't mean to interrupt," said the man who'd just opened up the door to her at-home office without knocking. "But it sounds like you might be having a little trouble." This part came through while he was looking right at Gina before he looked over at the couple. "Maybe I can help."

Donna's shoulders sagged with relief. Scott seemed to grow an inch or two from not being the only one with a Y chromosome in the room. As for her? It took just about everything Gina had not to let her Sicilian out. What in the hell did he think he was doing, walking in on a client meeting like this? It was beyond very not okay.

"Ford, can I have a word with you out in the hall?" she asked, digging her nails into the palm of her hand to help keep her voice steady.

"Before you do," Donna said, batting her eyelashes at Ford, despite the fact the man who'd put a gigantic ring on it was sitting right next to her. "Can I ask you one question?"

Ford's gaze ping-ponged between Donna and Scott and then he slid on his uber-neutral cop face. To anyone not paying attention, he would have looked completely together and in control. However, from her spot by the window, Gina got a good look at him in profile, and there was no missing that as he held his hands behind his back in an at-attention stance, he was tapping out a fast beat on his thumb. That little tell of nervousness shouldn't have cooled her annoyance at his butt-in-ski ways, but who was she kidding? The fact that he rushed in—requested or not—to try to help was kind of endearing.

Donna held up the envelopes. "Which color makes you think of eternal bliss?"

Ford blinked. He blinked again. His finger tapping on his thumb went into overdrive. Gina wasn't rooting for him, not after he'd barged in on her business, but she had to admit if only to herself that she was pulling for him. He could do this. He could make the whole thing right with one word. Pink or yellow, it didn't matter.

He cleared his throat.

Gina held her breath.

The thumb symphony stopped, and he said, "They're both really nice."

Donna's hopeful expression crumbled back into indecisiveness. Gina, however, wasn't confused at all. She was going to have to be one more in a long line of Lucas who found out how they looked in an orange jumpsuit.

"Can I speak to you out in the hallway now?" she asked, but the timbre of her voice perfectly detailed that this was not a request.

She didn't wait for an answer, just shot a quick smile in her clients' general direction and strode out into the hallway. She waited by the door until Ford walked through, but as soon as he did, she closed it behind him and got within whispering distance but stayed out of touching distance because, even as annoyed as she was, the urge to do that was just under the surface.

"What in the hell do you think you're doing?" she asked.

One eyebrow went up in the universal sign of male superiority. "Helping?"

"Is that what you call it?" Her entire body felt hot and tight at the same time. "Funny, I'd call it interfering with my business and making my job even harder."

Ford snorted, a dismissive sound that told her exactly what he thought of her business. "Come on, I've been listening to her waffle for half an hour. I figured she just needed a push."

Of course he did. Wedding planning was just simple women's work, after all. Not something that needed experience and education.

"And you came by this idea from your vast experience as a wedding planner?"

Something in her voice must have alerted him to the very vital mistake he'd made. "No, but—"

"Oh," she interrupted. "It was from your degree in hospitality and unpaid internships with some of the most demanding wedding planners in Harbor City?"

Seriously, those days had been fourteen-hour hells of grunt work and abuse.

"No, but—"

She verbally plowed forward, shoving his mealy explanation to the curb. "The only other thing I can think of is that because you have a dick you think that means you know all the answers to anything, whether you have experience in that area or have been working with a set of clients for months and know how to slowly maneuver them one way or another because if you don't do it a certain way, they get stuck in a loop of indecision?"

Ford kept his mouth shut. Good to know he had a sense of self-preservation.

"Look, this may seem like just a silly job to you from the outside, but it's serious. People pin a lot of hopes and dreams on their wedding day. Being a wedding planner is about organization, psychology, negotiation, and crisis management. Do not think for a second that coming in uninvited and thinking you could do my job without even an idea about what it entails was the right thing to do."

She inhaled a deep breath, ready to launch into another wave of words. It wasn't just Ford who didn't take her seriously. Her brothers didn't, either. What they didn't realize was that she was a small business owner who always found a way to make what sometimes seemed like the impossible happen. Her job was a challenge every day, and even though it drove her a little batty sometimes, she loved it.

"You're right," he said, the words coming out fast but true.

She nearly choked on her righteous indignation. "Excuse me?"

"I shouldn't have assumed. You're right."

Her brain was on a loop of *what the hell, what the hell, what the hell* as she tried to figure out what play he was making with this quick retreat. Whatever game he was running, and he had been doing so since he sweet-talked her into letting him park his cute ass on her couch, this acknowledgment of her competency was part of it.

She glared at him through narrowed eyes. "What's your move here?"

"No move." He shook his head. "I just wanted to help."

"Next time, ask first. This is my business, and it might not seem like much to you, but I'm going to build this company into something great and lasting—but first I have to go maneuver Donna and Scott into the yellow so their invites don't look like birth announcements."

She stalked over to the door, and her hand was on the doorknob before his voice stopped her.

"I have no doubt you'll make it happen."

The unexpectedness of his words was what made her pulse kick up. It wasn't because of the look in his eye when he said it, as if he really believed it. What he thought didn't matter to her. Still, her heart was thrumming when she walked back into her office and suggested the yellow to Donna and Scott.

...

"Come on, swing it like you mean it." Ford stood back and watched as Gina lifted the sledgehammer and let it come crashing down against the wall in the hallway. Her plan was to take out the wall and open it up to the library, which was filled with bookshelves and huge windows that looked out into the backyard and brought in the most sun during the day. They would take care of the demolition, and a guy who specialized in old home restorations would come in and complete the new arch where the wall had been.

It was a good plan, and it meant that he got to watch Gina go after the drywall like a woman on a mission.

Something about the way she set her full lips into a straight line and let out a deep breath before she swung away made him forget a little why he'd been camping out on her uncomfortable couch for the past two days in the first place.

That spring that poked him right in the lower back was what was keeping him up late at night. It sure wasn't wondering what Gina was doing upstairs when he followed the soft patter of her footsteps across the ceiling, or trying to imagine what she was wearing as she slipped between her sheets, or contemplating if her dreams kept circling back to that night in the hotel. There was no way his desperate need for a vat of coffee every morning was because of that. It was the spring jutting up to jab him in the kidney.

He took a drink of the sanity-maintaining brew and watched as Gina brought the sledgehammer down on the non-load-bearing wall, leaving a gaping hole.

"Should I even ask who you're picturing on that wall?" he asked.

Gina sat the sledgehammer down on the dusty hardwood floor and grinned at him. "Probably not."

"So, what happened to the fourth handyman you hired to help?"

She'd been telling him about three handyman nightmares since they started working on the wall. The woman had the worst luck.

"Sylvia?" Gina said, her voice thick with disgust. "She split with the deposit money for parts unknown."

He picked up the sledgehammer and positioned himself in front of the wall. "Did you file a police complaint?"

She rolled her eyes. "Yes, but it was five bills. Your brothers in blue aren't going to be knocking themselves out to track her down."

"And that's when you said fuck it, I'll do the demo myself?" He swung the sledgehammer, slamming it against the wall with a satisfying blow that may have had more than a little to do with his lack of satisfaction in other parts of his life. He was a detective, not a spy, and this undercover stint was starting to make him twitchy.

The Luca brothers were planning something, a move of some sort, and if he could just figure it out then he wouldn't have to be lying to a woman he was genuinely starting to like. Gina had been cracking him up over the past few days with her self-deprecating sense of humor, and she was smart, the kind of person who could judge running her own company and taking on a massive home renovation project. Plus, she had legs he couldn't stop watching.

"Nah." She shook her head as she reached up and pulled her hair into a ponytail, the move giving him a great view of her tits as they pressed against the T-shirt, which today featured a sloth doing yoga. "I gave up on hiring a handyman for demolition after Julio."

"What happened with him?"

"He came in, took one look at the place, and gave a quote so outrageous that I knew he just wanted to walk away from the place and never look back."

Ford took another couple of swings with the sledgehammer before setting it down on the floor. There were now enough started holes that it was time to move on to the reciprocating saw to cut out large pieces of drywall. Taking out an interior wall wasn't difficult, but it could be time-consuming. And messy.

"Too much work?" he asked before taking a swig from his coffee.

She shook her head again, sending her pulled-back wavy hair swinging in a way that had him wondering how it would look fisted in his hand as she was naked beneath him. *Shit.* What in the hell was wrong with him? She was the job, not a possibility. There were rules, and he didn't break them.

"Something about these old houses freaks most folks out," Gina said, seemingly oblivious—thank God—to where his thoughts had gone. "I was lucky to have gotten Juan to sign on for the real renovation work. His waitlist is a million years long for an older home like this. He's the best and he knows it."

He plugged in the reciprocating saw, needing something to do to keep his hands busy so he'd stop thinking about how much he'd like to be touching Gina instead. "If it's so difficult, why bother with it at all?"

"Her bones are strong." She ran her hand over the detailed scrollwork on the staircase banister. "She just needs some touch-ups."

"It's a makeover story, huh?" He smiled.

"No way." She handed him a dust mask and grabbed one

for herself. "She's perfect just the way she is, she just needs someone to love her like she deserves."

"You sound like my sister Fallon with her car."

Gina's eyes went wide with excitement. "What's she got?"

"A 1970 Pontiac GTO convertible."

"Ohhhh, that just sounds sexy."

Sexy? He liked the way she said the word.

"You like cars?" he asked, and suddenly he was searching his brain for any tidbit of knowledge he had about cars, which was pretty much nil beyond where to put the gas in and the number of his mechanic.

"I don't really know anything about them, but I know what makes me stop and say damn yes I will have some of that." She punctuated the remark with an exaggerated wink and slipped on the dust mask.

And Ford shifted his stance because he knew exactly what she meant, but he sure as hell wasn't thinking about the house or a car.

• • •

Gina had held out as long as she could—there was just something about working alongside Ford that made even something as tedious as refinishing the stairs enjoyable—but when she swore she heard her stomach over the sound of the sander, she had to give in to the inevitable. "Okay, that's it," she said after she clicked off her sander and took off her dust mask. "I need food."

He slipped his mask off and stepped closer to her. "Sounds like a plan."

Ford reached over and tucked a stray hair that had slipped from her ponytail behind her ear. He probably didn't mean anything by it, but it sent a shiver of awareness across her skin. Then he stepped back, lifted the hem of his T-shirt, and brought it up to wipe his face, exposing the hard planes of his abs and sending her thoughts to the four corners of the earth for the three-point-two seconds it took him to let his shirt drop back down in place.

"There's just one problem," she said, struggling to remember things like breathing and—oh yeah—eating. "I haven't been to the grocery store this week."

He gave her his cock-eyed grin that she'd gotten a little too used to seeing over the past few days.

"Pizza or Chinese?" he asked, taking the sander from her hand and walking it over to their makeshift supply table.

"I think they should combine both," she teased, finding her bearings now that his pheromones weren't close enough to whisper sweet nothings in her ears. "I'd scarf down a General Tsao's thin and crispy."

The look of pure horror on his face had her giggling so hard that she didn't pay attention to where she was stepping on the stairs, and her foot landed on the wrong spot on the third step from the bottom. The wood did a weird shimmy as it creaked and sank underneath her. Her scream was barely to her lips when Ford's strong arms wrapped around her. In the next heartbeat, she was pressed up against his chest. Would it really be that bad if she just melted into him? Or nibbled his ear? Or—

Regina! Snap out of it.

"You can put me down now." Or never, she was good with that, too.

"Yeah," he said, his voice sounding lower, rougher than usual. "Are you okay?"

The moment her feet touched the floor, her answer changed to a needy no, but she managed to shove the truth back before she said it out loud. "That step is all wonky. It's on the never-ending fix it list."

Ford took a closer look at the step. "I could fix it."

"Yeah?" She should be looking at the step, but instead she was checking him out. Again. "Juan has some specialty parts on order to do the repair."

"Let me know when they're in and stay off of it until then." Then he grabbed his T-shirt collar behind his neck and yanked it over his head. "Let me just go grab another shirt, and I'll be good to go get food."

He just needed a new shirt? She was more worried about her panties after that show of abs and shoulders. A woman could get used to having him around: rescuer, fixer, hottie—now that was a dangerous combination.

An hour later and they were seated at the neighborhood pizza joint with a half-eaten pepperoni pizza and a mostly empty pitcher of beer between them, and she was getting the inside scoop on one Ford Hartigan, twelve-year-old middle school cop.

"You really were the hall monitor?" she asked, although she already knew the answer.

Ford nodded as he took a bite of pizza.

"Did that mean you let your brothers off easy when they skipped class?"

He scoffed. "No way."

"So you've always been about the rules." Color her completely not shocked.

"For the most part," he said and took a drink of his beer. "How about you, did you know you wanted to be a wedding planner?"

She shook her head. "I love to organize things and knew I wanted to be an event planner, it's why I double majored in business and hospitality management, but the wedding part just sort of happened accidentally when my cousin needed help with her nuptials. Turns out, I love helping people plan for their big day. Once the house gets done, I'll be able to meet clients in the salon and display past wedding pictures to help give people ideas. Then, if everything works out, I'll be hiring employees and maybe even franchising out. Not too bad for sort of falling into it."

"So, you weren't the type of girl who planned her wedding in the second grade?"

"Not even close." Even as a kid, she'd known she was different. Maybe she couldn't place her finger on it, but she knew it was true. She took a drink of her beer before the memories could take hold. "I was too busy following my dad around to job sites, which brings everything full circle, since he was a contractor and now I'm up to my nose in renovations."

"Speaking of which, you have something…" Ford leaned forward, reaching across the table and swiping a bit of foam from the tip of her nose. "Got it."

Heat burned her cheeks. "Damn thing always gets in the way."

"I like your nose." He sat back in his chair, crossing his arms, and his gaze never left hers. "It gives your face character."

"Oh yeah, that's just what everyone says."

His eyes narrowed, and he got that look on his face that all but screamed incoming lecture, which was the last thing she wanted when they were having such a good time.

Rushing in before he could say anything, she said, "What's your favorite movie?"

His grin made her heart hiccup. "Anything with explosions."

"Ugh, action movies? Really?" It wasn't a total shock, but it wasn't what she'd been expecting from someone as committed to getting to the bottom of things as he was. "I would have pegged you as a film noir guy."

"You don't like action movies?" he asked, popping the last of his pizza crust into his mouth.

"Not usually." Sure, the eye candy was nice, but there was more to a good movie than a buff dude.

"You've obviously been watching the wrong movies," he said, standing up. "It's time to fix that."

Oh, this sounded like a very not good idea. Still, she asked anyway, "What do you mean?"

"Time to find out where you're hiding a TV in your house so we can start your education."

"I just watch on my laptop." *Brilliant conversational skills, Regina. When are you hosting that banter class again?*

"Well, that's part of the problem, but we'll make do." He tossed a few bills on the table. "Come on, I know just what to start you with. It's a classic about a cop who flies to L.A. to see his family for Christmas and a bunch of German terrorists take over the building."

"Sounds like fun," she said, not bothering to hide the sarcasm in her voice because that plot sounded ridiculous.

"You have no idea." He pressed his hand to the small of her back, not pushing her bodily but pushing all of her hello-I-want-to-do-naughty-things-to-you buttons. "Now come on, we have a date on the couch. I'll even share my Ice Knights blanket with you."

And that's exactly where she found herself later that night, surreptitiously taking sniffs of the blanket that smelled just like him while explosions lit up her laptop screen and the cop from New York jumped off the roof of a skyscraper using a fire hose as a bungee cord—so in other words, totally different from comedy movie nights with Lucy and Tess, but a helluva lot of fun, not that she was going to admit this to Ford.

"This guy is nuts," she said as she sort of but not really—okay, really—snuggled a few inches closer to Ford.

"He's saving a skyscraper full of civilians."

"And his estranged wife." It was an important detail.

"You didn't tell me your favorite action movie is really a romance."

He looked at her like she'd just told him that she alphabetized her books by author's first name instead of last name. "Not in the least."

"You really think he'd be breaking that many rules and regulations for just anyone?" Men. So blind to the obvious. "Come on, if it was just a building full of strangers, he totally would have handled it by the book."

"He's a cowboy," Ford said as if that explained everything.

"He's doing it for love." She looked up at him, and somehow the inches she'd scooted closer had become much more, because their noses practically touched. His gaze dipped down to her mouth. Her pulse sped up. "Trust me," she continued, her voice breathier than it had been a moment ago. "Love is my business, I know of what I speak."

"From personal experience?" he asked.

The rough timbre of his voice and his proximity had her losing IQ points by the millisecond. She tugged her bottom lip between her teeth, hoping the nip of pain would bring her back from the edge of making a major mistake—one she never wanted to repeat. Handsome men talked pretty but they rarely meant it, not when it came to her. Trusting Ford was the last thing she should do, no matter how easy it was starting to become.

Forcing herself, because it was the last thing she wanted, Gina put a metaphorical chastity belt on, took a deep breath, and got up from the couch. "And I think that's my cue to head up for the night."

"You'll miss the end if you go now."

Oh man. It wasn't the movie she was worried about missing. "Let me guess, he beats the bad guys and gets his wife back."

"Plus, she punches out the dickhead reporter."

Ten points go to the fictional cop's wife. "Now that's a twist I'm almost sad to miss, but I have a client meeting tomorrow morning." And she didn't trust herself not to try to jump him on the couch, so she concentrated on moving her feet away from him instead of her hands on him. "Good night, Ford."

"Sweet dreams, Gina."

If he meant frustrated dreams of a naked Ford Hartigan, then yes, she would totally be having those. Thank God her sense of self-preservation kicked into gear before that could slip past her lips, and she hustled out of the room and up the stairs, knowing she was skating on a fault line when it came to Ford.

But she couldn't seem to stop herself from falling a little bit for him anyway.

Chapter Eight

"I've got news."

Gina turned her attention away from the gorgeous pink-and-orange sky to the man standing in the open doorway that led out to the back porch, where she sat with a spiked lemonade and enjoyed the last moments of what had been a beautiful April day. Ford's face was set into grim lines as he crossed over to her, a brown beer bottle in his hand.

"It's about your grandpa."

"They confirmed it was him?" It wasn't like she hadn't been prepping for it. She'd known he was gone and wasn't coming back since she was a little girl—and seeing the ring had only confirmed what had been whispered about for years. Still, the news stung.

"Dr. Dev was able to make the ID." He stopped next to where she sat, his hair sticking out every which way as if he'd been running his hands through it repeatedly since six this morning. "Can I join you?"

She nodded. "Just be careful, a few of the boards aren't in great shape. Stick to the edge by the banisters."

Ford walked around sat down next to her on the step, close enough that his knee touched hers. They sat in a comfortable silence, watching the too many tufts of weeds fighting for supremacy wave in the spring breeze. A squirrel darted through the yard, on the run from a pair of cardinals chirping at it from a tree in the next yard over. The tulips someone had planted eons ago had bloomed into a bright line of pink and yellow that followed the fence that could use a fresh coat of white paint.

Sitting there, Gina let out a deep breath of acceptance. Her grandpa wasn't coming back, but the home he'd grown up in was starting to come into its own, and that would have to be her memorial to the man who'd been a criminal and, sometimes, a bad man, but a good grandpa to a little girl who knew from the start that she wasn't like the other kids.

Ford broke the silence. "Did your brothers figure out the funeral arrangements?"

"Turns out he didn't want any." She took a drink from her lemonade, the pink drink the perfect mix of tart sweetness and vodka to go with the end of a very long day with a sad, if expected, coda. "He was pretty specific about it, and my grandma is adamant about adhering to his wishes."

"Weren't they divorced when he disappeared?"

"Separated. They didn't divorce, they just lived separate lives. Too stubborn and too Catholic to divorce."

"Is she taking it hard?"

She pictured her grandma, who'd FaceTimed her from bingo the other night to let her know the cards were hot. The woman was a shark. She had to have been to keep up with Big Nose Tommy Luca.

And when Gina had broken the news to her about probably finding Grandpa in the attic, her grandma had gotten a faraway look in her eyes before blinking it clear.

"I think she grieved for him decades ago, like the rest of

us."

"Still, I'm sorry."

"Thanks." She fought the urge to lay her head on his broad shoulder as if she had the right. She didn't usually get this comfortable around people so fast. Something about being burned too many times for that. But Ford just had this way about him that made her feel like trusting him was the right thing to do. "You know, you're not so bad for a cop."

He gave her a lazy grin that turned the air in her lungs into champagne bubbles. "I guess I'll take that as a compliment?"

"From someone with my last name? You totally should." Luca. She'd never figured her last name to be one of the barriers to her hooking up with the right guy. Not that her last name overrode the big nose or her bulgy eyes in that department, but it sure didn't help. And thinking of her last name… "Any update on the cause of death and if someone is lurking in the shadows to make sure he or she can't get tied to Grandpa's death?"

Ford froze, his bottle halfway to his lips, for a second before setting it down on the porch. His unflinching gaze slid over to her. "Not yet."

She chewed on that for a second, considered it against her initial distrust. It tasted different now that she'd spent some time with him. Ford was dependable, solid, and beyond normal chit-chat about her family, he never asked about her brothers. Maybe she'd gotten to be too cynical. Maybe it was time to stop expecting the worst from him.

She took a sip of her spiked lemonade and looked out at the solar lanterns hanging from her neighbor's fence that were beginning to flicker on. "No one is going to be coming after me." There really wasn't, she knew it in her gut.

Ford pivoted on the step so he faced her and gave her a teasing wink. "You think this whole situation is a farce so I can get close to you?"

She snort-laughed, and it wasn't a pretty or nice sound. "Definitely not that. But it wouldn't be outside the realm of reality for someone to use me to get what they wanted."

"Explain," he said, his voice hard.

What? She was supposed to roll over and expose her soft, vulnerable underbelly to the guy who was only sitting beside her because it was his job? She shouldn't do that, but the words came out anyway.

"When you look like I do, you get used to people treating you as if you were just a punchline and not an actual human being. So yeah, people have tossed me into the boys locker rooms, walked away from me mid-sentence when someone hot walks into the room, and—oh yeah—sent me to a hotel room when I hadn't been invited. Stuff like that has happened to me for pretty much my entire life. I guess that's why my brothers are so overprotective of me."

She let out a shaky breath but refused to give into the nerves and the worry and the anxiety that ate away at her stomach lining whenever she had to confront the ugly reality of her life—no pun intended.

Ford didn't say anything. He just looked at her with his head cocked to the side as if he couldn't comprehend what she was saying. Really, why would he? He was hot, sexy, and had the kind of sense of humor that snuck up on a person. Then, he picked up his beer and drained it in one long swallow, tapping his thumb against the label after it was empty, a warm flush creeping up his cheeks.

"About the hotel—"

She smiled at him. She couldn't help it. The guy was obviously embarrassed by that night. "You're not to blame."

"Still—"

Stomach cramping up at the idea of hearing an insincere apology meant to spare her feelings, Gina cut him off. "Don't worry about me," she said with more bravado than she felt.

"My life has gotten a lot better since I've accepted who I am and said a collective fuck-you to the assholes of the world."

He raised a dark eyebrow. "Accepted who you are?"

"An undateable." She shrugged.

"That's not right."

She shrugged again. There was no arguing with the truth, and she was done fighting against it. It sucked, but it was what it was. "The world is a visual place. People judge others on what they look like, from skin color to age to physical ability to prettiness, within seconds of meeting. You know it's true. They've done so many studies to show how beautiful people have more opportunities than those with average looks—or less-than-average looks."

His hands were on her knees in the next breath, and he pivoted around so they faced each other. The fierceness of his expression made her catch her breath. His fingertips gripped her legs, and his thumb pressed into her inner thighs, sending jolts of electricity along her skin.

"You are not ugly."

Pretty people always said stuff like that, but she knew the truth. "My eyes do this bug-eye thing."

"They're big. So what?"

That wasn't what she meant and he knew it, so she went on. "Have you seen my nose in profile, I *am* Big Nose Tommy's granddaughter."

"Lots of people have big noses or some other perceived beauty flaw, so what," he said, leaning forward so their faces were so close. "It shouldn't change how you see yourself. I wish you saw the woman I see when I look at you."

Now he was just being stubborn. She knew what she looked like and how that impacted how others viewed her—every woman did. And his words hurt. They shouldn't have, because he was just trying to be nice, but the kind lies only lead to hope and heartbreak. "That's sweet of you to say, but fibs don't help. I don't look like a woman most men want to date and I know it. What helps is accepting it and moving on, not dwelling."

He didn't blink, just stared her into silence with the intensity of his gaze. "I believe there's someone for everyone."

A dangerous warmth spread through her. Not the burn of embarrassment that she was way too intimately familiar with, or the needy heat of desire. This was hope. If he believed something so ferociously, then maybe it could happen. It was a pretty thought, but not the kind a woman like her could afford to have.

"Detective Hartigan," she said, forcing a cheerful teasing into her tone that she didn't really feel. "I never would have guessed that you're a romantic."

"I guess I'm full of surprises." He let go of her legs and leaned back before picking up his empty bottle as he stood. "Want another lemonade?"

"I'm good." Any more and she'd follow through on the naughty ideas having his hands on her had inspired.

"All right." He rubbed his palm against the back of his neck, looking like he wanted to say something but not really knowing what it was. "I guess I'll see you inside."

Gina mumbled in agreement and followed him with her gaze as he walked across the porch, picking his way around the weak spots, and then disappeared inside.

Only once the door was shut behind him did she let go of the breath she'd been holding.

It came out as a sigh. She couldn't help it. She was the nerd in the teen movie who'd become friends with the hot, popular guy, only to do the one thing she wasn't supposed to—start falling for him.

• • •

"It's a doohickey," Gina said. "Who needs one of those?"

Okay, she knew it wasn't anything but the most gorgeous piece of reclaimed and restored ceiling tin that she'd ever seen. Just looking at the center wreath surrounded by a square of leaves on the silver tin surface made her heart speed up. It was beautiful. She just wanted to pet it. But with all of the other renovations and getting her wedding planning business set up for success, she didn't have the money to add amazingly gorgeous tin ceiling tiles to the list of must-haves. Instead, it was relegated to the list of somedays. Therefore, calling it a doohickey when Ford held it up at the Wooden Barber Hardware Shop on Main Street made saying she didn't want it an easier lie to utter.

The look Ford gave her told her exactly what he thought of that statement. It was kinda cute, that you're-full-of-shit smolder of his. Who was she kidding? It was totally hot.

"Think of what this will look like in your office. You can dazzle the Donnas and Scotts while they pick between pink and yellow envelopes and get them to make the decision you already knew they should make all the faster."

He had a point. She looked at the price per square foot written on a handmade tag affixed to the shelf where the tin sheets were stacked. Ouch. Her bank account would reach out and slap her if she even thought about it.

"It's gaudy." She barely managed to not flinch after letting loose with that fib.

The truth was nothing at the Wooden Barber was gaudy. The store was as if Ace Hardware and Restoration Hardware had an illicit affair, and the baby that resulted was this heavenly mixture of practicality and beauty in a specialty hardware store.

"Are you nuts?" Ford's eyes nearly bugged out. "It fits in perfectly with the Victorian era of the house and will be a real wow moment."

"You've been watching too many design shows." Because they had totally shown him the light.

"That's a lie." He snorted and looked down the aisle at another couple, who were discussing the pros and cons of a reclaimed stained glass window. "You know I only watch action movies and cop dramas to laugh at all of the shit they get wrong." He reached up and tucked a strand of wavy hair that had fallen from her ponytail behind her ear. "Get the tin ceiling—at least for your office, but it would look great in the rest of the main floor, too."

It would. She nearly winced knowing how amazing it would look, because it wasn't to be. She was a practical business owner and she had priorities she had to follow. Being a grown-up really sucked some days.

Too bad there wasn't any way around her bank balance. "Not gonna happen, Officer Bossy."

Ford took a hard look at her, the intensity of it making her face heat up. She wanted to press her hands to her cheeks but refused to give in to that old insecurity.

"Is it because of the price?" he asked.

Of course it was. "Nope."

He slid on his cop face. "You know I trap people in lies for a living, right?"

"So?" She wiped her suddenly clammy palms against the sides of her worn jeans and nibbled on her bottom lip.

He stepped in close, his next words brushing against the shell of her ear and sending her heart rate into overdrive. "I know you're lying."

"How's that?" Damn, she sounded breathy.

"Because you're gonna make your bottom lip bleed if you chew on it any more."

She immediately stopped nervously gnawing on her lip. "Fine. I want it, but I can't afford it."

He smiled down at her. "Good thing you don't have to."

It took a second for his words to penetrate the lust fog limiting the visibility in her brain to almost nothing. "What are you talking about?"

He took out his phone and opened the calculator app.

Wait a minute. How did he remember the dimensions of her office ceiling? Realization hit. This trip to the Wooden Barber was a setup. He'd planned the whole thing.

"It's my housewarming gift to you," he said as he finished his calculations and started putting squares of stunning tin into their cart.

She watched, vacillating between oh-my-God-yes and this-is-a-big-no-no. "I can't accept that."

"Why?" He didn't slow his pace. "Your friends don't give you presents?"

"Is that what we are?" she asked, not liking the word to describe them and really not liking the reason why. "Friends?"

"With handyman benefits." He gave her a wink. "Don't forget that part."

"Like that's gonna happen," she said with far too much despair in her voice that had nothing to do with his skills with a hammer. Oh God, she was in so much trouble.

He grinned down at her. "Good, I'd hate to be the only one."

As he finished adding the tin squares, Gina pushed down the giddy hope bubbling inside her—the one that made her want to believe that there could be something more permanent about what was going on between them. As if that was possible. As if there was a Cinderella moment in her future. She wasn't waiting for Prince Charming, and no fairy godmother was going to give her a makeover. She was who she was—and that was Miss Right Now and Not Miss Forever.

She'd better remember that, or there was nothing but trouble ahead for her.

...

Guilt buying? Ford? Yeah, he was doing exactly fucking that. He hated lying, but was doing it anyway with Gina, and that was exactly why he was handing over his debit card to the clerk at the Wooden Barber. The only other choice was coming clean about why he was staying with her. He couldn't do that. There were rules that had to be followed in an investigation, and giving up the goods to a civilian was a rookie mistake and he sure as hell wasn't a rookie. He was an asshole who was starting to think too much about a woman he should see as only a source, a way get the information he needed to stop the Espositos.

"So why did you join the police department?" Gina asked as they carried the two boxes of tin ceiling tiles back to his car.

Ford's grip on his box tightened. "Everybody needs a job."

"Bullshitting doesn't suit you," she said with a laugh.

Using the act of balancing the box in one hand while he pulled his car keys out of his pocket as cover for the unease creeping up his spine, he bought a couple of seconds. "You know me so well?"

"Enough to know when you're dodging."

He popped the trunk open. "It's a boring story."

She rolled her eyes. "I don't believe that."

Ford put his filled-to-the-brim box in the trunk and then took the half-filled box from Gina and set it next to the one he'd carried. She was staring at him, her arms crossed and a small smile playing on her lips. It was the curl of her lips that did him in. The need to make sure that smile stayed in place had him opening his mouth.

"I had a friend in high school, Jake, who was in the wrong place at the wrong time. He was crossing the street and a drunk driver blew a red light, hitting him hard enough that it knocked him out of his shoes." He let out a breath, clearing the mental image of what the scene must have looked like from his head. "The driver didn't stick around to see if Jake was still breathing. He peeled away, leaving burned rubber and a dead seventeen-year-old at the corner of Phillips and Granbury."

"That's horrible," she gasped. "Did they find the guy?"

He closed the trunk with more force than necessary. "No."

"I'm sorry." She stepped close and wrapped her arms around him, holding him tight.

It wasn't a long hug, more of a quick squeeze, but he felt it all the way down to his center. And when she let go, he missed the feel of her touch immediately. He had no fucking clue what was happening to him. Why her? Why now? But the answers to that didn't matter, because the fact of it was something was happening.

She went to take a step back, but he grabbed her hand, stopping her. Surprise and heat flared in her eyes. Yes, his entire body answered, and he stepped close, dipping his head as he did so.

A loud wolf whistle from a passing car barely registered, but Gina jolted back at the sound, her face flushed as she nervously chewed her bottom lip, a protective arm slung across her belly.

Shit.

Ford searched the street, wanting to mop the street with the dick who'd put that look on Gina's face and stopped the kiss before it could happen. "I'm sorry."

"No, it wasn't you, I just..." Her words died off.

He intertwined his fingers with hers. "What?"

"It's nothing." She tried to smile, but it didn't take.

"Doesn't seem like nothing." Sure, he was pressing, but

no one should be able to put that lost, beaten-down look on her face.

"Sometimes old hurts come back to slap you in the face, that's all."

"Gina," he said, using the same comforting but authoritative tone he employed when interrogating nervous witnesses. "I want to understand."

She swallowed and lifted her chin and pulled her hand free from his, obviously determined to brush whatever was going on under the rug. "It's nothing. Don't worry about it."

"Was it the guy in the car? Do you have history?" His gut clenched at the idea of that. Possessiveness wasn't the best look for a guy in his position, but he couldn't deny that's what had him grinding his teeth in frustration.

"A history?" Her cracked laugh was as disbelieving as the look on her face. "No. I have no clue who that was." She walked around to the passenger side of the car. "Look, let's just go home and put up this ceiling."

"You can't avoid this story forever." Not if it made her react like she just had. This was important, and he wanted to protect her from it.

"Yes," she said, opening the door and sliding inside. "I can."

・・・

The next week was all hammers and nails—and not in a way that would reduce any of the frustration building each time Ford laid eyes on Gina. So far, he'd helped take out a wall in the hall so it could be widened, knocked out some primo avocado-green laminate countertop in the kitchen, put up the tin ceiling, and helped Huey, the plumber who seemed to owe a great debt to the Luca family—Ford didn't want to know for what—renovate the master bath. That last one meant traipsing through Gina's bedroom multiple times a day, which was its own kind of hellish torture for his imagination.

The woman might love organization, but it didn't show in her bedroom. It was impossible to miss the black lace panties on the floor near the laundry basket, the rumpled pillow and half-made bed, and the warm vanilla scent of her that seemed to linger in the air. He'd spent way too many hours at night on that poor excuse for a couch staring at the ceiling and picturing her wearing only the black lace panties, dabbing perfume on her wrists and between her perfect tits. It was not what he should be pondering during the long, sleepless nights, as his captain would have told him if he wasn't chewing Ford's ass out already.

"So you've got nothing," the captain said during their usual late-afternoon call.

"You knew this was a long shot." Ford left out the part about the captain being the one to come up with this cockamamie plan, even though keeping it to himself was about to kill him. So, he took a second to inhale a deep breath and watch Gina through the window as she put another coat of white paint on the backyard fence.

The pinch in his shoulders eased, and his blood pressure dropped from the red zone as he watched her work her paint roller.

Then she bent over to get more paint on the roller, and the calming breath he'd inhaled came out as a frustrated groan that he hoped the captain took as annoyance about the lack of results. "Her brothers haven't been around all week."

"You need to find a way to change that."

Well sure. He'll just teleport the Luca brothers over from wherever they were. That would totally work. Clamping his mouth shut before that thought could spill out, he tapped his finger and thumb together to the count of twenty and only then gave himself permission to speak.

"Her grandmother's birthday party is tomorrow. I'm her date. The whole family will be there."

"If that comes up empty, then I'm calling your operation."

And there it was. The captain couldn't have been any clearer with his meaning, and the blame for the lack of results landed with a loud thud at Ford's feet. It was a response that anyone could have seen coming, but that didn't make it any easier to take. That's why his gut did that clench and shimmy thing, because the failure that was all but assured was going to get pinned to him.

It wasn't because the end of the operation meant no more Gina or hearing the silly songs she sang to herself as she brewed coffee in the morning or the mind-melting view of her ass in those black yoga pants she always paired with ridiculous novelty T-shirts.

That part didn't matter. It couldn't. He was one of Waterbury's finest, and she was a Luca. There had to be regulations written down forbidding that kind of fraternization. So after tomorrow, that was that.

His grip tightened on his phone, and he turned away from the window. "I understand, sir."

"Don't worry, Hartigan. You'll still be in the running to stay on the task force, but I have to tell you that bringing in some hard intel would go a long way to helping you there."

No shit, Captain Sherlock. "Yes sir."

And that was the little breath of hell that hung over him for the rest of the afternoon, right up until an incoming text message made his phone buzz as he and Gina were sanding down the intricately carved banisters for the main staircase. She'd been telling him some of her wedding planner horror stories—who knew ducks could shit that much—and explaining that despite the craziness of it, she was ready to start working with her newest client next week. Continuing to listen, Ford pulled out his phone and glanced down at the message.

> Mom: *Don't forget to pick up the pastries from the bakery before you stop off for family lunch today.*

Great. Lunch was in an hour. He rammed his fingers through his hair and tried to work out how he was going to explain to his mom that he wasn't coming. Kate Hartigan was not going to be happy, and she wasn't going to be shy about telling him. "Oh hell."

"Did someone run a red light?" Gina asked.

God, didn't he wish. "It's my mom."

The teasing look in her brown eyes softened. "Is everything okay?"

"Yeah, I just forgot to tell her I couldn't make Saturday family lunch today. It's pretty much a standing event for the entire family, and not going means you better be in the hospital." He stared at his phone.

Gina started sanding again. "Why can't you go?"

"I'm not leaving you here alone." *Yeah, or is it that you know your time pretending to be Mr. Fix It with Gina is almost over?*

"Then I'll come with you."

As if it was that easy. Bringing the uninitiated to a Hartigan family event was not something to be undertaken lightly. "Trust me, that's the last thing either of us want to do."

She stopped sanding and looked up at him, her smile too cheerful to be real. "Don't worry, it's not like you have to pretend I'm your girlfriend with your family."

And there it was, the famous Ford Hartigan charm thrilling women everywhere. *Fucking A, Hartigan. Get your shit together.*

"It's not that."

"What is it, then?" she asked.

"My family can be a lot to handle—especially all at once." How in the hell did he explain it to her?

First, there was the sheer number of them. Then there was the whole volume aspect, because they were not a quiet family. Finally, there was the fact that his mom wouldn't stop pestering Gina with questions about every aspect of her life from the moment she walked in the door.

The Hartigans were not for everyone.

As the family saying went, there was the red Irish, the black Irish, and the so-much-trouble-they-got-kicked-off-the-island Irish—the Hartigans were all three. Yeah, there was no way he could subject Gina to all of that.

"You really think they're crazier than mine?" she asked, her tone so full of disbelief he would have thought he'd just told her that coffee wasn't the best thing ever invented.

He nodded. "Yes."

"Well, the only way to settle this is to compare." She tapped her finger against the tip of her nose and made a series of little harrumph sounds that reminded him of being at the doctor's office. "You're already locked in for my grandma's party tomorrow. I'll meet your people today, and then we can compare tomorrow night."

"What about your brothers, will they be there?" he asked, keeping his tone neutral.

"They'll be there. I keep trying to schedule a bowling night with them, but they're being cagy on dates."

"Are they busy next Friday?" he asked, part of him hoping they weren't, not because he particularly wanted to hang out with them but because that was the night the Espositos' big deal was going down, according to Kapowski's informant—and with each day he was hoping more and more that his time with Gina would be a bust for the investigation.

"No clue, but I'll ask," she said. "Don't think you're getting out of this bet, though. The one with the more normal family buys the cannoli."

"I don't like cannoli." Because that was the most important thing to note about what she'd just said. *Is it a wonder the woman hasn't fallen at your feet in worship?*

Gina gasped and slapped her hand over her mouth. "What a horrible thing to say. You obviously have never had Vacilli's cannoli. Don't worry, you'll understand the error of your ways after you buy the cannoli tomorrow night."

"That's not gonna happen." It couldn't. There had to be an SOP about it.

"We'll see," she said with a grin that lit up her whole face, giving her a kind of gleeful radiance. "Now get a move on, we don't want to keep your mom waiting."

She dropped her sandpaper onto the table where all their supplies were laid out and bounded up the stairs, while Ford stood there watching with his mouth hanging open. Had he agreed to take her to the Hartigan family lunch? He didn't think so, but there she went to change.

Maybe she'd do just fine dropped into the pushy, loud-mouthed, crazy mix that was his family.

Or not.

Chapter Nine

Ford hadn't been lying about his family. They were even more of a cliché than hers. Huge Irish family, far too loud and friendly, and firefighters. Well, except Ford. He was the odd man out in this craziness. More quiet but no less affectionate. And a cop. Which his brothers teased him about incessantly.

His family was totally overwhelming, but in a good way. It reminded Gina of the last Luca family christening—loud voices, lots of food, and too many people crushed into a space that would always seem too small no matter how big because the personalities of those inside were just that large.

Ford had introduced her to his parents first, Kate and Frank Sr. He was a bear of a man with a shock of orange hair that was probably visible from space, and she was an Amazon of a woman who was so pretty it was kind of hard to look her in the face and remember what to say.

Thinking of what to say wasn't a problem with the oldest Hartigan, Frankie, because the towering ginger firefighter rarely stopped talking, so Gina didn't have to think about what to talk about. It wasn't like he rambled, it was just that he was so charming that people couldn't help but hang on what he was saying and encourage him to offer up more. Frankie's twin brother, Finian, had dark hair instead of red, but otherwise he looked almost exactly like Frankie. He talked almost as much, too.

Maybe being a firefighter just made them chatty—especially compared to Ford. That was her working theory, anyway, right up until she met the Hartigan sisters.

Fiona was ten minutes older than Ford, and Faith six and a half minutes younger. She found that out because Kate had taken her by the arm almost as soon as Gina had walked through the door and was delivering the best introductions that veered right up to the edge of the TMI line and then fell right over it.

"So, the doctors told us we wouldn't have any more kids after the terrors over there." She nodded at Frankie and Finian, who just grinned at their mom's description of them. "I'd always wanted a big family, though, and boy did that fertility treatment take."

"Mom," Ford groaned. "She doesn't want to know that."

Gina fought to keep a straight face at Ford's obvious discomfort while his mom was giving up all the goods.

"What?" Kate said, waving a hand at her youngest son. "It's not like I told her about the injections and the timing of certain things and the little cup your father had to carry around with him."

"Moooooooooom!" That from all of the Hartigan siblings at once.

And that was it for Gina. She couldn't stop the giggles at the matching looks of horror on the siblings' faces. Okay, the Hartigan crazy was definitely strong, but it was a different brand than the Lucas'. Theirs was heavier and a little darker, for obvious criminal-enterprise reasons. But the Hartigans? They were just the best kind of a mess, and she was enjoying the hell of it.

Kate lifted her shoulders in a nonchalant shrug and rolled her eyes at her children. Frank Sr, who was watching a hockey game on TV with one eye and the goings-on in the kitchen with the other, raised his glass—thankfully not *the* cup—in mock toast.

"Anyway, we weren't expecting any more after our triple helping of trouble, but then came our sweet Fallon."

Ford's next-to-youngest sister, an emergency room nurse whose resting facial expression promised she would put up with exactly zero amount of bullshit, shook her head at her mother's description. Someone near the stove, it was too crowded in the kitchen to know for sure who, mumbled something about Fallon being sweet as long as she got her way. Kate either didn't hear it or decided to ignore it, because she kept going.

"Then the Lord blessed us with Felicia and—"

"I was so small, they knew it was time to stop," Felicia said as she walked around the massive kitchen table, putting down plates while her fiancé, Hudson, followed a step behind, laying down the napkins.

Everyone chuckled at what had to be a long-told family joke, because unlike the rest of the towering Hartigans, Felicia was pocket-sized.

"Don't listen to them, Matches," Hudson said. "You're the perfect size."

A mournful cat wail sounded from the cat carrier in the corner at the sound of Hudson's voice. He laid down the last napkin and squatted down to the carrier. She couldn't hear what he said to the kitty inside, but it must have done the trick because the yowling stopped.

"Now, Gina," Kate said, steering her toward the table. "Why don't you tell us about yourself. Do you have any siblings?"

Ford stiffened beside her, and Fallon gave her an appraising look that said without words that she knew exactly who Gina's family was, but Gina was saved from answering that question by the calming, computerized voice of Alexa announcing the first timer was up.

"Oh, dinner's done. Everyone sit down."

What happened next was a prime example of controlled chaos as people crowded into the kitchen and sat down at the table. She ended up next to Ford as the beaming Kate looked on. Everyone was pretty much elbow-to-elbow but no one complained, instead everyone just got to passing the platter of ham, a huge bowl of garlic mashed potatoes, trays of veggies, and more around the table.

"So, Gina darling, when did you two start dating?" Kate asked.

Embarrassed at being singled out, Gina lowered her gaze to her plate. "We're not."

"I knew it," Frankie said with a teasing laugh as he poured gravy on his potatoes. "She's way too normal for Ford."

Okay, well, in the realm of descriptors that had been used to describe her looks, normal was one of the nicer ones. She pushed the peas around her plate and concentrated on keeping the expression on her "normal" face neutral.

"Remember Olive?" Finian asked.

Fallon cocked her head to one side and squished up her mouth for a second. "Is that the one who corrected everyone's grammar?"

A collective groan filled the room. Frank Sr let out a disgusted snort mid-drink, which made the milk go down the wrong pipe. He started coughing hard enough that everyone was hollering at him to hold up his arms while Kate whacked him on the back until he told her that he wasn't going into the dirt today and she could just calm down already.

"No, that was Patrice with the grammar," Felicia said

from her spot at the end of the table next to Hudson. "Olive was the one who hated hockey."

"Better to hate hockey than to root against the Ice Knights," Fiona said.

Gina turned to Ford. The tips of his ears were red, but he continued on eating his peas and potatoes as if he wasn't getting the business from his family. It was good-natured, yeah, but still it had her tensing up on his behalf.

"Oh, like what's-her-name who had a Cajun Rage tattoo?" Faith asked with a sneer.

Gina almost dropped her fork. A Rage tattoo? This was Waterbury. They were Ice Knights fans. The Rage were the Knights's biggest rivals. For hockey fans in and around Harbor City, rooting for the Rage was like declaring you hated indoor plumbing.

"You dated a Rage fan?" she asked, looking at Ford like he'd grown a second head. "That's just wrong."

She thought back to the Ice Knights blanket she'd given him. That wasn't just a blanket, it was a promise of loyalty. Ford turned to her, a chagrined expression on his face because he must have known that he'd done wrong by dating a Rage fan.

"It wasn't my finest moment," he agreed with a good-natured chuckle and then turned to his family. "But I'm not the only one here who's had some crazy dates." He looked at Finian. "Remember the woman who kept showing up at the firehouse in nothing but a trench coat?" His attention moved down to his sisters, who were giggling at how red Finian's ears had turned. "Or the guy who told Fallon he didn't believe in women having college degrees? Then there was the guy who took Fiona on a very romantic date to Chuck E. Cheese's?"

By the time he got that last bit out, everyone at the table was laughing. Then the stories really started. Faith recounted how she thought she was going on a date and it turned out to be a vacation timeshare pitch. Frankie told a story about a woman who spent an entire dinner date talking about her love of sloths. Felicia and Hudson tag-teamed the retelling of how they'd gotten together because he was helping her land another man.

"How about you, Gina?" Frankie asked. "What's your worst date?"

Still giggling a little, she went over her very limited dating history for some small disaster nugget she could share, and her gut dropped—because in that instant, she realized that *she* was probably the nightmare part of the date. Her smile froze, and her lungs stopped working. Then, she felt Ford's hand on her thigh. He gave her a squeeze. It wasn't sexual, it wasn't a come on—it was reassuring, as weird as that seemed. The tension seeped out of her, but she still didn't have any dating horror stories to share.

She was saved from the moment of exquisite awkwardness by an ear-piercing yowl, a loud clatter, and a flash of orange sprinting across the crowded kitchen table, headed straight for Felicia and Hudson.

"Honeypot!" Felicia yelled.

Hudson made a grab for the one-eyed cat, but it juked and avoided him, landing one paw in the bowl of mashed potatoes before sprinting onward. After that it was just total chaos.

Food went flying. Chairs fell over backward as everyone jumped up and tried to catch the crazed feline. Frankie reached for the furball, but the kitty blasted past him, taking a detour through the gravy boat, knocking it over and sending the brown liquid splashing across the table.

By the time Hudson managed to capture Honeypot, it looked like a tornado had landed in the Hartigan kitchen.

A piece of ham had somehow ended up hanging from the ceiling fan, Finian had applesauce splattered across his shirt, and Ford had a glob of mashed potatoes on his cheek. It wasn't until she reached up to wipe it off that she realized quite how close she was to him. Really close. Like feel-the-heat-of-him-against-her-nipples kind of close. Then he gave her that super hot half-smile and all forebrain function ceased and she gave in to the wonderful want of it, as he started to lean down and she raised herself to her tiptoes to bring her right in line with his mouth. Her eyes started to flutter closed, she tilted her head, and—

Kate Hartigan's voice cut through the lusty haze surrounding them. "So, you two aren't dating?"

Gina leapt back like Ford was kryptonite, which—let's face it—he was starting to feel like. "No ma'am," she said, unable to meet the matriarch's eyes.

"Huh." Kate said in a tone that translated to *that's a bunch of B.S.* "We'll see about that."

Mortified to infinity not only at Kate's misunderstanding but at her own behavior, Gina prayed for what felt like the billionth time this week that the earth's crust would open up and suck her into its bowels of molten magma.

When that didn't happen, she followed Honeypot's example and hustled across the room. She picked up the empty cat carrier and took the long way around the table to avoid Ford as she carried it to where Hudson and Felicia stood with the cat.

It was always a better choice to deal with a demon cat than her own personal horndog demons.

• • •

Getting stuck with kitchen duty was best avoided at all costs—especially when his mother was looking at him like that. He knew that look on Kate Hartigan's face. He'd seen it every time he tried to get away with something and she managed to pull the truth out of him with the skill of a senior interrogator. That she was focused on him right now instead of the potato paw prints covering the counter meant there was no escape.

"So," she started, her voice light, as if she wasn't about to deliver a punch. "You and Gina, you're just friends?"

"In a way." His fingers were tapping against his thumb, and the tips of his ears burned.

"What way is that?" she asked.

"It's complicated." Understatement of the year right there.

"Yeah, so much so that he's not sleeping at his apartment," Fallon said as she loaded another stack of plates into the dishwasher.

He shot his sister a dirty look. She just grinned back at him, no doubt all too aware of how she was stirring the pot.

The thing was, no matter what his family thought, there was no way he could tell them everything about the situation with Gina—in no small part because he couldn't understand it himself. Watching her may be his job, but it didn't feel like one, and that was messing with him in all of the ways he never wanted.

"You're living with her but she's not your girlfriend?" his mom asked.

"I'm not *living* with her." No, he was spying on her, a fact that was burning a hole in his gut, even if it was better that it was him than Gallo. He hated lying to her.

His mom crossed her arms and leaned back against the kitchen counter. "Where are you sleeping?"

"Her house." Not that he'd call it sleeping. It was more like staring up at the ceiling and imagining what she was doing alone in her bed while that damn couch spring did its best to cripple him.

"But you're not living with her," Fallon said, accepting a tower of bowls from Finian. "It's just an extended pajama party?"

His brother snort-laughed. "Doubtful there are any PJs involved."

"Shut up, Finian."

"Boys," his mom said in that voice that said cut the shit now. "So, help me understand what's going on, because she seems lovely and she's an Ice Knights fan."

"It's complicated." Figuring out world peace would be easier than finding a way out of the mess he'd made for himself. "It's work."

"Just work?" she asked.

He nodded as he snagged a bunch of paper towels from the counter and started to sop up the lake of gravy Felicia's practically feral cat had knocked over. "Yes."

"So, the fact that the room crackles when you two are in it?" Fallon asked as she closed the fully loaded dishwasher.

He rolled his eyes at his sister. "That's not scientifically possible."

"Oh Ford," his mom said, taking the gravy-soaked paper towels from him and dropping them into the trash can under the sink. "Denial is more than a river in Egypt."

She wasn't wrong. Then again, Kate Hartigan rarely was—and if you asked her, she'd say she never was. And he no idea what to do with that, because falling for Gina Luca wasn't something that fell under any heading in his book of personal rules and regulations.

"Am I interrupting?" Gina asked from the kitchen doorway.

All the frustration and confusion swirling around inside him settled as soon as he looked at her.

"Not at all, honey," his mom said. "What can I get for you?"

"Actually, I just got a text from Juan that the special order to fix the wonky stair is in, but he can't pick it up before they close." She held up her phone. "Do you think we can swing by on the way back home and get it? I told Juan that you said you'd agreed to fix the step so he could tackle something more pressing on his list, like the front porch."

"Not a problem," he said, more than ready to get back to the Victorian with its creaks and leaky faucets and—most importantly—her alone.

"Great." She flashed that smile at him, the one that did funny things to his breathing. "I'll just go tell your dad goodbye."

She ducked out and every eyeball in the room except for the ones in his own head zeroed in on him.

"Go home, huh?" Finian asked, picking up on the one thing Ford had been hoping his family would miss. "That's what you boys in blue call work? Maybe I *did* pick the wrong line of work."

After flipping his brother off—behind his mom's back, of course—Ford issued his goodbyes as Gina came back into the kitchen and did the same with his mom and siblings. It was strange to watch. The other women he'd brought home had all been more than a little freaked out by the crazy that was the Hartigans, but Gina had taken it all in stride. Next time, she'd be yelling at the TV during the hockey game like the rest of them.

Next time, Hartigan?

Where in the hell had that come from? There wouldn't be a next time. Like he'd told his mom, it was just work. And that's what he kept telling himself, even as he checked out the way Gina's ass looked in those jeans as she walked up to the customer service desk at the big box hardware store. He reminded himself again when she did that thing where she twirled her hair around a finger while she waited for him to ring up the order. She did it a lot and probably wasn't even aware of it. However, since it *was his job* to watch her, he'd seen her do it repeatedly. It always made him want to reach out and run his fingers through her wavy hair, curl it around his fist, draw her in for a kiss, and then—

"You ready to go?" she asked as she carried a box that had to weigh at least forty pounds.

"Let me," he said, reaching for the box.

"I can do it."

"I know you can, but you don't have to." He took the box and led the way out to the car parked closer to the dollar theater in the shopping center than the home improvement store. People were lined up at the ticket booth. The marquee read: *One night only! Jaws.* For a man who couldn't wait to get back to Gina's place not that long ago, the idea of spending a few hours in a darkened theater sounded pretty damn good.

"Up for another movie night?" he asked, jerking his chin toward the theater marquee.

"The shark movie?" She held out her hand palm-up in the universal sign for *give me your keys*. "I've never seen it."

He shifted the box of supplies and pulled the keys out of his front pocket—a more difficult task than usual after watching her walk around in those jeans. "What do you watch at the movies?"

"Mostly comedies, some indie movies." She took the keys and, as soon as they were in range, clicked the open-trunk button on the key fob.

"Let's expand your repertoire."

She gave him a teasing smile. "Big word for a detective."

"I'm not always going to be a detective," he said as he loaded the box in his car's trunk. "I'm going to be the youngest police chief in Waterbury's history."

She raised an eyebrow and cocked her head to the side. "Yep. I can see it."

So could he. He'd been planning his career path out since high school. So far everything had gone according to plan because he'd followed the rules—written and unwritten, like the one that said no fraternizing with anyone with ties to the Esposito crime family. That Gina's tie was tenuous wouldn't matter to the review board. It made him look like a guy who blew off the rules. But this didn't count as fraternizing. He was on the job. It was totally different.

Keep telling yourself that, Hartigan.

Silencing that internal voice, Ford closed his trunk and turned to Gina. "Movie night, my treat?"

"I thought you were going to fix the wonky stair tonight."

That stair was one of the few things still on his personal-handyman list. For some reason, he'd been dreading the arrival of the supplies Juan had ordered. "Maybe I'm putting that off because I don't want your handyman list to be finished."

Shut the fuck up, Hartigan, before you confess to all the dirty things you think when you hear her get into bed at night.

Gina's cheeks flushed. "I don't suppose you have any candy we can sneak in with us."

"That's against the rules," he said, knowing she was just giving him shit and playing along. "I'll get the popcorn, though, extra butter with M&Ms mixed in."

"Not an offer I'm going to turn down. It's a date." Her cheeks turned pink the moment the words were out of her mouth.

He knew exactly where her mind was going, and he liked it. Not that he'd admit it out loud to anyone, but a date with Gina sounded pretty damn good. Since he couldn't have that for real, he might as well let Hollywood help him pretend.

"That it is," he said, sliding his palm across the small of her back and keeping it there as they walked across the parking lot and to the movie theater, as they stood in line for tickets, and while he carried the popcorn on their way to find their seats.

And when the lights went down, he moved the arm rest between them into the upright position. "To make it easier for you to reach the popcorn," he said when she gave him a questioning look.

By the time the great white's fin was spotted for the first time, his arm was resting on the back of the movie seat and they were sitting so close that if she dropped an M&M it wouldn't be able to fall between them.

The fact that he'd already seen the giant shark menace the summer swimmers at least a million times wasn't the reason why the action on the screen was just background noise. Instead, he was tuned in to the way her shoulders tensed whenever the music changed, how her eyes widened as the action picked up, and how she giggled and shrugged when she caught him watching her reactions. When the police chief declared they were going to need a bigger boat, Ford was curling a strand of her wavy hair around his fingers and feeling every bit like a horny high school kid with no clue what to do next. And when the credits started on the screen, neither of them moved. They just stayed pressed against each other in the darkness as everyone got up.

Maybe he turned to her first, maybe it was her tilting her face upward, but before the first gaffer's name scrolled by, his mouth was only an inch from hers. Her full lips were parted, and her hand dropped from the popcorn bucket to his thigh.

All thoughts of the dangers of fraternization and his captain's warnings scattered. He dipped his head and her eyes fluttered shut just as someone in the row behind them passed by, accidentally jostling them in the process and sending what was left of the popcorn flying.

Gina grabbed the bucket before it hit the floor and sat back in her seat, that open, needy look on her face disappearing. "Sorry, I guess I crowded you."

She was giving him an out. He should take it, but he

didn't.

Instead, he cupped the back of her head, bringing her toward him, and kissed her.

Electricity shot through him the moment his lips touched hers. And when she opened underneath him, it was all he could do not to move his hands to her hips and pull her across the seat and onto his lap so he could rock her against his straining dick, deepen the kiss, and finally give in to the want that had been building since the night of the wedding.

Some sane part of him pushed its way to the forefront, though, and reminded him of where he was and who he was kissing. Breaking the kiss wasn't something he wanted to do, but he had to anyway.

They sat there staring at each other for a second, and the sight of her kiss-swollen lips made him want to give back into the insanity of kissing her, but he held on to his fast-fraying control. "I'm sorry, I shouldn't have."

"It's okay, it was just a kiss," she said, avoiding looking at him as she stood up and brushed the stray popcorn kernels off of her. "Didn't mean a thing, right?"

His gut clenched at the declaration as he stood up—because kissing Gina was starting to mean something to him, and there wasn't a damn thing good about that.

Chapter Ten

Ford futzed with his tie the next morning, cursing whoever invented the damn things. He hated ties, but wearing them wasn't optional for detectives on Waterbury's force, so he'd gotten used to them. Now, after nearly five years of wearing one almost every day, he couldn't get his fingers to work right to make a Windsor knot. Why the muscle memory amnesia? Probably the lack of sleep after that almost kiss yesterday at his parents' house. Cockblocked by his own mom. That wasn't right.

And as soon as they'd gotten back to Gina's house after that kiss in the movies, she'd disappeared up the stairs, and he'd spent another night staring at the ceiling and wondering if tonight she was wearing the black lace panties.

"My grandma will think you're up to something if you wear a tie."

He turned and saw her standing in the open door to his makeshift room. She was wearing a retro-styled pink dress that was so sugary sweet all he wanted to do was dirty it up. Fuck. That was not where he needed his thoughts to go.

"It's her birthday party, right? You're dressed up."

"Thank you." She did a quick curtsy while giving him a teasing wink. "Still, a button-down shirt for you is fine. The tie makes you look like a cop."

He checked out his reflection in the mirror above the cold fireplace. It was just a regular plain navy tie. It wasn't like it was emblazoned with the department's logo. "I *am* a cop."

"Don't remind me." She snagged the tie from his hands and dropped it onto his freshly made couch bed.

"So, you're saying you're not going to introduce me to everyone as your boyfriend, Detective Hartigan?"

She looked at him like he'd just told her that she had ants crawling up her arm. "Oh God no, and don't mention it to my grandma, she's liable to curse you."

Luckily for him, Grandma Luca did not do that. Instead, she grabbed him with surprisingly strong hands for an elderly woman and kissed him on both cheeks in greeting. Then she took Gina by the arm and led her into the kitchen for what the older woman called girl talk.

That left him alone to navigate Grandma Luca's crowded living room. He recognized several of the people carrying around little plates of food, but most were new faces, which could be a good thing. Who knew what the Luca brothers had told these people in passing that might turn out to be valuable information? At this point, he didn't have anything to lose.

He was about to approach a scrum of people near the TV when Rocco—who was wearing a tie—strolled up to him.

Rocco handed him a glass of what smelled like bourbon and delivered what probably looked like a friendly slap to Ford's back that landed with enough force to leave a mark.

"I suppose you think you're fooling people?" Rocco asked, the smile on his face not reaching the man's eyes.

So that's how this was gonna go, huh? Okay, he could play

that game—especially if he could goad Rocco into revealing more than he wanted. After all, wasn't that why he was here in the first place?

He gave Rocco his best you're-full-of-shit-and-we-both-know-it smile. "I'd never expect to pull anything over on a guy like you."

If the sarcasm landed, Rocco didn't show it. "She's too good for you."

There was no need to ask who the *she* was because for once in his sorry, low-level-criminal life, Rocco was right about something. "I'm sure she is."

"No, I mean it." Rocco let the friendly veneer slide off his face. His eyes narrowed, his jaw squared, and an intense concern turned his already dark eyes to an almost black. "She's got a good heart. People look at her and they make judgments. They always have. It's not fair, but neither is life. That doesn't mean I'm gonna let some pretty-boy organized crime detective just fuck with her head, though."

And that accusation was way too close to the truth of how he'd ended up in her house to land without anything other than near-lethal force. Guilt burned like an iron poker pressed to his side. Ford's cheeks hurt from holding the fake smile, and he had to consciously loosen his grip on the glass in his hand. Then, like an unexpected answer, he spotted Gina weaving her way through the crowd, a huge smile on her face that didn't falter until she spotted him with her brother.

"Everything okay?" Gina asked when she got to them.

"It's perfect, sis," Rocco said. "Just having a little heart-to-heart with your boy."

She didn't look convinced, but she seemed to let it go. "You busy next Friday? It's past time I kick your and Paul's asses in bowling."

Rocco's gaze cut to Ford, the vein in his temple bulging. "Sorry, sis, we're booked that night." He kissed her cheek and started to walk away. "I've gotta go talk to Mikey. We'll catch up soon."

His trouble detector going crazy, Ford was ready to follow up with Rocco about what had him so busy that night when Ford's phone started to vibrate in his jacket pocket. He pulled it out, took one look at the number, and knew there was no way to blow off this call to question a guy who would never give him a straight answer anyway.

"I gotta take this," he said, hating all the reminders he got about who he was and who she was any time they walked out of her house.

Her smile faded just the tiniest bit, and she seemed to curl into herself, drawing an invisible protective shell around her shoulders. "Don't worry about it."

That wasn't the way this was going to go. Dipping his head, he gave her a quick kiss on the lips. It was a simple thing, easy, really, and it hit him like a Mack truck because when he lifted his head there was no missing the restored brightness of her smile that just made him want to kiss her again and again and again until it was the only kind of smile she ever had.

Before he could do that, though, he forced himself to walk toward the relative quiet of the front porch under the suspicious watch of her brothers, who stood next to their grandmother in the living room. No doubt his captain on the other end of his ringing phone would approve of the kiss as a way to solidify his cover story with her family.

Ford hadn't kissed Gina because of that, though.

He'd done it because he couldn't stand the truth that whatever was building between the two of them couldn't happen because the real reason why he was in her house and in her life was always there, lurking in the background. The revelation had him swiping his thumb over his phone's touchscreen with more force than necessary to answer the call.

"Give me a second," he said as he stepped out on the porch and did a quick visual sweep to confirm he was alone out there. "I'm not at the best place where I can talk."

"Good, because you only need to listen," the captain retorted. "Your clock is just about up. The ME's report came in. No obvious signs of trauma from what was left of Big Nose Tommy Luca. The ME says without that, and considering the factors surrounding where the body was discovered, he probably starved to death after getting stuck in the wall."

Of all the awful ways Gina's grandfather probably had imagined going, a slow death by starvation probably hadn't been what he'd pictured.

"A cleaned-up version of the report needs to be shared with the family," the captain went on. "That means your time is up. I sure as hell hope you found out some intel."

Oh he had. He knew Gina's favorite color (pink), her irrational hatred of action movies (that really needed to be changed), and that when he looked at her, something happened to the air around him, making it hard to breathe. But about her brothers or the Esposito crime family? "Not yet."

"Too bad. Getting information about the Espositos was the kind of thing that could make a detective's career."

Bile coated the back of his tongue with chalky guilt. "Understood, sir."

"Well, you've got one last night. Make the most of it." The captain hung up without saying goodbye.

Ford didn't let out the frustrated growl tickling the back of his throat. He swallowed it. This was the nature of the life he'd chosen. He did the hard thing because it was right and the rule of law mattered. The Espositos hurt people and needed to get taken down. If that heroin hit the streets, no telling how many lives could be ruined. He'd gone into this knowing he was lying for the right reasons.

Just as important, he was the only detective on the task force who was right for this case working with Gina. Exactly why that was the reality of the situation wasn't something he wanted to examine. He was just doing his job, and now his time was just about up.

Determined to make the best of what time he had left, he went back inside the house, focused on his job almost as much as the woman in the pink dress who smiled every time she looked his way.

A few seriously unproductive hours trying to pump the Luca family and friends for information later, and he was standing with Gina in her kitchen, which was lit only by the dim light above the sink. She'd just gotten done telling him about how her grandma had tried to give her the talk about how to hold onto a man during their girl talk session. Her eyes were bright with laughter. And she was smiling. He fucking loved that smile.

"I never thought I'd hear my grandma say the word blow job," she said, shaking her head. "That wasn't completely awkward at all, but she sent me home with homemade cannoli, guaranteeing it would make everything work out in the end."

And there it was, the swift kick to the balls delivered via ricotta and pastry shell. "And she's not wrong," he said with a forced cheerfulness the he wasn't feeling at all. "I'm gonna be out of your hair after tonight."

Gina handed him one of the mini-cannolis, but her gaze didn't meet his. "You heard back from the medical examiner?"

He took a bite of the cannoli but didn't taste a damn thing. "They believe it was natural causes."

Gina didn't visibly react so much as he felt her emotion as she processed the news she'd been expecting—probably since her grandfather disappeared years ago. It hadn't been totally unexpected, he knew, no matter what cock-and-bull story he'd fed her about the possibility of someone coming to clean up after her grandfather's death, but that didn't change the facts.

"So," she said with a melodramatic sigh, recovering herself, because the woman was nothing if not incredibly resilient. "I'm losing another handyman."

He nodded, more than willing to play along if that's how she wanted to frame their goodbye. "Afraid so."

"I'll kinda miss my fake boyfriend," she said with an exaggerated pout.

Unable to stop himself, he leaned in, needing to be closer to her. "You're fake breaking up with me?"

"Yep." She gave him a sassy grin. "If I don't get to use of your hammer, you're no good to me."

...

Gina couldn't believe the words that had just come out of her mouth. It must have been the sugar talking. It was totally the sugar talking, plus the two glasses of wine she'd drunk at the party and the confirmation of what she'd already known in her gut about her grandfather.

But she wasn't the kind of woman who could get away with a double entendre like that. He was just so damn close that her pheromones kind of took over her brain, which was probably not scientifically possible, but it's all she had for an explanation right now.

She looked up at him through her lashes, anticipation making the air electric around them. "We never got to finish what we started in the hotel that night."

What was coming out of her mouth? This wasn't her. This was some other woman who thought she had a shot with a guy like Ford.

"We shouldn't do this." But he plucked the half-eaten cannoli out of her hand and dropped it into the box where he'd just put his.

"Am I still in possible danger?" she asked, her hands going to the buttons of his shirt, slipping the top one free.

He shook his head as he looked at her fingers working on button number two. "No."

"Are you still on the clock?" Her hands were shaking with nerves, but the button slipped free.

She slid her fingers down to the third button, wondering if she was sex-drunk and possessed by a woman with ten times the confidence she had.

All she knew was that she didn't want this man to leave her house for the last time without letting the tension that had been simmering between them boil over. Some could argue that made her desperate. Others might say it made her assertive. She didn't give a flying fuck. This was her last chance with Ford, and she wasn't going to waste it.

Her fingertips brushed over the third button of his shirt, but his hand covered hers, stopping her. Her breath caught.

"No, I'm not on the clock." His words came out with the rough edge of a growl, hard and wanting, that thrilled something inside her.

He brought her hands down to her sides, his strong fingers encircling her wrists, but he didn't let go and he didn't walk away. Instead, he stood there looking down at her, desire and need making his green eyes turn even darker.

Heart hammering against her ribs, she gave into the pheromones and the sugar and the wine and the lust that kept her up at night. "So why shouldn't we finish what we started? Afterward, we go back to our normal lives. No commitment. No tomorrow. Just one night to do what we didn't in the hotel, then you leave at dawn and that's that."

"Because this can't ever be more than that," he said.

Didn't she know that all too well. "Exactly."

He looked for a second like he was going to argue with her, but in the next breath his hands were on her hips, pulling her close, and his mouth was on hers in a kiss that should have set every flammable can of paint lined up against the kitchen wall ablaze. It was hot and demanding and so achingly desperate. It was as if they couldn't get enough of each other and they both knew tonight was it.

He tasted of bourbon and cannoli, need and satisfaction—and she couldn't get enough as she reached back for his shirt and yanked it out of his pants, desperate to feel him and not the cotton covering his skin. He broke the kiss with a groan when she slid her hands under his shirt.

"I need to see you," he said, reaching behind her for the light switch.

"No." That couldn't happen. She didn't want to break the moment with brightly lit reality. She grabbed his arm before he could reach the switch and lowered it so his palm was on her leg right at the spot where her dress stopped. Excitement sizzled across her skin, and desire swirled through her, hot and demanding. She wanted this—wanted him—so bad. Watching his face in the soft light spilling into the kitchen from the foyer, she slowly slid his hand higher, under her dress and to the inside of her thigh. "You need to feel me."

"You have no clue just how bad," he said, gliding his fingers up her inner thigh. "Open your legs for me."

"Like this?" She widened her stance so her feet were shoulder-width apart.

"Not quite." In a flash, his hand was gone and she wanted to scream her frustration, but then he had his hands on her waist. "Hold on."

She did, her hands on his shoulders as he picked her up and whirled her around before sitting her down on the counter, so close to the edge that she had to hold onto him to keep her balance. Then his hands were on her thighs again, pushing her pink dress higher and higher up her legs. An impatient man would have just shoved it up and out of the way, but not Ford. He inched the hem up slowly, his gaze locked in on each millimeter of skin as it appeared. He was going to make her nuts. All she wanted was for him to just touch her already, and he was ogling the freckle above her kneecap.

"You're killing me," she groaned, her grip on his shoulders tightening as he did this circle thing with the pad of his thumb over that freckle that made her legs shake.

"You don't like this?" He nudged the fabric up a little higher. "It sure seems like you do."

It wasn't that she didn't, it was that she wasn't used to it. With most guys, it was lights off, clothes shoved aside, and then it was prime time, not all of this teasing slowness that was making her core ache and her nipples harden to stiff points without even being touched. Like it? What Ford was doing was fucking addictive. "I guess I'm used to a fast rush."

That made him stop completely. His gaze rose from her exposed legs to her face. The lust in his eyes was so intense she had to look away.

He cupped her chin and angled her face upward so she had no choice but to look at him. If she thought he'd been intense before, it was nothing compared to now. "I'm not other guys."

She shook her head no in agreement, the ability to actually form words having left her.

"I need you to say it." He ground out the words. "Say my name."

"Ford." It came out like a breathy plea, which it was, because she was about to combust here.

"That's right, and I'm gonna make you come so hard,

Gina Luca, that you're going to remember my name when you're a hundred years old and can barely remember your own." He dropped his hand back down to her legs and spread them wide, the move dragging the bottom of her dress up to the top of her thighs. "Now you gotta lift that sweet ass of yours up for me."

The idea to question him didn't even occur to her. All she knew was that her entire body tingled with anticipation and the ache between her legs got stronger each time he touched her. She dropped her hands from his shoulders to the counter behind her, lifted her butt off the counter, and balanced her weight on her palms as he glided his hands under her dress—there was just something thrillingly dirty about seeing his big hands disappear under what was now her very small skirt.

Her heart was racing as his hands moved higher to her hips and he hooked two fingers around the waistband of her panties and yanked them down. She nearly closed her eyes at the feel of the cool air against her slick folds, but she was so glad she didn't, because then she would have missed Ford's nearly comical expression of exasperation when he pulled her black lace panties down her legs.

He let out an agonized groan and shook his head as he balled the lace up in his hand. "These damn things have been tormenting me."

Okay, that made no sense. "My panties?" she asked as she lowered her weight back to the counter, her dress spread out beneath her.

He looked down at her underwear in his hand as if they were the answer to a question that had driven him to the edge of a cliff. "The idea of you wearing this scrap of lace has been one of the things keeping me at night, and now I finally got to take them off after dreaming up a scenario for what would happen next."

Oh my. Yes. She wasn't sure at first, but now she really

liked where this was going. "What was your idea for after you took them off?"

"You think I only had one?" He gave her that cocky half smile of his that always left her out of breath. "Pull up the front of your dress."

There wasn't much to pull up because as it was it only barely covered her, but she did. "Is this what you wanted? Or was it this?" She spread her legs wider.

His answering groan did naughty, naughty things to her.

"Yes, to all of it."

...

One imagined outcome? Ford had millions, but with the real woman in front of him so wet he could feel her desire on the fabric still balled up in his hand, there was only one thing he wanted to do first. Hands on her ass, he lifted her up higher as he pulled her right to the edge of the counter. Fuck, the look in her eyes right now was almost enough to make him nut in his jeans. He had to take a step back because he wasn't about to rush through this.

"Your dress," he said, trailing his fingers across her supple skin to her thighs, so very close to where he wanted desperately to be, but not touching her there. "Unbutton it."

Her tongue wet her bottom lip as her fingers went to the teeny-tiny buttons that went up the middle of her dress. For each one she freed, he dragged his fingers a little bit up her thigh.

"That's it," he said. "I want to see all of you."

What felt like millions of minutes of exquisite torture later, but was probably only twenty seconds, her pink dress was unbuttoned. What a sight. The front of the dress was pushed up to her waist, showing her glistening folds between her widespread legs, and her dress hung open and had fallen off one shoulder, exposing one tit with its hard nipple pressing against the sheer black lace of her bra. It was a sight he'd never forget, but what made it truly memorable was the look on Gina's face. Her full lips were wet and parted slightly, her cheeks were flushed with desire, and her eyes as she watched him watch her promised there was so much more to come.

He'd never seen someone so beautiful in his entire life.

"You aren't going back on your word, are you?" she asked, bringing one hand up to her exposed boob and pushing the cup of her bra down. "Promises were made." She rolled her nipple between her thumb and finger, pinching and tugging it taut. "Something about a mind-blowing orgasm that would stay with me for the rest of my life." She let go of her nipple and slid her hand down over her stomach to the tight, dark curls at the apex of her thighs. "Or do I need to take care of that myself?"

Lust blasted through him like a rocket explosion. Watching her touch herself was more than he could take. He was between her legs on the next breath, spreading her folds with his fingers as he took his first taste. She moaned and moved her hips as he worked her with his tongue, teasing and playing with her hard clit and her soft folds. Up and down, circle left, circle right, he took his time, enjoying her every reaction, the way her body tightened when he did something she liked and how she cried out when he did something she loved. She was fucking magnificent, and he couldn't get enough, so he kept going, nice and slow, driving her to the edge and leaving her teetering there in horrible ecstasy.

"Oh my God, Ford."

The heated desperation in her voice brought out the caveman in him, the one who wanted her to always remember this moment, to remember him. He slid his fingers inside her slick passage, plunging inside, and then made a come-here motion with one finger when he withdrew. Her thighs shook against his ears and she grabbed his hair, keeping him exactly where she wanted him.

"That's it," she cried out. "Right there. Don't you fucking stop."

Like that was going to happen, when she was so close that she was holding him tight enough to be on the verge of making him bald. One more lick, a suck, a stroke of the nerves just inside her entrance, and she came with a loud scream of *yes* that he could hear even though his head was caught between her clenched thighs that were acting like earmuffs.

All of that was totally worth it, though, when he stood up and saw her coming down from the high of her orgasm, while he could still taste her on his lips.

It was a phenomenal sight. And the night had only just begun.

...

Gina might have had to give up on ever thinking again, because her brain was a giant pile of mush—very happy, very satisfied, dopamined-up mush. When the world came back into focus, she had to laugh. Ford stood in front of her, his hair standing straight up—oops—and a look of such male pride on his face that she knew she had to fix that right away or he'd be unbearable.

"Tell me you have a condom."

His expression went from I'm-stud-of-the-week to I'm-stud-of-the-year. *Men.* But he grabbed his wallet from his back pocket and took out a condom.

Hoping her jelly legs would hold her, she hopped down from the kitchen counter and swiped the foil packet from him. "Take you pants off and sit down."

One eyebrow went up in question, but being the smart man that he was, Ford took off his jeans and sat his fine ass down on the kitchen chair.

"I'm at your mercy," he said, his hot gaze tracking her every move.

Still on the orgasm high, she considered making him squirm. After all, it wasn't every day that she had a man like him sitting half-naked in her kitchen. The temptation he offered was so much better than the possible satisfaction of dragging it out, though.

She slipped her dress the rest of the way off, unsnapped her bra and let it fall to the floor, and then walked in her heels to his chair, where she tore open the condom wrapper and rolled the condom on his hard, hot dick. His quick inhale of breath when she touched him probably put the I'm-the-stud-of-the-week smile on *her* face, and she didn't care. They could co-own the moment. She was a giver that way.

So when she put her hands on his shoulders, stepped wide so she straddled him in the chair, and then lowered herself down onto his cock, it was for both of them. Okay, the second she made contact with the head of his dick, that changed to being all about her, because oh my God had she had a drought and this was never going to happen again, but she'd had the best intentions to be a good sharer. Moving her hands from his shoulders to the back of the chair because she wasn't sure she wouldn't leave nail imprints on him despite the fact that he was still wearing his shirt—*poor planning on your part, Miss Gives The Orders Regina*—she took him all the way in.

"Fucking A, Gina." The words came out half groan and half growl while he grasped her hips.

He was very not wrong. This was so damn good. She rocked forward, swiveling her body a bit and changing the angle as she fucked him—and that's what it was, *uninhibited fucking*, the kind that only happened when she wasn't worried about what weird expression was on her face or how her stomach looked at the moment or if her body was making a weird noise.

For some reason, she was too overwhelmed by sensation to figure out at the moment, none of those usual thoughts happened when Ford touched her. They both just *were*. Later, she'd examine that, but not now, not when the man she'd spent the past week dreaming about was making that tormented growly rumble that did things to her very minimal—at the moment, okay, really any time she was around Ford—sense of control.

He reached up and cupped the back of her head, bringing her mouth down to his. Her body's response was a huge hell yes when his tongue swept into her mouth in the kind of overwhelming kiss that made her think oxygen was totally superfluous.

Sensation shot through her, pleasure making every nerve in her body vibrate. All of it grew with each twist of his tongue around hers and each undulation of her hips as she rocked against him until she couldn't take it any more. Everything inside her tightened and expanded in the same breath, and her orgasm washed like a wave over her, and she broke the the kiss and threw her head back with his name on her lips.

His hand dropped from her head to her hips again, and he gripped her tight, pumping her up and down on him in a series of short, hard thrusts before he came with a harsh groan.

Minutes, hours, days later, her brain came back online. "Wow."

Ford's tired chuckle brushed across her bare shoulder. "Seconded."

They stayed like that for a moment before the realities of the situation demanded attention. After they'd both gotten up, he'd disposed of the condom, and she'd gathered up her clothes, he followed her up the stairs to her big fluffy bed, which felt a lot smaller with Ford in it.

He told her stories about being the smallest brother in his family. She told him about being the tallest girl in her class. They laughed and swapped more stories and fell asleep snuggled against each other. At o'dark hundred, she woke up to Ford kissing that spot on her neck guaranteed to make her entire body zing, and that led to a whole lot of fun before sleep overtook them again. And once the sun finally did break through the night? Ford did what she'd asked earlier and left after a sweet goodbye kiss.

And that, she figured, was that.

Chapter Eleven

Wednesday night was Paint and Sip night with the girls. With the exception of last week, when she was in virtual house arrest/protective custody/Lustville, Gina never missed it. Tonight, she almost ditched, but that would have led to more questions than she wanted to answer, so she put on her big-girl panties—not the little black lace ones—and made her way down to Evanston Avenue and the art studio that sat above the hardware store down the block from Marino's Sports Bar. It had seemed like her best option, right up until she walked in and faced down the two women in the world who knew her best.

"You look different." Lucy cocked her head to one side and gave her a long up-and-down look while she sipped her rosé. "What have you been up to? Was being up to your elbows in house renovations code for finally getting naked with someone tall, dark, and epically talented with his tongue?"

Gina stopped herself from looking at her reflection in the mirror behind the counter, where Larry, who owned Paint and Sip, was serving up small plastic cups of the best cheap wine money could buy. Did she really look that different? It had been two days. Surely they couldn't see that spot at the base of her neck where Ford had nipped her.

Trying to be as subtle about it as possible, she adjusted the neckline of her T-shirt to make sure the collar hadn't slipped. "I don't know what you're talking about."

Lucy didn't look convinced. In fact, she looked even more suspicious as she peered at Gina through her signature glasses with the bright red frames before turning to the third in their little trifecta. "Do you believe her, Tess? Because I don't."

Gina and Lucy turned to Tess.

The much shorter, auburn-haired florist didn't hesitate. "Nope."

"Well, sorry to ruin it for you, but there's nothing to tell." Okay, that was a straight-up lie to her best friends, but it wasn't like there was a possibility of her seeing Ford again, so why bring it up? "What are we painting tonight?"

Lucy dropped her gaze down to Gina's neckline. "Aardvarks drowning in the ocean."

"Interesting," Gina said and sat down in front of one of the large canvases with a few swooping lines drawn in pencil on it.

Tess and Lucy exchanged a she's-totally-full-of-it glance and joined her.

"Liar. That's not interesting, it's totally preposterous. Even Larry wouldn't have dreamed up something so ludicrous." Lucy turned and gave their instructor a cheery wave as she sat down. "No offense, Larry."

The balding man in the Stay Weird apron splattered with several years' worth of dried paint just rolled his eyes. After two years of the three of them being here every Wednesday night, he'd either learned to put up with Lucy's brash ways or how to pretend like he had.

Tess sat down at the canvas next to Gina's, putting her plastic cup of wine down near her paint brushes and a second cup next to the last canvas in their row. She was too distracted wondering why the normally one-glass-and-done Tess was double fisting it to realize she was under attack until it was too late.

Lucy snagged her shirt, pulled the collar just enough to reveal the hickey Ford had left, and cried out in triumph. "I knew it wasn't just home renovations last week. You were shacked up with a dude. Finally!"

Gina force herself to take a measured sip of her rosé, even though she just wanted to chug the bottle. Paint and Sip night was not the place she wanted to have this discussion.

"It was the wedding guy," Tess said with a gasp.

"Oh my God, say yes. Say it was the wedding guy, because he sounded so flippin' hot."

"Who sounded hot?" asked a woman from behind her.

Gina turned to see who was moving in on their conversation and almost fell off her stool. The plastic cup slipped in her grip, but she managed not to drop it. Some of the pink wine did slosh over the side and landed smack dab in the middle of her shirt, because why only be humiliated once when you could get a second helping for free? It was the universe's version of an embarrassment buy-one-get-one-free sale.

"There you are, Fallon," Tess said, grinning at Ford's sister. "Lucy and Gina, this is Fallon Hartigan. She's the emergency room nurse I was telling you about who helped me out when I couldn't find my way around the hospital during deliveries the other day. We started talking about the total dumpster fire of dating in the modern age and trust me, she is one of us—totally single and slaying it."

Gina didn't even bother wishing that the ground would

open up and end her misery now. It was too late for that. Disaster was bearing down on her like a midtown bus with busted breaks. There was no way she was gonna get out of the way in time. She was about to be a bug on the windshield of life.

"Nice to meet you, Lucy. Hey Gina," Fallon said as she sat down. "So, tell me about the hottie."

Oh hell. Gina downed her rosé. She was gonna need it.

"Oh, it was at this guy at a wedding Gina planned the other weekend," Tess said, her face taking on an excited glow. "She got put on a kiss cam with a total babe of a cop in front of everyone. I swear I would have died, but she ended up kissing him. What was his name, Gina? It was a car name, wasn't it?"

"Ford," Gina and Fallon said at the same time. Of course, Gina said it with resignation and Fallon with more than a hint of surprise.

A heavy hush fell over their little group as Tess and Lucy looked from Gina to Fallon and back again. Then, they scooted their stools closer. They must have spotted something in her face because Tess handed Gina her still-full cup of rosé without a word.

Lucy zeroed in on Fallon. "You know him?"

"He's my brother," she said, giving Gina an assessing look that all but screamed they'd be talking about this later.

Tess gasped. Gina took a big drink of the second cup of wine, wondering if maybe she'd get lucky and it would be poisoned. This was so not how she expected tonight to go. Come on out to Paint and Sip night, it'll be fun, they said. Yeah, sure. More like total mortification. At least she hadn't told her besties that she'd slept with Ford this week—although sleeping was pretty much the last thing they'd done. She had muscles she'd never known about that were still a little sore.

Lucy let out a loud laugh and clapped her hands together

with joy. "You banged her hot brother?"

And that earned them a glare from Larry and some curious looks from the other women at Paint and Sip night.

"What? Ugh. No. Tell me no more," Fallon said, slapping her hands over her ears. "Hearing uptight Ford get called hot is bad enough, please do not let me hear about what he's like in bed."

"If they even made it to a bed," Lucy said in her version of a whisper that to almost everyone else in the known world was a normal volume.

Twin dots of fire zapped Gina's cheeks. They had. Eventually. But she wasn't just going to announce that in the middle of Paint and Sip. Not that this whole thing wasn't awkward enough as it was, because it very much was.

Fallon fake gagged. "I need a time machine so I can leave myself a note at the door to warn me not to come in."

If she figured out how to do that, Gina so wanted in on it. "Don't worry, I'm not commenting on what happened."

"But something *did* happen," Lucy pressed.

What was the use in denying it at this point? Lucy and Tess would see right through any lame attempts at lying. And Fallon? She'd been at that Hartigan family lunch, so if she hadn't seen the almost-kiss herself then she'd probably heard about it. No one in that family—besides Ford—struck Gina as the kind to keep any tidbit of gossip to themselves. So she might as well fast forward from the fun stuff to the reality of the situation now.

"But it's not going to happen again," she said, her tone more cheerful than she actually felt about the whole thing.

Tess gave her a sympathetic shoulder squeeze. "Oh, I hate that."

"It doesn't matter." And if she said that enough, it would become a reality. "I'm fine with my life the way it is. I don't need a man to make me happy."

That last part wasn't a lie. She didn't. She had a home that would—eventually—be exactly how she wanted it. She owned her own business helping people celebrate their own happily ever afters. She had friends who, despite their nosy ways, were the best she'd ever had. She had family—okay, they were more than a little strange, but they were still her family and they loved her. Really, what more could she ask for? Sure, having someone to share her life with on a more intimate basis would be nice, but she didn't need it. She was fine just the way she was.

"No, you don't," Lucy said with a nod of agreement. "But it does help if you want to keep your feet warm at night."

"I can get socks for that," she retorted.

So what if she was picturing big thick ones that smelled of warm cedar, just like Ford did.

"Ladies," Larry said, his unexpectedly deep voice cutting through their giggles. He stood in front of the room, paint brush at the ready. "Class is starting." That was their usual Wednesday night cue to shut the hell up. "Tonight's painting subject is the naked mole rat sunning itself on a settee."

"Okay, I take it back," Lucy whispered in her totally loud way. "Painting a drowning aardvark wouldn't be *that* weird for him."

...

By Tuesday, the box of supposedly bleach-enhanced Chapstick left on Ford's desk in the squad room had been swapped with a new kind of supposed gift. There, on his stack of case files, was a brown paper bag with eyeholes cut out. Ford stared down at it. The fuckers had even done a half-assed job of drawing a pair of women's open lips below the eyes, with an opening cut into the middle. Fury, hot and immediate, rushed up from his toes, and his gaze locked in on Gallo and Ruggiero, who were watching him.

"You two don't know who happened to leave that, do you?" Ford didn't bother to try to hide the anger burning in his gut as he grabbed the latest anonymous so-called gag gift from the stack of case files on his desk and crumpled it into a tight ball that he flung into his trash can.

Gallo just grinned his shit-eating grin and shook his head. "Nah, but it looks like someone hit a sore spot, huh, Johnnie?"

"Probably a PTSD reaction to his last assignment," Ruggiero said, his voice thick with fake sincerity. "You'd think for that kind of hazard duty he would have at least brought back some useful information."

"Sure," Gallo said. "But you can't be too hard on him. Hartigan probably barely made it out of there with his virtue intact."

He knew what they were doing. The dipshit duo had gotten yanked into the captain's office a few hours ago for a reaming loud enough that everyone in the squad could have written direct quotes. The pressure was building for results, and the organized crime task force had gotten almost nothing beyond the date of the heroin delivery. Without a time and location, that bit of news was worthless.

Ford had spent the last two days interviewing CIs, tracing down warehouse owners on the waterfront, and every other idea he could think of to actually use some detective skills to uncover the information they needed. Gallo and Ruggiero had been hitting the streets as well.

They'd all turned up shit.

So yeah, it's possible the two detectives were just taking out their frustration on him any way they could. But that didn't mean he wasn't pissed off regardless.

"What's wrong?" he asked, closing the distance between his desk and where Gallo sat on the corner of Ruggiero's desk.

"Did the captain chew you a new one for the task force's lack of results? I mean, sure, you might wish that was because of one operation that didn't pan out, but you've been in charge for months and working the Espositos for years."

The entire squad room went silent. Even the precinct's admin assistant stopped typing. Gallo got red enough in the face that Ford wondered if the portly detective was about to have a heart attack.

"You don't know what the fuck you're talking about, Hartigan." He stood up and took what he probably thought was a threatening step forward. "Maybe if little pukes like you did their jobs right, we'd have something to nail those bastards on. Instead, we just got some weak-ass story about how the brown-bagger doesn't know anything about what her brothers are up to."

For as quiet as the squad room was before, it totally disappeared at that moment. "What did you just call Gina?"

"A brown-bagger." Gallo puffed up his chest and put a swagger in his step as he took the last two steps before stopping just inside Ford's personal bubble. "Why, would you prefer grenade?"

"You need to shut the fuck up, Gallo." And *he* needed to mentally remind himself grown men did not lose their shit on their superiors at work. Besides, Ford wasn't the hot-headed stereotypical kind of Irish. He liked rules and order. He was just about to turn and walk away when Gallo jabbed his finger into Ford's chest.

"Why, what are you gonna do about it? I'm point on this task force, so you need to remember that, sit your ass down, and do what I tell you, unless you want to be stuck with Butterface duty again."

Ford's fist connected with Gallo's nose before Ford had even realized he was taking a swing at the other man. Gallo stumbled back, but like the bull of a cop that he was, he kept his feet planted. He let loose a roar of fury and came right at Ford.

The older detective may have been putting perps behind bars since before Ford even dreamed about the academy, but the donuts and the laziness had done their job. Ford easily sidestepped Gallo, spun on the ball of his foot, and followed up with a right hook that landed on the sweet spot of the older cop's jaw, leaving him wobbly on his size ten rubber-soled shoes.

Gallo raised his right fist, but Ruggiero grabbed his partner before he could throw a punch. No one grabbed Ford. There wasn't a need. The sight of Gallo with the look of murder on his face as his partner held him back was enough to bring him back reality. He'd lost it and slugged a superior officer—definitely a violation of a dozen regulations. Ford *never* lost it. But this time he had, and in doing so he'd tried to knock his direct supervisor's head off.

And surprisingly, he didn't regret a single action.

"Ford. Gallo." The captain's yell cut through the chaos of the moment. "My office right the fuck now."

Chapter Twelve

Ford accepted the beer Frankie handed him as he paced the length of his brother's deck. Anger and adrenaline were still pumping through his veins, making his steps jerky as he moved from one end to the other while Frankie watched, an amused look on his face.

"Damn. Mr. By the Book got suspended." Frankie took his phone out and started thumb typing. "I'm gonna have to put this information in our family group chat."

Annoyance eating away at his stomach lining, Ford whirled around and shot his brother a glare. "That's what you're taking away from this, that I'm suspended with pay for the next week? Not that the moron who was leaving all of that shit on my desk and being a disrespectful asshole only got a three-day suspension?"

"No, I got that part," his brother said as he sat down in one of the Adirondack chairs that Frankie had been forced to paint lime green with yellow polka dots after losing a bet with Finian. "And I also got the part about how you've got it bad for this chick."

"Did you inhale too much smoke at the last fire you responded to? Because your thinking is messed up." Got it bad. That was fucking ridiculous. Gina was funny, smart, and yeah, being around her pretty much turned him into a horny teenager, but that didn't mean he wanted any more than the one-night-only sex—which had been pretty damn phenomenal—that they'd both enjoyed. "I don't have it bad for her."

"Uh huh." Frankie started typing again. "Sure you don't."

Ford's phone buzzed, but he sure as hell wasn't going to look at it. He had the jackass texting right in front of him, grinning at him like he was some TV shrink about to solve all of Ford's problems.

Pissy? Me? Not at all since I walked out of Gina's house at the crack of dawn, thank you very much.

"What does that mean?" Ford asked, taking a seat in the other obnoxiously painted deck chair and taking a long drink from his beer.

"Well, Mr. Detective, using the information you provided as well as my own keen observational skills, I noticed that you couldn't stop looking at your"—he made air quotes—"'just friend' as she gave you the hey-good-lookin' eyes during family lunch. Then, you defended her honor to the point that you broke police rule nine hundred and forty-six and tried to clean the clock of a guy who happens to outrank you. So, by putting on my Sherlock hat, I was able to deduce that you have a major hard-on for one Gina Luca." Frankie's phone buzzed in his hand, and he glanced down. "Felicia agrees, and since she's the only one of us in a committed relationship, I'm gonna declare that means I'm one hundred percent correct."

Ford glared out at the pristine backyard. "You're an idiot."

"Not when it comes to women."

Okay, Frankie may have made the rounds a few dozen

times among Waterbury's single women, but that didn't make him a relationship sage. "If that's the case, then why is Felicia the only one of us in a committed relationship?"

"Are you kidding?" Frankie waved his hands over his body like a gameshow hostess showing off a prize. "You want me to limit the ladies of Waterbury's access to all this ginger firefighter hotness? I'm not that cruel."

Ford laughed. He couldn't help it. Even when he was in a shitty enough mood to eat nails, Frankie's good-natured lack of humility always cracked him up. The man really was a menace to the women of Waterbury. How in the hell he managed to stay friends with 99 percent of the women he dated was a mystery to Ford.

He couldn't even get Gina to call him. Not that he'd called her.

He couldn't initiate contact. But if she'd called, that would have been a different story. Too bad she hadn't called. And the fact that she hadn't told him just about everything he needed to know about her thoughts about things after their night together. And now he was stuck twiddling his thumbs for a week.

"What am I going to do?"

Frankie looked at him like he had two heads and neither of them had a brain. "Go tell her you're into her."

"Not about Gina." Because there was nothing he could do about her, they'd both known that going into the other night. That's probably what made it seem like more than it was and why he couldn't seem to stop thinking about her. "What am I going to do about the suspension?"

"Dude." Frankie shrugged. "I have no clue on that one. I'm a man who loves two things in this world and they both start with F—fighting fires and fucking."

Ford snorted. "You're so classy."

"No, but I am honest about who I am and what I want."

His brother turned a very un-Frankie-like serious gaze on him. "Maybe you should try that."

No detective work was necessary to figure the meaning behind that piece of advice out. Ford took another drink of his beer and tried to think of a way around the obvious, but there wasn't one. There were good guys and bad guys. Cops and robbers. The two didn't mix.

"Her grandfather was Big Nose Tommy Luca. Her brothers are Rocco and Paul Luca."

"So?"

"I'm a detective." He had no clue how to be more plain about the impossibility of it all than that.

"Are you trying to say that the wedding planner who blushes every time you even glanced in her direction at family lunch is actually a member of a dark crime family and does wet work as her side hustle?" Frankie didn't even try to hide how funny he thought the idea was. By the time he got the words side hustle out, he was working so hard to hold back his laugh that his shoulders were shaking.

"No, you oversized smart-ass. She doesn't have anything to do with them."

"I see," Frankie said and then took a long, slow drink of his beer. "So, what does your job have to do with a damn thing when it comes to you having a good time with a woman who wants you?"

It sounded ridiculously simple when his brother put it that way, but Frankie didn't understand. "There are standards we're expected to keep as detectives and regulations we have to meet in regards to who we associate with."

"And wedding planners are on the list of those to be shunned, huh? I think I understand now why cops' divorce rates are so high."

That wasn't it at all, and his brother knew that. "Go screw yourself, Frankie."

Frankie let out a loud laugh. "I love you too, man."

After that, the conversation turned to the Ice Knights and what a total shit trade the team had made when they'd made a play for Zach Blackburn. The defenseman nicknamed the Harbor City Hooligan had made so many boneheaded plays during the season—contributing to the Ice Knights missing the playoffs—that the Post had just named him the most hated man in Harbor City.

By the time Ford finished his single beer and gotten into his car for the short drive home, he wasn't even thinking about Gina anymore. Which was what made it even more of a mystery as to how in the world he'd ended up parked outside of her house wondering if she'd answer if he rang the doorbell.

· · ·

Gina had to stop staring at the couch in the front room that had the Ice Knights blanket folded perfectly and resting underneath the pillow Ford had used. Really, it was getting creepy.

She needed to go in there, pick them up, and stuff both back in the storage closet. That's really what she should do.

Instead, she did a one-eighty and walked to the front door and picked up the watering can so she could water the plants out on the porch. She swung the door open and stopped dead in her tracks. Ford was standing at the bottom of the porch stairs, looking damn good for a man whose facial expression said he couldn't decide if he should turn back or go forward. She knew how he felt. Her heart was going a million miles an hour, but her feet weren't moving an inch.

"Hey," she finally managed to get out. "I wasn't expecting to see you again."

Why oh why couldn't she have found the extra time to

wash her hair today? The frizzy mess was contained in a bun on the top of her head, but strands kept escaping and sticking to her lip gloss. Add to that the well-worn jeans and a shirt that declared to all she didn't do mornings, and she was definitely not looking her best.

He did that slow, half-smile thing that made her lungs go tight. It wasn't fair. "I wasn't expecting to be here."

Okay, that took some of the tingly excitement out of her metaphorical sails. "Then why are you?"

He shoved his fingers through his hair but, because it was him, it all just fell back into perfect place instead of looking a mess. "I wanted to see you."

And BAM she was back up to teetering on the edge of something fantastic. Why did he do this to her? He made her feel excited and scared and nervous and sparkly—yes, it sounded dumb, but it was true—and at home all at the same time. She didn't understand it, just like she couldn't quite grasp why after everything they'd agreed to he'd shown up on her porch saying he wanted to see her.

He climbed the first two steps, his hand on the recently sanded banister and all of his intense focus on her. "Can I ask you a question?"

If there was a time in her life when she'd ever wished she was a Rizzo from *Grease*, this was it. To have that confidence and bravado and chick balls. Instead, she was a Frenchie, forever the goofy sidekick. She knew this. Still, she dug deep to find her badass inner Rizzo. "Depends on what you want to know."

"Are you involved in anything illegal?"

And that was pretty much the last thing she'd expected him to ask. The preposterousness of it made her laugh out loud. "Well, I have a lead foot. Does that count?"

Ford didn't laugh. In fact, his jaw seemed to tense even more. "So, no running numbers or delivering messages or wet work?"

"I don't even know what that last one means." She shook her head. She was a wedding planner, and the only kind of wet work she dealt with was being sure to keep extra tissues on hand for the mother of the bride. "Why are you asking me this, Ford?"

The stubborn man didn't answer. Instead, he vaulted up the last three steps to the porch and strode toward her, right across the spot on the porch marked with a big red X so Juan would know which boards needed to be replaced.

"Wait, Ford, watch out for the—"

She spoke too late. The wonky board that always felt like it was about to give way when she stepped on it finally did. The crack sounded, then a snap, and then a crash as Ford fell through the porch up to his hips.

"Oh my God," she yelled, dropping the watering can in her shock. It bounced once and fell over onto its side, all of the water inside spilling out and rushing right to Ford, soaking him. "Are you okay?"

He looked down at the boards surrounding him, a few of which had broken off into sharp points but none of which were close enough to pierce him. "I'm a little scraped up, but I'll live. It looks like for the most part it was a clean break," he said. "But don't come any closer. I don't want you to go down, too."

He braced his hands on the boards closest to him, but they started to creak as soon as he put his weight on them. Oh, this was not going to go well. The more he tried to get himself out, the worse it seemed to get. It was like her house was trying to eat him.

"I need to get help," she said, pulling out her cell phone from her back pocket with shaky hands.

Ford continued to survey his situation. "Who are you going to call?"

"The fire department," she said, already scrolling for their non-emergency number. "They got one of my cousin's kids' head free after he'd gotten it stuck between two banisters at my grandma's house."

"Do not dial that number," Ford said, each word coming out as a staccato punch. "I'd rather live the rest of my life in this hole than have you call the fire department."

"That makes no sense." That wasn't rhetorical. It really made no sense at all. If she hadn't seen him fall through the porch herself, she would have figured he'd banged his head hard to be talking such bologna.

The vein in his temple pulsed, and he squared his jaw with enough force that it made the muscles on the side of his face bulge out. Ignoring her question, he tested out the boards within reach, each of which wobbled under the pressure. Finally, he let out a frustrated huff.

"My brothers and my dad are firefighters. I would never hear the end of it if they had to come pull my ass out of a hole in a porch. They'd stop and take pictures before they did it. They'd probably call my mom and FaceTime her during the process. I could save the entire family from a deranged serial killer, and they'd all still be telling the story of the time I got stuck in a hole on your front porch."

After having lunch with his family, she had to admit he wasn't wrong. They wouldn't do it out of meanness, but they'd totally give him a hard time for a good long while. And she could understand why. Ford was always so damn sure of himself that seeing him in this situation was something to savor for a little bit.

"I don't know," she said, letting her finger hover over her phone. "Calling the fire department seems like the standard operating procedure here. I know how much you love following protocol. Remember when you refused to start painting the hallway until you'd stirred the paint for exactly thirty-five seconds?"

"That's what the guy at the paint counter recommended to achieve the best sheen," he declared as he crossed his arms across his chest as if the truth of the statement was obvious.

Which it was. Just not in the way he was thinking. "Like I said, you always follow recommended protocol."

"Not in this case," he shot back.

"Ford Hartigan, are you breaking the rules?"

"I seem to be making a habit of it whenever I'm around you," he groused.

Now this was something worth exploring, and since he didn't seem to actually be hurt apart from his pride, she put her phone away in her back pocket. "Well, since I have you trapped, you've got to tell me everything." She was being an ass. She knew it, but how often did a woman like her have the hot guy she lusted after trapped in her porch? This was a situation that needed to be savored like a fine wine or a greasy cheeseburger when she had a hangover from savoring too much of that fine wine. "Why are you here instead of at work?"

"I punched a fellow detective who happens to outrank me."

Whoa. It took a few seconds for his words to sink in. "That doesn't sound like you."

His face darkened, and for a second she didn't think he'd answer. Finally, he grumbled, "I had my reasons."

"Don't suppose you'll tell me?" Because she was dying to know what in the world could push someone like By The Book Hartigan to punch a superior.

He just held her gaze.

Wow. Throwing punches at another detective. She would have to follow up with Fallon about that, because Mr. Tight Lips wasn't going to give up any of the goods, which was really too bad. Of course, it wasn't enough of a reason to let her house eat him, no matter how nice it was to have him around again.

"Then I guess I've got no choice but to free you." Sticking close to the outside wall of the house like Juan had warned her to do, she went to the end of the porch where there was a ladder she'd used to put up the hanging plant baskets.

She carried it back and laid it down so that it spanned not only the hole Ford was stuck in but also several feet past it in both directions, giving him something to brace his arms on that wasn't dried-out wood from the last century. Was it bad that she totally scoped out his forearms when he pressed his palms onto the ladder and lifted himself out of the hole? Well, if it was, too bad, because she had to get her thrills where she could.

By the time he was standing next to where she stood close to the door, his T-shirt plastered to his chest because of the water from the watering can, she was having to stuff her hands in her pockets to keep from reaching out and running her hands over him to make sure he was really okay. He looked okay. Correction, he was Ford Hartigan—he looked way better than okay.

Regina, this is not the time to go there.

But she couldn't help it. Being so close to him that she could smell the warm cedar of his cologne and feel the sizzle of the air around them discombobulated her.

"If I take you out to eat, will you agree not to sue me?" She regretted the words as soon as they were out. Why did she always make dumb jokes when she got nervous?

He gave her that cocky half grin. "Is there cannoli involved?"

Of course, the mention of her favorite pastry sent her brain right back to that night in her kitchen. Did he mean… He couldn't… She looked up into his face. There was no missing the heat in his eyes as he watched her. Oh God. He did.

She swallowed hard and nodded. "Most definitely there will be cannoli."

Chapter Thirteen

They walked into the bakery. Scratch that. Ford did his best I'm-not-shoving-you-but-I'm-totally-shoving-you move to get into the tiny storefront of Vacilli's Bakery so Gina wouldn't have to be elbows-to-asses with a bunch of sugar-crazed Waterbury citizens desperate to get their pastry on.

"What is with these people," he muttered under his breath—but not enough under his breath, going by Gina's giggle and the dirty looks he got from the other people crowded into the bakery.

"You haven't had their cannoli yet."

"But I've had cannoli. Remember?"

Pink splotches appeared on her cheeks. "You got distracted."

"I can't imagine why. Maybe it was when you took your dress and—"

She cut him off, "Ford!"

He was almost as disappointed as the old man in line ahead of them whose face fell when Gina interrupted and then grumbled something about young people not being any fun.

"You know, in some places it's illegal to be as sexy as you are. I'm a police officer. I know these things."

She rolled her eyes. "I know very well that that's not true."

"You know every law in every state in the U.S.?"

Her gaze faltered, dipping down to the floor. "No, I know for a fact that I'm not that sexy."

"You couldn't be more wrong." Her smile lost that joking quality and went stiff. He couldn't help but think that she was recalling whatever it was that someone had done to her to break her trust so completely that she wouldn't tell him about that day at the Wooden Barber. But he knew better than to push. She'd tell him eventually. He could be patient—for her.

"What's so special about this place? Cannoli is cannoli."

"No. There is cannoli and then there is Vacilli's cannoli. The main bakery is in Harbor City and has been there for decades. I would love to get to go to the Harbor City one someday and spy on them making the cannoli. They opened this one a few years ago."

"Wait, this isn't grand-opening crowded?"

"Are you kidding?" She laughed and patted him on the arm like he'd just asked if the Ice Knights were a hockey team. "This is barely a Saturday morning crowd. You should be here the day before Easter. I've seen old ladies shove little kids out of the way to move ahead in the line."

Once they finally made it through the twisting line and got their cannoli, he had to admit it was pretty amazing. Just not as amazing as watching the woman he couldn't stop thinking about practically have an orgasm in front of him after taking her first bite.

Up until that moment, he hadn't realized he could be jealous of a pastry—but he was.

. . .

Going to the grocery store with a guy was weird. Gina had to walk slower, listening to her latest audiobook was verboten, and going through the tampon aisle was…awkward. Still, she'd never had a better time tapping melons—not a euphemism.

"Have you really never bought a cantaloupe?" she asked.

Ford shook his head and knocked on the melons as if he was executing a search warrant. "Never."

She took the fruit from him before he busted it in the middle of the produce section. "Then what's in your fruit bowl?"

"If I had one?" He scrunched up his face as if he were really pondering it. "Junk mail."

Could he have given any more of a dude answer? No, he couldn't. "And yet, you seem like such a normal person."

"My hours can be unpredictable, so I do a lot of takeout." He pushed the cart a few feet to the pineapples, giving them a suspicious once-over. "Speaking of which, the captain asked me to come in tomorrow."

"That's good, right?" she asked, almost sounding convincing.

His suspension was T-minus a few days away from being over. Not that she was counting the hours down. The happy home renovations while playing house time had to end at some time. The clock was always clicking down with them—something she couldn't afford to forget.

Someone cleared his throat behind her.

"If that means you'll be keeping better company, Gina, it sure does."

Shit. Gina flinched. She knew that voice. She turned to see Paul standing there with a basket of Roma tomatoes, a large bulb of garlic in his hand, and a scowl on his face directed at Ford.

Her brother puffed up his chest and kept his focus on Ford even as he addressed her. "This guy bothering you, sis?"

She had officially had enough. Turning to Ford, she pasted her best please-play-along smile on her face. "Do you mind going to grab the eggs for me?"

He didn't look happy about it, but he swallowed whatever he'd been planning to say to her brother and dipped his head down to plant a kiss on her cheek before heading off in the direction of the eggs.

She waited for him to clear the produce area and spun around, hands on her hips, to confront her brother. "Really, Paul? What is your problem?"

"I don't trust him."

She bristled at the unspoken reason for that. "Why, because he's spending time with me and who in their right mind would do that?"

That got Paul's attention. He blinked at her as if his brain was trying to catch up with her verbal left turn. "Don't put words in my mouth."

She snorted. "I don't have to when they're written all over your face."

It was the same look of surprised disbelief, followed by an almost-verbal curiousness about how in the world she and Ford had ended up together—the sexy cop and the woman with the schnoz.

"He's a cop," Paul said, sputtering just enough for her to know that hadn't been his first thought.

"Yeah, well you and Rocco are the only ones still up to your neck in the old family business, so I'm not worrying about it. Maybe being around him will get you two knuckleheads to finally see the light and move to that island you're always talking about."

"We're thinking about it, but we're both a little young for retirement." Paul cracked a smile, the same one that had always cheered her after a bad day dealing with people saying shitty things about her.

Her anger abated enough for her own lips to curl up before the reality of what he'd said hit her. Damn it. She wasn't going to encourage this nonsense. "Yeah, well in your line of business, there's no guarantee you'll get any older."

He glared at her. She shot him a dirty look right back. Other shoppers avoided them.

Finally, Paul leaned down, a deceptively goofy look on his face as he asked, "Why are we fighting, sis?"

Dammit. Why did he have to do that? It was just disarming. Still she stuck to her guns. "Because you insulted my boyfriend."

Paul cocked his head to one side and gave her an assessing look. "Is that what he is?"

"No." Because as much as she'd like it to be true, she knew it couldn't be. "But we're something."

"Is he good to you?" Paul's face got a dark look to it that she'd never seen before but had heard people who'd crossed him whispering about.

"Yeah, he is." Her heart did that fluttery thing again. "So why don't you stop doing the overprotective thing? I can stand up for myself."

"Old habits are hard to break." He smiled ruefully. "Anyway, you know it's just because we love you."

Isn't that what he and Rocco had always said when she'd come home, beat down after another day of being teased at school? At home with them, she was just Gina, their annoying little sister. She'd never told them the worst of it or how she'd gotten her nickname. Some humiliations couldn't be avenged, not even by a pair of brothers willing to take on all comers.

"I love you too," she said, giving her brother's arm a squeeze. "But I'm not that girl barely making it through the school hallways without crying anymore."

"Grandpa would be proud of you." Paul looked over at

the cantaloupe she and Ford had been checking out earlier. "He always told me and Rocco you'd be the one in the family to make the best choices. He wasn't wrong. Look at you. I'm proud of you, sis."

And this had officially gone to a place her conversations with Paul didn't usually go. It made her stomach hurt. "Everything okay?"

"Always." He smiled at her, and it almost reached his eyes. "Who knows, maybe Rocco and I are getting ready to follow in your footsteps."

"You two want to be wedding planners?" She grinned. She couldn't even imagine what that would be like. "Or dating a cop?"

His laugh was all the answer she got, because that's when they both spotted Ford coming their way with a blue carton of extra-large eggs. "Talk to you later, sis."

"When are we going to have that bowling night?"

"How about Thursday? Bring your boy," he said. "Rocco'll be by before that, though. We've got a surprise for you."

That did not bode well. "You know I hate surprises."

"Not from us. Ours are always good." He gave her a quick kiss on the cheek. "See ya, sis."

Then he walked away, clearing the produce area before Ford made his way to her side.

"Everything okay?" Ford asked.

"Yeah, fine." She watched the back of Paul's head until he turned down the cereal aisle.

Something was off, but she couldn't put her finger on it.

She was rolling it over in her head when Ford handed her a cantaloupe with the worst thunk sound possible, and she turned her attention back to teaching him the correct cantaloupe tapping technique.

. . .

Losing had never been as hard as it was right now as Ford tossed his bright yellow bowling ball into the gutter with enough skill to make it look like an accident when it was anything but. Growing up Hartigan pretty much equalled competitive to a fault. However, if he wanted to make some sort of connection with his thick-necked opponents, kicking their asses wasn't the way to make that happen.

"You're so far back, Hartigan, that you need to go find you a St. Christopher's medal," Rocco said from his spot closest to the overflowing plate of nachos and pitcher of cheap beer.

"Stop trying to stir up shit," Gina said as she walked up to the line, her hot pink ball at chin level, and chewed her bottom lip raw, staring at the pins at the end of the alley like this time she was going to get a strike. "Silence, please. I'm gonna do it this time."

The woman had a lot of positives—the sweet curve of her ass, the sound of her laugh, the way her smile made her eyes twinkle—but amazing bowling skills weren't among them. Gina was straight up awful. Her brothers were even worse. That meant that Ford was trying not to eat his tongue in an effort to play as badly as possible in order to not sop up the spilled beer on the floor with them.

Gina threw her bowling ball down the waxed alley. Oh, some people rolled their balls—not Gina. The hot pink ball landed with a thunk a few feet in front of her and did its drunken wobble down the alley toward the pins that were not shaking in fear. The ball smacked into five of them, knocking them over. It was pretty close to her high roll of the game. She did a little shimmy dance move, threw her arms in the air, and turned to face her brothers and Ford at the table with a smile that lit up her whole face.

Maybe there was some asshole out there who could look

at her and not return her grin. Ford was a dickhead, but he couldn't stop the ends of his lips from curling upward. Her no-good brothers did the same.

"I told you this was going to be my game," she said, seemingly forgetting that she had a second turn in this frame and making her way back to their table. "And you guys thought I was crazy for insisting Ford join us for our monthly game. He's my lucky charm."

The look Paul cut at Ford behind his sister's back would be enough to kill a weaker man. For all Ford knew, that was the loan shark's favored glare when it came to collecting past-due debts.

"That may be so," Rocco said from his spot in the booth overlooking the lanes. "But you have another turn."

She swiped her mug off the table and took a quick drink. "Having the game of my life really worked up a thirst."

Then she took off back to the bowling ball return.

"This Friday's a go," Paul said in a low voice to his brother.

"You sure?" Rocco asked.

Paul nodded.

"What's on Friday?" Ford asked, his attention caught by the date they were talking about.

"None of your fucking business," Paul retorted.

Ford shrugged and took a drink. He could have pushed more. The Luca brothers were in it up to their necks, and all he needed was for them to get comfortable enough with him over beer and bowling to make a couple of slips.

Sure, as he told his boss, the likelihood of that actually happening was about as good as a vegan voluntarily eating at a Brazilian steakhouse, but if there was even a chance he was taking it. After all, he was in it to win the war against the Espositos, taking the entire organization down, not just win the battle of the Luca brothers. But judging by the men's body language and fuck-you stare in his direction, he wasn't going to get anywhere with a direct attack. He'd just take this intel back to the task force and let Kapowski run it by his informant for more detail. He could take another run at the brothers if needed after that. Until then, he'd do what he could to protect Gina from any fallout that may rain down on her because of her brothers.

At least that's what he was telling himself as he ignored his targets and zeroed his attention onto the way Gina filled out her jeans, to the point that he didn't see Paul move at all, let alone with enough time to dodge the man's palm before he smacked it against the back of Ford's head. The other man hadn't used a lot of force, just enough to send his message.

"Gina might like you, Hartigan," Rocco said, his attention focused on his sister and his body language deceptively relaxed. "But don't think I won't smack that look off your face, cop or not."

"What look?" Ford asked, as if he had any hope of selling that level of bullshit.

Paul glared at him. "The one that says you are having particular thoughts about her."

All true, but it wasn't like he was creeping on her. Gina liked him. He liked her. It wasn't like anything could happen between them. Not really. There might be fun, but that was it. He was an investigator. She was a Luca. It didn't get any simpler than that, which was part of the appeal. Letting go and living in the moment with her wasn't a problem because there'd never be any more to it than that. Still, the way her brothers treated her as if she wasn't able to take care of herself rankled.

"She is her own woman," he said before adding more quietly, "and she doesn't seem to mind my thoughts."

Rocco snorted his obvious disagreement. "She also thinks she's having a great game and that the three of us aren't throwing it."

The shock at that announcement must have shown on his face, because both brothers started laughing and Rocco poured beer into a mug and pushed it across the table to Ford. And here he thought he'd been the only one purposefully playing like shit. Now this put the Luca brothers in a different light—one that seemed all too familiar. The Hartigans were competitive, loud, and stubborn, but they always looked out for each other, even if that meant pretending that Felicia's banana bread was edible.

"She's our sister," Paul said. "But she sucks at bowling."

"So, you roll gutters once a month?" Was it wrong that he wanted them to say no, to stay in the total-asshole-criminal lane and not the older-brothers-determined-to-put-a-smile-on-their-sister's-face lane?

"It actually helps on league night," Paul said with a shrug. "It takes more control than you'd think to miss."

Giving into that brother solidarity bond, Ford raised his glass in a toast. "Now, I can believe that about playing on league night."

Rocco and Paul clinked their glasses against his. How often had he seen similar behavior between one Hartigan sibling or another? A million would be on the low count. They loved Gina, and there was no doubting how she felt about her brothers. So for an instant he put away his badge.

"Since you guys gave me a warning," Ford said. "Now it's my turn to give you one."

"Oh yeah, what's that?" Rocco asked.

"She'd be brokenhearted if you two got caught up in something that's way above your pay grade." Ford shot a hard look at the brothers, hoping like hell they'd understand his veiled words. "Life in your line of business always ends up in one of two ways: jail or an unmarked grave. I'd hate for her to spend decades wondering if your bodies would ever be recovered. Why don't you guys spend this Friday looking for a new line of business and make your sister happy."

Rocco and Paul didn't flinch. They just continued to look at him with that dead, mile-long stare that those connected with the Espositos had mastered. It gave nothing away. Then, as if they were mirror images, they each grabbed their beer mugs and downed the contents in one long swallow. Then, they turned without a word and watched Gina's bowling ball swerve down the alley before ending up in the gutter just shy of the pins.

After that, they went through the lineup with each of them rolling total crap until it was Gina's turn again. If she knew they were letting her win, she didn't let on. She just wiggled that perfect ass of hers, smiled as if she didn't have a care in the world, and had the time of her life—which was way better to observe than Ford had imagined.

"They'll never find your body, you know," Rocco said, falling back into his mob-connected loan shark persona.

Ford puffed out his chest and scowled at the brothers. "Excuse me?"

"Fuck with Gina…" Rocco paused as he turned to look at Ford straight-on and laid his meaty forearms on the table, then leaned forward on them. "And they'll never find you. It doesn't matter where we are at the time, we'll come back and hunt you down."

Out of all of that, there was only one thing Ford needed to address. "I'm not fucking with her."

One of Paul's eyebrows went up. "You're going with that, instead of the fact that we just threatened a police officer?"

"Yeah." Why that put a radioactive turn in the pit of his stomach, he had no idea. They were just playing it for the moment, nothing more.

"Why?" Rocco asked.

"What does it matter?" Defensive? Him? Yeah, he sure the hell was.

Rocco sat back in his chair, his face settled into a you-owe-us-five-Gs glower. "She likes you."

"Yeah." Ford took a gulp of beer.

"You like her?" Paul asked.

He downed another drink but refused to think about his answer before the truth came out. "Yeah."

The Luca brothers turned to each other. Something passed between them, one of those silent conversations a person could only have with someone they'd known forever. Finally, Paul shrugged and Rocco shook his head.

"Don't fuck it up, then," Paul said. "And everything will be fine."

"Your turn, Ford," Gina called out from her spot by the ball return, close enough to watch them with curiosity but not so near that she could overhear what they were saying as the balls crashed into pins on the other lanes.

Without a word to her brothers, he got up and went over to retrieve his ball.

"Are they giving you a hard time?" she asked, giving him a soft hip check.

Yeah, that wasn't something someone with any testosterone would ever admit. "Why would you say that?"

"Because my brothers are as overprotective as they are predictable," she said, amusement giving her words a light lilt. "Take throwing this game, for instance. They've been doing it for years, as if I didn't realize they play in a league and could wipe the floor with me."

And so much for Gina not realizing what he and her brothers were up to. Really, he should have known better. "So why do you go along with it?"

"It makes them happy." She shrugged. "We do weird things when we care about people. You know?"

Yeah, he did.

And this time when his ball landed in the gutter, it wasn't

on purpose. It was because he glanced over at Gina before letting go and she pursed those pink lips of hers and blew him a kiss, punctuated with a wink.

Turns out it was easy to send a bowling ball into the gutter when his mind was already there.

...

Almost a week after his suspension, Ford walked into the squad room. Everything looked the same—the burned coffee, the surly suspect handcuffed to a desk, the tower of paperwork in his inbox—except for Gallo's face with its large purple bruise that was the same size as Ford's fist.

Gallo gave his version of the stink eye as Ford walked by on his way to the captain's office. What was he supposed to do? Fall down on his knees and beg for forgiveness? Not fucking likely. He stopped at the corner of Gallo's desk, picked up the crumpled paper towel sitting next to the detective's coffee mug, and handed it to him.

"You got a little something right there." Ford made a wiping motion on his own chin right where Gallo's bruise was.

Gallo dropped the paper towel and flipped him off.

He slapped his palm over his heart. "Oh man, does that mean we're not forever besties anymore?"

Ignoring the curious looks and occasional glares from the others in the squad, he walked over to the captain's office and knocked on the door.

"Enter," came the captain's gruff response.

Ford walked in and closed the door behind him. The captain didn't look up from the report he was reading. It wasn't an unusual move. The man liked to make people cool their heels, wondering what kind of hell was about to get rained down on them. It had never worked on Ford, but he'd grown up with Kate Hartigan bringing down the heat, so it would take a whole lot to make him sweat in his shoes.

Hands clasped behind his back, he stared straight ahead. "You wanted to see me, sir?"

"You've been seen with Gina Luca," he said, eyes still on the report. "Do I need to remind you that your operation was terminated and that it is a serious violation to go rogue?"

He gritted his teeth. Cops were some gossipy assholes sometimes. "No sir."

The captain still wasn't looking at him. Instead he took out a red pen from his top drawer, uncapped it, and started to circle and cross out various words on the report. "Are you sure? I can't have a detective going wild on me—especially when the whole thing looks as suspicious as this does."

"I'm not tracking, sir."

"You aren't known for picking the runt of the litter to date, Hartigan." The captain capped his red pen, set it down next to the now-bloody report, and gave Ford a hard look. "Gina Luca is so far off your usual radar that you'd need the Hubble Telescope to find her."

For a second, all Ford could hear was white noise. Was this what it was like for Gina? Being judged every day, before she'd even opened her mouth, about what kind of person she was based on how she looked? An angry burn ignited in his stomach at the absolute unfairness of it all and at himself for never really grasping it before. She'd tried to tell him, and he'd just played it off, telling her she wasn't ugly, as if that declaration was enough. She wasn't. Not to him. But others? How she looked was all they saw.

"There are no regulations against a detective having a personal life," Ford bit out.

"Yet there are against fraternization with undesirables."

"Gina is a small business owner and respected member of the community."

"And…" The captain paused dramatically. "A Luca."

If he hadn't made the same argument to himself not a week ago, he would have been more pissed. As it was, he had to go with the facts. "There is nothing in regulation three hundred forty point six that forbids a personal relationship with a citizen in good standing, no matter their last name."

"True, but if she crosses even one tiny line, that's going to reflect poorly on you, which will reflect poorly on the task force, which will reflect poorly on *me*, and then you and I are going to have a real problem. Do I make myself clear, detective?"

"Crystal," Ford said, feeling as if he was eating a few shards of it. This whole meeting was bullshit. He was a good detective. He'd never let personal feelings interfere with a case. Ever.

"Good, because the only thing keeping me from busting you back down to the street is the fact that you're a good detective who always follows the rules. Don't make me regret my generosity." The captain turned his attention back to the report and uncapped his red pen. "Now get out of here until Monday. I suggest you spend the time between now and then figuring out how to show Rodriguez that you're not a hotheaded Hartigan like your brothers."

"Rodriguez?"

The captain let out a put-upon sigh. "Evelyn Rodriguez is coming in from the one-four to take over the task force in preparation for the Espositos' heroin shipment this Friday."

Now that was the first bit of good news he'd heard since he walked into the squad room. Rodriguez had a reputation as someone who got results the right way.

"Gallo and Ruggiero?" he asked.

"Moving to white collar." The captain started circling and crossing out again. "Now get out of here."

Ford did, driving not to his house but back to Gina's.

He parked in the driveway of her Victorian and looked up at the behemoth. Most of the inside work that needed to be done was near completion, and now Juan's crew was erecting the scaffolding that would be used to repair and paint the outside. The fact that he even knew that should weird him out. This wasn't his house. He didn't live here.

No, Hartigan, you just spend almost every night here and act as a handyman for free.

The voice in the back of his head wasn't wrong. He hadn't been back to his house for a week now. He had clothes hanging in the closet and a shaving kit under the sink. He wasn't sure how that happened. There hadn't been a plan. There hadn't been a talk. There hadn't been a list of house rules written and agreed to. He'd just accidentally moved in. What in the hell was he doing?

"Hey," Gina called out from an open window in the front room. "You coming in or what?"

Yeah, he realized. He was. And he was staying.

• • •

Gina shouldn't have let Lucy do her hair. It looked great—the woman had magic defrizzing fingers—but it was pulled back and twisted into a deceptively casual knot that left her face totally exposed.

Sure, it wasn't that Ford didn't know what she looked like, but having her hair back was like giving up a security blanket that she could sort of hide her big honking nose behind.

"We could stay in," Ford said from his spot by their open bedroom door.

Her hands flew up to her hair. "It looks that bad?"

"No, you look that hot. I don't think anyone but me should see you in that dress."

A smile—one of those goofy ones that made her look like

a fool falling in love—spread across Gina's face. She couldn't help it. Ford may tell everyone that he wasn't the charming Hartigan, but he was full of shit. The man managed to charm his way into her heart—and panties—every single day. She needed to be careful, she *knew* that, but she didn't want to. For once in her life, she was going to take her friends' advice and believe that she'd get to live the fairy tale she'd never expected—at least for a little while longer.

Her stomach growled. And dinner. She'd also get dinner.

"You promised to feed me, so no staying home tonight," she said as she crossed over to him and hooked her arm through his.

"And cannoli for dessert."

"The actual pastry this time." Last time, there'd been, well, a different kind of cannoli. Oh God, she'd never look at her favorite dessert the same way again.

"I have an order already waiting for us at Vacilli's. We can pick it up on our way home from the restaurant."

Home. She couldn't get over the thrill hearing him call the Victorian that gave her, even though part of her knew it would just make everything hurt more later when he left for good. She'd deal with that when it happened. Not tonight.

...

Crossing the bridge over into Harbor City at night after dinner out meant being surrounded by sparkling lights, people everywhere, and the big-city excitement that always sped up her heart rate. Gina had no interest in ever living on this side of the harbor—even the idea of what rents were gave her a heart attack—but visiting sure was fun.

"So where are we going?" she asked Ford after they'd parked his car in the garage and turned right on 85th Street.

"It's a surprise," he said, taking her hand and intertwining his fingers with hers.

"I hate surprises." She knew she could trust him, but still the anxiousness of not knowing what was going to happen next had her feeling twitchy. "I've had too many bad ones."

"Well, not tonight." He stopped. "We're here."

She looked up at the building and gasped. The original Vacilli's. The bakery in Waterbury was one of the franchises, but this was the real one. The windows were dark and the closed sign hung in the door, but she could still see the displays of pastries that made her mouth water. Everyone had a weakness, and hers was most definitely this. Even if she couldn't go inside, this was pretty amazing.

Then the bakery's door swung inward. An older man in an apron stood in the now-open doorway. "Detective, welcome." He turned to Gina, and a confused look flickered in his eyes for the briefest of seconds before he recovered. "And you must be Miss Luca. I understand you are a big fan of our cannoli."

"Like you wouldn't believe," she said, pushing back the familiar angry embarrassment of someone's first reaction to seeing her because she refused to let that ruin whatever Ford had planned.

"Good," the man said. "I'd hate to share the recipe with someone who didn't love them."

Recipe? Share? The only message her brain sent back was that the man's words did not compute. "What?"

The man laughed, and a real warmth filled his gaze as he looked at her. "Yes, you're here for a very special couple's baking lesson. Didn't the detective tell you?"

She turned to Ford the sneak and waggled her finger at him. "No, he's very good at keeping a secret."

"Well then, surprise," the man said. "I'm Conrad Vacilli. Come inside so we can get you set up with espressos, and I can show you how to make the most famous cannoli in

Harbor City."

Gina couldn't believe it. All the times she'd talked about how much she'd loved the Vacilli's cannoli, he'd been listening, really listening—so much so that he'd made this happen. Warmth spread through her chest, expanding outward until she couldn't believe she didn't have light shooting out of her fingertips.

She leaned forward and brushed her lips across his. "Thank you."

Ford winked at her and gave her that smile that made her stomach do the flippity-flop thing, and they walked inside the bakery together to learn the secret to making the best cannoli in the tri-state area.

Chapter Fourteen

Gina had flour on the tip of her nose, and Ford wasn't about to tell her. She'd had a perma-smile on her face for the entire drive back to Waterbury and had chattered excitedly the entire ride to her house about this detail and that detail for making cannoli.

As the street lights lit up the inside of the car as he drove down her street, he couldn't help but sneak peeks at her smile, her eyes, the joy that lit her up from the inside out. He had no idea how so many people missed it when they saw her, but Gina Luca was beautiful.

Once at her house, he followed her inside, carrying the results of their baking lesson in a white Vacilli's box, while she continued to rave about techniques and ingredients. He walked behind her so he could watch her ass sway from side to side in that yellow dress she'd put on that clung to her curves. He'd spilled a bag of flour at Vacilli's watching her move around the kitchen in that dress. It had not been his smoothest moment, but those seemed to be few and far between when he was with Gina—and that was saying something.

The woman just did things to him. She shook things up. And he liked it. A lot. Probably too much.

He should probably be worried about that. He wasn't. He was too busy wondering how, when they'd first met, he'd missed how her eyes twinkled when she smiled, how the curve of her high cheekbones perfectly highlighted her dark eyes, and how the nose she hated so much gave her a unique look that was so much her own that she redefined what beautiful could be.

"And the mixer," she said as she closed the front door after he'd walked through and flipped the deadbolt. "I cannot believe how big it was." She paused for a breath as she leaned back against the door, and her eyes went wide when she looked at him. "What's wrong?"

Not a damn thing. Everything. That he wasn't touching her. The fact that she still had clothes on.

"Ford?"

His name on her lips snapped something in him. The Vacilli's box hit the hardwood floor with a thump. His determined footsteps echoed in the foyer as he crossed over to her. She let out a soft mewl when he pressed his body against hers. He cupped her face in his hands and took her mouth like a man who had just discovered the meaning of life, because that's what he'd just realized. Gina. She was his meaning.

He couldn't get enough of her because there was no such thing. The curve of her breast. The dip of her waist. The roundness of her ass. God, she was so sweet everywhere.

He broke the kiss, gliding his lips down the long column of her neck as his hands were busy with the hem of her dress, pulling it higher and higher, desperate to feel her soft skin.

Her hands were in his hair, holding him close as he kissed along the line of her exposed collarbone. He raised his hand and brushed the back of his knuckles down the long column of her neck to the collar of the thin material of her dress. Her answering moan tipped him over the edge.

He grabbed her hips and turned her around so she faced the door and made quick work of the zipper on the back of her dress. There was no slow teasing between them, not tonight.

"Take it off." He barely recognized his own voice in the gruff command.

She turned around and reached for the light switch.

"Leave it on."

She hesitated but left it alone. Then, she let the yellow dress slide off her body to pool at her feet, her eyes on him, a sexy come-hither upward curl on her full lips. "Like what you see?"

"'Like' isn't the word I'd use." He curled a hand around her wrists and pulled her arms up above her head, pinning them to the door with one hand. "'Obsessed with' seems about right."

Eyes watching her face for her reaction, he brushed the back of his knuckles over her hard nipples, pressing against the pale pink of her sheer bra. "'Can't get enough' comes to mind."

Desire swirled in the dark depths of her hooded gaze, and he pinched her nipple through the material, and she let out a needy moan. "'Want it all' is definitely correct."

He put his leg between hers, moving it so that his thigh rubbed against her panty-covered mound. "The question is, what do *you* like?"

He unsnapped the front clasp of her bra and sucked her nipple into his mouth, raking his teeth over the hard nub. "Do you like that?"

"Yes," she said, her voice breaking.

Rolling her other nipple between his finger and thumb, he moved his leg away from touching her. She let out a frustrated groan that he felt down to his balls. He cupped her breast, rolling his thumb in circles around her nipple again and again before taking his hand lower, stopping only when he got to the top of her panties. She pushed her hips forward, silently begging for his touch. Poor Gina. She was as lost as he was. He kissed the spot where her shoulder met her throat, that pulse point that was always so sensitive to his tongue, his lips, his nipping teeth.

"Are you wet for me?" he asked against her flushed skin.

She let out a tortured moan. "Yes."

He slipped his fingers beneath the elastic of her panties, brushing against the tight curls at her apex but not going any farther. "Do you want to fuck me?"

"Yes." She bucked against his hand, undulating her hips in an obvious effort to get him to touch her where she needed him.

But he wasn't going to do that. Not yet. He needed her to understand what this was about. They weren't just fucking. Not anymore. This was more. "Do you want me to fill you up and make you mine?"

Lip caught between her teeth, she nodded. "Yes."

"I want you to be mine." It was a declaration, a promise, a prayer. He picked her up and headed for the stairs. "No one else's."

...

It was just talk, the kind of out-of-your-mind, turned-on-beyond-belief talk that didn't stay true in the light of day, but Gina wasn't going to think about that now. Not with Ford touching her like that and looking at her like he really meant it—like he'd fallen for her the way she had for him. And that's what it was, and that's what made this so good and so bad at the same time. She loved him. There wasn't any two ways about it. Ford Hartigan didn't have to make her his, she already was.

"Be careful of the wonky step," she said as he carried her up the stairs.

His grip tightened on her. "You don't have to worry when you're with me."

He brought her into the bedroom and set her down near the foot of her bed. Then, he started to unbutton his shirt, and her jelly legs decided it would be better to watch the show from the bed. Her legs were smart.

Totally unconscious of the fact that she was in her underwear while he was doing a strip tease—even if he probably wasn't thinking of it that way—Gina took in the moment, packing it away in her memory bank for a night probably not that long from now when Ford would be gone.

His shirt went first, followed by him reaching behind his head and yanking off his undershirt. That gave her an unobstructed view of his muscular chest and arm-porn-worthy biceps. She meant to stay on the bed, really she did, but her legs—smart legs, remember—had other ideas. While he flipped off his shoes, she was next to him, tracing her hands across the expanse of his shoulders, circling his flat nipples with her tongue, and lowering herself to her knees to better follow the happy trail leading from his belly button to the button of his jeans.

When he reached to unfasten it, she swept his hand aside and did it herself, watching the exquisite anticipation that made his nostrils flair and darkened his green eyes. She pushed his jeans down, then his boxers, and wrapped her hands around the base of his hard cock, stroking up and down.

"Gina," he said, the rough edge of his voice sending a thrill through her.

She cupped his balls and took a slow lick of the swollen head. "Yes?"

"You're not being nice."

Up and down she stroked. "Really? I thought I was being very nice."

The vein in his jaw ticked, visible proof of the tenuous hold he had on his control. "This is about you tonight."

"And this isn't?" she asked, twisting her grip as she moved her hand up and down his length.

He closed his eyes and said on a harsh exhale, "No."

Silly men. "You don't think I get turned on watching you fight off an orgasm?" She leaned forward and swirled her tongue around the head of his cock, relishing the salty pre-come at the tip. "Because I do." She took him in deep before letting him go. "I do a lot."

He shut up after that—unless she wanted to count the rumbling sounds of approval as he threaded his fingers through her hair and held her in place while he moved his hips back and forth with slow, precise movements that had both of them on the edge of sanity. She did not want to count that. Instead, she slid her hand between her legs and underneath her panties.

"Fuck," he said, his voice tight. "Are you playing with yourself?"

Since her mouth was busy, she just nodded.

"I want to watch you." His hands in her hair held her in place as he took a step back. "Show me."

Whatever wanton woman had taken over her body was more than willing to comply. She stood, slid her panties off, and got up on the bed. Ford watched, fisting his dick, as she spread her legs. Everything was so sensitive that it only took a few strokes with two fingers around her clit for her to be on the verge of coming.

"Yes, that's it," he said, moving closer to the edge of the bed. "Don't hold back."

She didn't. She couldn't. Fingers slick with her arousal,

she touched herself, bringing herself closer and closer with each movement until there was no holding back. The vibrations started, and in the heartbeat before her orgasm hit, she realized that Ford wasn't watching what she was doing with her fingers, he was watching her face.

...

There was no coming back from this. Ford knew it. Watching Gina come apart was almost more than he could take.

He grabbed a condom from the drawer in her bedside table and tore the wrapper open with more force than necessary, but he was using all of his conscious effort to stop himself from sinking deep within her without any protection. She opened her eyes and looked at him with lazy satisfaction in her gaze as she watched him roll on the latex.

"I think I might be done," she said, even as she caressed her tits.

He grabbed her ankles and pulled her down to the edge of the bed. "We both know that's not the case."

"That's true," she said, lifting her legs straight up.

Now that was an invitation he wasn't about to ignore. He stepped to the edge of the bed, brought her ankles to his shoulders, clutched her hips in his hands, and in one bold push, buried himself to the hilt inside her. They both let out an appreciative moan, along with a little bit of "oh my God" and "yes please." She squeezed his length and swiveled her hips in a way that had him counting back from a bazillion to keep from coming right then and there. Then, while he was still trying to stay away from the point of no return, she dug her heels into his shoulders and used them to leverage herself as she rocked against him, taking him in and out as pleasure built at the base of his spine.

He wanted to take it slow, but she felt so fucking good.

Holding onto her hips and lifting her up, he thrust forward and withdrew, again and again. She tightened around him as she begged him not to stop and then came hard on his cock. The heady scent of sex filled the air around them as the tingle in his spine spiraled out to his limbs, his balls tightened, and he came.

It took a minute for his vision to return so he could see the content, blissed-out look on Gina's face, her cheeks flushed and her brown hair a disheveled mess around her head. He'd never seen a woman more beautiful.

He should tell her. He should tell her this wasn't just for fun for him. He should tell her… "I'll be right back."

For the love of Mike, Hartigan. Man up.

Yeah, talking about his feelings like that wasn't in his makeup. So, he wimped out and went to the bathroom to clean up. By the time he got back to the bedroom, Gina's eyes were closed and she was breathing evenly. Great. He'd had his chance and he'd blown it. Next time the opportunity presented itself, he wouldn't hesitate. He'd tell her everything.

An image flashed in his mind of being in the captain's office and the conversation that had sent him to her door in the first place and all the lies of omission he'd told to get inside. Well, not everything—at least not yet. All he had to do was figure out how to make sure she wouldn't hate his guts if she ever did find out the whole truth about how he'd ended up on her doorstep.

Chapter Fifteen

Gina couldn't stop singing to herself. At the grocery store, she was humming along with some classic Supremes and executing some pretty bad—not in the good way—dance moves in the produce section. At the card shop with a wedding client looking at invitations, she hadn't even realized she was singing along with the latest bubblegum pop hit until her client joined in. And now, here she was in the kitchen making coffee and shaking her ass to the music coming from the front of the house, where Juan and his crew were putting the finishing touches on the totally renovated front porch that would no longer try to eat people. It was a great fucking day and a testament to the power of getting laid on the regular.

"Well, happy morning to me," Ford said.

She turned around to see him standing in the kitchen doorway wearing only his jeans. Her breath caught. She could look at his broad shoulders and washboard abs all damn day. His dark happy trail led right to the waistband of his jeans, which were unbuttoned and hanging onto his hips by some invisible force. God, would she ever get used to that sight?

Or even better, would she ever get used to that bubbly feeling that filled her when he said her name or looked at her like he was really seeing her and not just a caricature? Being around him was better than just the contact high of hanging out with someone so hot she thought she might go up in flames. Being near Ford was like getting to feel the sun on her face after a long winter, and it was about the happiest and most hopeful feeling she'd ever had.

"Coffee?"

"Not exactly what I'm in the mood for," he said as he walked over to where she stood by the coffeemaker. "But I do have to head out pretty soon, so I can head back to my house and change before my shift."

She poured a cup and handed it to him. "They don't allow half-dressed detectives?"

"No, that's totally against the rules."

"They need to rethink that one." She leaned in and inhaled his clean man scent before giving in and kissing the love bite she'd left last night, right where his shoulder met his neck. "I'd confess to just about anything if it meant I got to see you looking like this again."

He set his coffee down on the counter and reached behind her to cup her ass, giving it a playful squeeze. "Is there something you need to confess?"

"Well, officer," she said, trailing her fingers across his chest. "I'm afraid I have been a very bad girl."

He let out a harsh groan and lifted her up, so she had no choice but to wrap her legs around his waist. Good thing that was pretty much all she wanted to do anytime she was anywhere near him anyway.

"Oh, Detective Hartigan," she said, curling her hands around his neck and leaning in to whisper in his ear. "I think you *like* it when I've been bad."

"You have no idea." He pressed her more firmly against

him.

She undulated her hips again, rubbing her cotton-panty-covered core against the hard evidence of just how much he liked it. "I think I do."

"Tell me you don't have plans tonight."

Mentally checking her calendar made her groan. "I have a pre-engagement party meeting with new clients tonight, but I'll be done by eight."

He let out a sigh and lowered her to the ground but kept his arms around her waist, holding her close. "You can't just tell them to book a restaurant and leave it at that?"

"No." Did the man not understand that her job was to facilitate and promote the fantasy of romance and its effervescent, everlasting qualities? "Some people like more of a public show than that."

"Why?" he asked, his fingers busy drawing circles on the rise of her ass in the most distracting of ways.

"Because they're in love," she said, desperately trying to put words together in a way that didn't end up with her saying *kiss me, you fool*. "And they want to share that with their family, their friends, and the whole world. Shout it from the rooftops."

Ford picked her up and set her down on the kitchen counter where everything between them had started and kissed his way down her neck, his hands sliding under her tank top to caress her breasts. It melted her in all the right spots and made her do that stupid happy sigh hopeful thing.

It was hard—like bypassing the emergency chocolate when she was PMSing hard—but she put her palms to his chest and pushed him back. "You've got to stop or you'll be late for work."

"Now who's the one who doesn't want to break the rules?" he asked with a teasing smile.

"Detective Hartigan, you have criminals to catch, which

means you'll have to wait until tonight to solve the mystery of what panties I'm wearing."

The look on his face confirmed she'd scored big. There was no doubt in her mind that he'd be wondering about her panties all day. Oops.

Then, he glanced over, and the I'm-gonna-sex-you-up look transformed into the curious expression he'd had before he'd checked out the back shed that hadn't been opened in forever and came out with six mousetraps. Used mousetraps. It had been nasty.

"What's that?" he asked, tapping the top of the box.

"No clue. My brothers dropped it off and told me not to peek."

Ford tensed. "Do they do that often?"

"Not really." Okay, it happened every once in a while, but it had always been a surprise for a family member—earrings for their mom's birthday, hockey tickets for her. Suddenly, though, seeing it through the eyes of a detective, the box Rocco had left started to look more sinister, and she hated that. Her family and Ford's work stayed separate. They had to in order to make this whatever-it-was work. "They don't bring their work to my house."

Curious face got replaced with cop face. "Work?"

It was a single word, but it carried so much meaning. They weren't lovers from different sides of the track. They weren't Romeo and Juliet—although thank God for that, considering how *that* ended. But her last name hung over them like a lead weight held up by a fraying rope. Someday, it was going to come down and land on them, no matter how hard they both wanted to ignore it. She may not be doing anything illegal, but that didn't mean she wasn't tainted.

What saved everything from going straight to shit was the fact that they'd been upfront and honest with each other since the beginning. They didn't lie to each other. Ever. It was the one rule that Gina needed people to keep, especially after what had happened that had led to her getting that awful nickname in high school. It had taken years to trust a man after that.

Ford pulled away and fastened the top button of his jeans, his gaze shifting over to the box before he spoke again. "Gina…"

She hated the way he'd just said her name. "Ford, stop. It's probably just a surprise gift for when the house renovations are done. Paul and Rocco like to do little things like that. It's nothing that should change this." She reached out and put her hand on his chest above his heart. "I trust you. I need you to trust me, too."

He glanced up from the box, then back down again before bringing the full force of his attention to her. "I do."

"Good, then we don't have anything to worry about," she said with more cheer than she felt at the moment, but so determined to make the best of what could be a weird situation when everything between them was so new. "I'll be done by eight. You want to meet up after?"

"Sure." He gave her a quick kiss. "Let's grab a beer at Marino's."

The nerves making her heart beat in a jerky pattern calmed, and she let out the breath she'd been holding. "Sounds perfect. I'll see you then."

He gave her a wink and walked out of the kitchen, giving her a perfect view of his ass as he did so. Damn. The man's ass was truly a thing of beauty. How had this happened to her? From Kiss Cam to flirty kisses in her kitchen and so much more upstairs, her life—an undateable's life—had taken a turn for the much better, and she promised herself that she'd enjoy the ride for as long as it lasted.

By the time Gina walked into Marino's, she wasn't humming any more.

Her newest clients didn't know what they wanted to do for their pre-engagement party, but they sure didn't want to do any of the eight million things that Gina had proposed. Some days, clients were the absolute worst.

She had to scan the crowd a few times before she spotted Ford in the back of the bar near the dartboards. He was standing with a bunch of guys that she could tell were cops even from across the room. There was just something about their stance, the way they scanned the crowd with suspicion, that gave them away in an instant. Of course, the fact that Marino's was one of the most popular cop bars in Waterbury made it a pretty solid bet that almost everyone in here either had a badge or wanted someone with one.

Just as she started toward the dartboards, Ford turned. She knew the moment he spotted her, and her step faltered in response to the uptick in her pulse and the way her bra suddenly felt way too tight. He started toward her, and she forced herself to keep walking, although swooning kinda seemed like a possibility. Good Lord, what was happening to her?

Oh Regina, you are in so much trouble.

She pushed the thought away to the very darkest back corner of her mind, determined to enjoy the limited time with Ford while she could.

"Hey there," Ford said when they met at the halfway point. "It was starting to feel like you were never going to get here. How were the happy couple?"

She rolled her eyes. "Pains in my ass."

He laughed. "Then that means you need a beer immediately. Why don't you sit here, and I'll go grab us some?"

"That sounds phenomenal." Almost as good as getting to

sit down next to Ford. "I'm gonna dip into the ladies' room, but I'll meet you back here."

The walk to the bathroom was a short one, but Marino's was crowded. She maneuvered around people, but with each step she couldn't shake the feeling that everyone was watching her, judging her—and finding her lacking. It made her skin crawl and her breaths come in faster and faster bursts. The free-floating anxiety reminded her of all the times she'd walked down the halls in school and heard the whispers and giggles behind her back. She tried to shake it off, but her anxiety just responded with a fuck-you that made her lungs pinch.

Maybe it was just a side effect of having the last name Luca and walking into a cop bar, but her skin was burning by the time she finally made it into the blessedly empty restroom.

She rushed into one of the stalls and shut the door behind her, shoving the lock in place. Only then could she finally take a deep breath. All of this time spent with Ford, waiting for the other shoe to drop, was really starting to get to her.

The outside door to the restroom swung open, letting in the sound of the band warming up in the main bar.

"Oh my God, did you see her?" a woman said. "I wonder if he lost a bet. You know how the guys in that squad are always pulling pranks."

"That at least makes sense. I mean, there's no way he'd pick her over you, Patrice," a second woman responded.

"I mean really, how do you even kiss someone when their nose is that big?" the first woman asked. "I wonder if it gets in the way during blow jobs."

The sound of the women's giggling filled the bathroom as Gina stood in the stall and prayed that they weren't talking about her, even though she knew in her gut they were.

"Oh well," the first woman said. "It's Ford's loss."

"I second that."

The door squeaked again, and the sound of the band filled the bathroom before the door swung shut. Gina stayed in the stall, strangely calm. This was familiar ground. Really, she was past due for a reminder of the way the world worked. She'd spent the past month in a kind of Ford-shaped cocoon and had forgotten just what the real world was like for the women who didn't fit into the mold of what society found acceptable.

She and Ford were never going to work out. They'd both known that from the beginning, which is why they'd promised each other not to think it was more than it was. Too bad she'd fucked that up by falling for him.

She opened the stall door and walked to the sink and, as she washed her hands, she considered the situation. The best parts of her day had become the moments she spent with him, laughing over things that probably no one else would find funny. Seeing him had become something that helped get her through a bad meeting with a client or the bad news of a renovation estimate increase from Juan. She looked at herself in the mirror under the unflattering-even-if-you're-a-supermodel florescent bathroom light, and the truth was written all over her face.

"You idiot," she told her reflection. "You love him."

Ugly girls from mobbed-up families like her should know better than to fall for hot cops like Ford Hartigan. It never ended well—and end it had to.

Mind made up, she walked out of the bathroom with her chin high. If anyone was watching as she made her way over to Ford, she didn't notice and didn't care. Fuck them. She was leaving.

"Everything okay?" Ford asked as he handed her a beer.

"I need to go home." She set the beer down on the table and pushed it over to his side. "Sorry."

"Okay." He pushed his chair back and stood. "I'll

drive, and we can swing back by and pick up your car in the morning."

"No." Dammit, her chin started trembling. She needed to get out of here. "I need to go by myself. I'll talk to you later."

She rushed out of Marino's, the warm late-spring air hitting her as soon as she walked out onto the sidewalk. Of course, it meant her hair was going to frizz immediately, but that didn't matter. Not anymore.

The bar door swung open behind her and Ford marched out, heading straight for her.

"What happened? Did I do something to piss you off?"

"It doesn't matter." She took in a shaky breath. "I just need to go home."

"Gina." He took her hand in his much bigger one. "Please talk to me."

Looking up at him, she saw everything she'd ever thought she wanted in a guy. He was kind, smart, funny, and he made her feel like she was someone special, someone who was wanted just for who she was. God, what an idiot she'd been to think that was possible.

She tugged her hand free.

"I can't do this any more, Ford," she said before she lost her nerve. "It's been nice to pretend for once that this thing between us was something that could happen. But we both know it can't, not for the long term, and I'd forgotten that until tonight. I can't afford to forget it any longer."

Ford narrowed his gaze, his green eyes crinkling at the edges with confusion. "What are you talking about?"

"Look, my family and your job don't mix." It wasn't *not* true. It just wasn't the whole truth, and at this point she wasn't sure she could give him that. So much for always being honest with each other.

He crossed his arms and stood looking at her like she was talking crazy. "It's a good thing I'm not dating your family, then."

Ugh. Why did he have to be so frustrating?

"You know what I mean," she said, her voice just below a shout, because if she was going to make an ass out of herself on the sidewalk in front of Marino's with people slowing their pace so they could listen in for a second before walking inside, then she might as well go total fishwife about it.

"No, I know that you're feeding me a bunch of bullshit right now," he hollered back. "What is this about?"

He wasn't going to let it go. He was too stubborn for that.

"Do I have to say it?" she asked, her voice cracking.

Ford's face softened, and he took a step forward, reaching for her. "I guess so, because I'm not getting it at all."

Avoiding his touch was the last thing she wanted, but she couldn't let him touch her. Not now, not if she actually wanted to get the truth out and be done with this horrible conversation. She took a deep breath, pushed her hair back behind her ears, lifted her chin, and stepped into the light coming off the red neon Marino's sign above the door. Might as well let him really get a good look.

"We both know I'm not the girl who ends up with a happily ever after with a guy like you, so I need to walk away now while I still can."

Chapter Sixteen

Ford couldn't think of a single thing to say. It wasn't just because he wasn't the charming Hartigan, it was because he really had no fucking clue how to respond with words to such an asinine comment.

So he didn't even try.

He simply closed the distance between them, took Gina's face between his hands, and kissed the ever-loving hell out of her. It wasn't a particularly nice kiss or a gentle one. He didn't mean for it to be.

When she opened her mouth in surprise, he deepened the kiss with a ferocious need that had him straining against his own sense of self-control. On some level, he knew they were standing in front of Marino's with people weaving around them on their way into the bar, but he didn't give a shit. This wasn't about those people.

It was about him and Gina.

So he kissed her like a man who believed that if he did it right, she'd forget that anyone had ever called her awful names or made her feel like she wasn't everything a man could want.

"Get a room, Hartigan," someone hollered.

The words cut through the haze of need surrounding him, and he broke the kiss.

"That is what I think about how you look," he said, his breath ragged exhales of frustration. "I can't be around you and not want to do exactly that. All the time. Even when we were on that damn Kiss Cam at the wedding."

Gina blinked away the wetness in her eyes. "You don't have to lie. I know what I look like."

That was it. He couldn't take it. If he didn't get this out now, he was going to explode. He grabbed her hand and pulled her around to the side of Marino's and into the walkway that led to the closed beer garden.

"Where are we going?" she asked, keeping pace with him on those long, amazing legs of hers.

He didn't answer her question. He couldn't. He didn't trust himself with words right now, not where they could be seen.

Inside the alley, he brought them both to a standstill just inside the wrought iron fence surrounding the beer garden. He gave the area a quick look-see. The ivy lining the walls was coming in, and flowers had started to bloom, but no one else was there. Thank fucking God, because he wasn't sure he'd be able to hold onto his control long enough to make them leave.

Still holding Gina's hand and with no intention of letting her go, he marched through to the back corner, where they could finally get the privacy he needed for this. Once there, he dropped her hand and stood to one side so he wasn't blocking her in. The last thing he wanted was for her to feel like she was trapped. She could go. He wouldn't stop her. However, he prayed with everything he had in that moment that she'd stay and listen to what he had to say, because she needed to hear it. She needed to understand.

"You want to know what I see when I look at you?" he said, unable to keep the rough edge out of his voice. "I see a woman who makes me absolutely insane."

"Thank you," she said, sarcasm thick in her tone. "What a compliment."

This woman was going to kill him. She had no idea what she did to him. Getting all emotive wasn't his thing. He was Irish, for the love of Mike. His people didn't do those crazy public declarations her clients seemed to love. So here he was, staring at the woman who'd turned his life upside down, with no fucking clue what to say. And yet, the words came anyway.

"I can't get through five minutes without thinking of that sweet mouth of yours, or the way when you laugh when you throw back your head and just let it go. The best part of my day is making you laugh and watching how your eyes seem to just glow with happiness. I think about how, when you look at me, you're really looking at me and not at a cop or one of the wild Hartigan clan. You see me." He took a step back, then another, and another, until his back was against the ivy-covered brick wall farthest away from her. "And when I look at you, I don't see a beautiful woman. I see *you*, and that's better than any fucking beauty queen. So, if you need to go home. I won't stop you."

Her head was angled away from him so he couldn't see her expression, as she walked away from him. One step. Two steps. Three steps. Each one leaving his blood colder than the last. Then, at the arbor leading into this isolated section of the beer garden, she stopped.

"You're gonna break me, Ford Hartigan," she said, her voice ragged and her back still to him.

"I won't. Trust me." And he meant it. He meant it completely.

She turned and the next thing he knew she was in his

arms, her mouth on his, her hands yanking at his T-shirt, pulling it out of his jeans. There was so much desperate need running through him that the desire flooding through his blood tipped him over the edge of sanity—or maybe it was the way Gina's lips felt on his, the way her tongue dared him to take them higher, or it could have been the way she seemed unable to all but attack him, too. He didn't care that they were in the empty beer garden at Marino's or that if they got arrested for indecent exposure it would be the least of his worries. He needed her now.

His hands went to her skirt, a flirty piece of red material that had swirled around her thighs when she'd stormed out of the bar. Reaching beneath it, he slid his palms up the outside of her thighs and over the generous curve of her hips. So distracted by the taste of her mouth, it took a moment for the reality of what he was feeling to make sense.

"You're not wearing panties."

"They seemed to slow things down," she said as she kissed her way down his neck, her hands busy with the button on his jeans. "This seemed smarter."

"You have the sexiest brain in the world." Hell, everything about her was sexy—the dip of her waist, the needy moan she let out when he glided his fingers inside her already wet pussy, the feel of her clenching around his fingers. "Jesus, Gina. You feel so damn good."

He loved seeing her like this, so wanton and free of all the baggage that she carried around all the time. It made him want to push her, give her everything, let her have more than she thought she could take, just so she could have it all. In and out, he moved his fingers inside her, rubbing and stroking the soft swollen lips as she stood there, legs spread, head back, taking it all.

She worked the button of his jeans free and slid her hand inside, curling her fingers around his hard cock. "I need you inside me."

"What, you're not going to come for me first?" He pushed a third finger inside her, twisting and turning them together. "I want to feel you come. Show me how you'd take my cock."

"Ford." His name came out like such a sweet plea.

Right behind her moan came the sound of Marino's customers—his fellow officers—passing by the walkway. Gina must have heard them, too, because her hips faltered.

"Oh no." He plunged his fingers deeper, added the pressure of his thumb to her clit, swirling it around the sensitive bundle of nerves there. "You don't get to stop. You just have to be quiet. Can you do that?"

...

Gina was going to lose her mind with Ford's fingers inside her and a bar full of cops on the other side of the brick wall she was leaning against. The voices from people walking by still echoed in her head, and for half a second a dark memory from her past tried to push to the front. A public place. A man she couldn't get enough of. Losing herself to the moment. The crushing weight of mortification afterward that knocked something loose forever. That recollection tried to take hold, but she shoved it away. This wasn't then. She could trust Ford. He'd never lie to her like that.

He must have sensed her hesitation, because he stopped that wonderful thing he was doing with his fingers. "Do you want to stop?"

She shook her head.

"Gina, look at me," he said. "I need to know you're okay with this."

Okay with it? That didn't begin to describe it. She wanted Ford more than she'd ever wanted anyone and she needed him right now. She lifted her head, never more sure of anything.

"I don't want your fingers." Her hands went to his jeans again, taking down the zipper with a ruthless efficiency born of desperate need. "I want you."

Something crackled and sizzled in the air around them as he stared at her, lust swirling in his green eyes. Then everything happened almost at once. His fingers were gone from her wet folds. He grabbed his wallet and pulled out a condom, rolling it on before she'd had a chance to process that he'd ripped the foil package open. Then his hands were on her hips and he spun her around so she faced the wall.

The thrill of anticipation zinged through her as she pressed her palms to the cool brick and spread her legs wide.

"I can't do slow and easy right now, Gina." He flipped her skirt up and exhaled a hiss of appreciation as his palm caressed her bare ass. "I'm gonna fuck you hard and fast. Are you ready for that?"

She had a response ready, a good one, but before she could say it, she looked over her shoulder at Ford and everything in her brain scattered. He stood there, his T-shirt rumpled, his jeans shoved down to mid-thigh, and his hand wrapped around his cock as he looked at her with an intensity that made this feel more like a claiming than fucking. Her core clenched in response, and she arched her back in invitation.

It was one he didn't turn down. He lined his cock up with her wet, swollen entrance and plunged inside her, so deep she felt him everywhere.

"You are so tight," he said, his voice raw with need, as he withdrew and thrust forward. "I can't get enough of this. I can't get enough of you."

Words. They were in her head but they were beyond her as she rocked back against him, meeting his every push forward and undulating her hips to change the angle so that with every forward plunge into her, he rubbed against that spot just inside her entrance that made her toes curl and the tight ball of energy inside her tighten and expand at the same time.

"Ford," she cried out, closing her eyes and letting her head drop. "Please."

She didn't know what she was begging for, she just needed it.

"Is this what you want?" His slid his hand from her hip to her abdomen and lower. He parted her tight curls with two fingers and circled her clit—soft and hard, fast and slow—until the only thing tethering her to earth was him. It was too much and not enough, and she needed it all.

The brick wall ate into her palms as she pushed against it and thrust backward to meet him. Again and again they moved together and apart until her thighs started to tingle and her orgasm hit her like a lightning bolt that exploded inside her, filling her with a blinding light and fullness. His hand came over her mouth to muffle her cries as he fucked her through her climax, his chest pressed to her back.

"Gina," Ford called her name in a guttural whisper and came hard inside her.

The world came back to her in bits and pieces, slowly, as if time or their location didn't matter. The feel of Ford against her. The smell of the flowers starting to bloom. The unconcerned chatter of people walking along the sidewalk on the other side of the beer garden. Ford kissed the back of her neck and withdrew, getting rid of the condom in one of the nearby trashcans as she stood and let her skirt fall back into place. They grinned at each other like they'd just gotten away with stealing the Hope Diamond, that post-sex high too strong to let reality intrude.

Once he had himself tucked away and fastened his jeans—necessary, if unfortunate—he took her hand and they walked to the beer garden's dark entrance. There he paused and looked around, making sure no one was heading their way from the sidewalk in front of Marino's.

"Okay." He started walking forward. "The coast is clear."

The fact that he'd bothered to make sure no one would see them come out of the beer garden probably looking every bit like they'd just screwed each other's brains out, that he'd protected her like that, made a comforted warmth spill through her.

True, he hadn't said he loved her in that speech of his, but he'd surely meant it. Why else would he have said all that?

She may not need a man in her life to make her happy, but with Ford holding her hand as they walked to his car, she was finally beginning to believe that she was going to get everything she hadn't let herself believe she wanted.

Chapter Seventeen

The Hartigan house was, once again, in total chaos. Gina kinda loved it.

"So, no Honeypot?" she asked Felicia, the smallest and quietest Hartigan who, unlike the rest of the brood, lived across the bridge in Harbor City with her billionaire fiancé, Hudson, and her one-eyed cat.

"No way," Felicia said, pushing up her glasses. "She has been banished from this and all future family functions. That was the edict that came down from on high."

"You mean Kate?" Gina asked as she spooned potato salad on her plate, since today's lunch was being served buffet style to accommodate everyone who wanted to watch the hockey game playing in the living room. The fact that it was the playoffs do-or-die time of the year was the only reason Kate had relented to the many pleas of her family.

"You can't go higher than Mom," Felicia said with a chuckle as she and Hudson made their way through the line behind Gina.

"How did you come up with the name Honeypot?"

Felicia's whole face lit up. "It's the kind of ants I study."

"I've never heard of them, what are they like?" That seemed like a nicer way of saying she'd always thought an ant was an ant was an ant.

"Don't ask," Hudson interrupted, his face an exaggerated mask of disgust. "They are gross."

Felicia turned to her fiancé with a teasing gasp. "How can you hate on the ant that brought us together?"

"Easily." He gave a mock shudder.

And that's pretty much how lunch went. She chatted with all of the various Hartigan members and those like herself who'd been brought into the fold, including the guy Fallon had brought, Kyle. He worked out of the same precinct as Ford but was still in uniform. When she'd asked how he'd met Fallon, he responded with a shrug of his shoulders and made a comment about cops and nurses always seeming to end up together.

"I know, he's an ass," Fallon told her later while they were watching the Ice Knights get killed in the second period. "But his dick is magnificent."

Gina almost choked on her bite of fried chicken. "You can't say that. Someone might hear." She looked around, but everyone's attention was glued to the TV.

"They'll live." Fallon shrugged and took a bite of her drumstick. "Trust me, with Frankie here, they have definitely heard worse."

That was probably true. Frankie seemed to have been born without a filter and, as he liked to put it, a humble bone in his body. The man was a certified mess, but a fun one. Looking around at the Hartigan clan, who'd made her feel right at home, Gina realized that Ford wasn't anywhere around. And that's when she got a gloriously delicious idea that involved *his* magnificent dick and a quickie in the farthest-away room with a lock. All she had to do was find him.

"I'll be right back," she told Fallon, figuring the kitchen was the likeliest spot. "I'm gonna go get some more water."

Mind made up, she walked out of the crowded living room, more than ready to keep looking until she found him. She didn't have to look far. Ford was in the kitchen with Kyle. They both had their backs to her as they loaded up their plates with more food.

Found ya. She was about to say something when Kyle spoke first.

"I thought the shit assignment you got to shadow the Luca girl for intel on her brothers was over?"

"Shut your mouth, Carlin," Ford said. "We don't discuss business outside the squad room."

Gina froze, trying to make sense of the words.

"And man, I thought Gallo had been exaggerating about how she looked, but he was most def not," Kyle went on, his back to her as he poured gravy over his mashed potatoes. "Bruh, you have taken one for the entire squad. You should be getting hazard pay."

The water glass almost slipped from her hand as realization set in. Shadowing her because of her brothers? She'd been an idiot. Again. He hadn't wanted her. He'd wanted to nail her brothers. All of the little questions about her family he'd peppered her with and the way he'd worked the room at her grandmother's party, it hadn't been because he wanted to get to know her, because he was falling for her like she had fallen for him. It had been because he was working a case.

"Yeah, he should be getting hazard pay." She barely recognizing the ragged voice as her own. "There has to be a regulation for it somewhere, I'm sure."

Both men turned, but she didn't bother to look at Kyle. He wasn't the one who mattered here. Ford was. And he looked as guilty as a kid caught with an empty ice cream container and a mouth smeared with Cookies 'N Cream.

Trust me, he'd said, *I see you.*

She had.

Now she was done.

Inhaling a deep breath, she turned and walked out of the kitchen. The world may have finally dropped open underneath her, but she hadn't fallen into the hole and she wasn't about to act as if she'd been raised without manners—even if she'd been raised by criminals.

"Gina," Ford called out. "Please, wait."

Refusing to stop, she kept going into the living room. Kate and Fallon took one look at her and their faces darkened with concern.

"What happened?" Fallon asked, rushing over.

Kate reached out to her. "Honey, are you okay?"

Not in the least. All the time she'd spent with Ford had been a fantasy, a fairy tale. But instead of getting a happy ending, she felt like her entire insides had been scooped out and she was just a hallow shell standing in the Hartigan's living room.

"I will be just fine," she said, her voice so much steadier than her legs felt at the moment. "Thank you very much for everything, but I have to go."

Not waiting for a response, because this empty feeling wouldn't last forever and that meant her emotions were a ticking time bomb, she turned and started toward the door.

Ford stood in front of the door, all the color washed from his face. "Gina, please hear me out."

Isn't that what she did last time after overhearing the badge bunnies in the bathroom? She'd known they were right, that he couldn't really be that into her, but she hadn't wanted them to be. So she'd listened to him. And there'd been other times when that itchy feeling at the back of her neck had warned her that this wasn't going to work out like she wanted. She'd ignored it. Listened to him instead.

After everything she'd been through, all the humiliations and embarrassments, she would have thought she had a super sense about it by now.

"Did Kyle lie about me being a job?" she asked, half-wanting to hear him deny it.

Ford opened his mouth, but nothing came out.

"Not fast enough on the cover story this time, huh? You probably should have held onto that gem of 'I see you' for another girl." Pain. It was everywhere. Her chest. Her throat. Her eyes. Her stomach. They all ached like she'd been hit by a truck. The need to get out of the Hartigans' house went from a need to a life-or-death necessity. She pressed through the bone-deep ache and walked to the door, stopping right in front of Ford, and looked him in the eye. "But believe me, now I see you, too. Please move."

He opened his mouth as if to argue, but he must have seen in her face that she wasn't going to listen. He stepped aside.

She walked out of the house without looking back, using all of her concentration to put one foot in front of the other until she got to the end of the block, where she called an Uber and wondered just how far away the driver would take her if she begged.

...

All of Ford's policing skills left him the moment Gina walked out of the house, because he couldn't detect his way out of a paper bag. First, he hesitated in the doorway, the click of her shutting it echoing in his skull, staring at it as if she was going to come back if he just stared at it long enough. When realization finally dawned, he yanked the door open with enough force that it bounced off the wall and shook the family photos lining the entryway and took off down the street. He had a fifty-fifty chance of picking the right direction and, of course, went the wrong way, correcting his mistake just in time to see Gina get in the back of a car with an Uber sticker and drive off.

You know where she's going. You can just go home and—

But the Victorian wasn't his home. It never had been. It was just the place that had felt like it because she was there. He forced his feet to work, to move one in front of the other, and get him back to his parents' house so he could figure out his next move—because he had no idea what to do next.

If he could just talk to her...but that wasn't his way. It never had been.

He didn't charm. He didn't emote. He followed rules and standard operating procedures. If there was a guidebook for what to do after fucking up this bad, he hadn't read it.

Fallon was waiting for him, her hands planted on her hips, when he walked through the front door. Kyle stood just behind her. It took everything Ford had not to punch the douchebag just for the satisfaction of watching him go down. That wasn't going to happen, though, because his mom was standing right beside the loud-mouthed dick. Faith and Finian stood right behind her, glowering at him.

"What in the hell did you do?" she asked.

Everything wrong, but he wasn't about to admit it. "What were you thinking by bringing that asshole here?"

Kyle let out an offended squawk. "I'm not an asshole."

Ford and Fallon turned on him as a unit. "Yes, you are."

Kyle's gaze went from Ford to Fallon and back again before he grumbled something that sounded a lot like *crazy fucking Hartigans* and stormed out of the house. The only thing better than watching Kyle walk out would have been seeing Gina stroll back in—a fact that landed like a punch to the kidneys.

"Don't let the door hit you on the way out," Fallon hollered after him, turning with a smile toward Ford. That moment of agreement at taking out the trash, though, disappeared faster than donuts in the break room.

"What did you do?" she asked.

He looked from his sister's pissed-off expression to his mom's concerned one and told them what he could. "My job."

"How's that?" Finian asked.

They weren't this dense. He was a cop, for the love of Mike. They had to understand the conflict here. "You know who her brothers are."

"So?" Faith asked, putting so much annoyance in that one word that it was like she'd just watched the best person in *her* life walk out the door. "That doesn't explain what *you* did."

What did he do? He tapped his thumb and finger together in a fast beat, not wanting to fess up because what he'd done was shitty—totally justified, yes—but totally shitty. Letting out a deep breath, he let the truth of just what he'd done into the light so they could all see the ugly of it all.

"I was assigned to watch her and find out if we could learn anything from the family angle."

His mom gasped and made the sign of the cross. "You mean this whole time you've been pretending to date her for a case?"

"No." He shook his head. "It was never like that—not once we started dating."

"Then spit it out before the girls throat-punch you," Finian said, looking like he just might deliver a blow himself.

Their mom cut a death glare at his brother and sisters. "There will be no punching in this house, thank you very much."

"Thanks, Mom," he said.

She turned her angry stare to him. "Save your thanks for God, who is obviously looking out for you, since I haven't boxed your ears yet. Now spit out the whole story."

So he did—well, as much of it as he could, from the Kiss Cam to the cover story to get into Gina's house to the suspension to the ice-pick-to-the-balls moment when Gina had walked into the kitchen and overheard Kyle the moron.

"You let that sweet girl believe her grandfather might have been murdered to get into her house?" his mom asked, shaking her head in disbelief.

His frustration at himself spilled out and his voice rose. "He was Big Nose Tommy, there was a high probability of it."

"But you highly doubted from the beginning that that was the case," Finian said.

"Yeah." In the beginning, it hadn't seemed like that big of a deal, but after getting to know Gina, having to admit it was like being hit with a haymaker of his own stupidity right in the nose.

Fallon shook her head. "And then after all of that was put to bed and you two got serious, you never told her?"

And there it was, the knockout punch. "No."

Everyone gathered in the entryway wore identical expressions that roughly translated to *there never was a dumber man than Ford Hartigan.* He couldn't argue the point.

The whole time, he'd figured it would be something Gina's rule-breaking family would do that would mess everything up. Instead, he'd done it all by himself.

"Well, what are you going to do now?" Faith asked.

Ford wished like hell there was a procedure manual for this. "I have no clue."

Chapter Eighteen

Ford had barely sat his ass in his chair Friday morning before his name rang out over the squad room.

"Hartigan," the captain yelled. "My office."

When he walked into the office and saw that the new task force lead, Rodriguez, was already there, he knew this wasn't just another meeting. The captain got introductions out of the way with his usual pondering efficiency, and then he and Rodriguez sat down.

Since there wasn't another chair, Ford remained standing. Judging by the look on their faces, having enough chairs hadn't been simply an overlooked detail.

"I understand you have a special in with the Luca family," Rodriguez said, her tone neutral, but there was no missing the calculating look in her eye.

"I did." Until he'd fucked it up like an asshole.

Not a muscle moved in Rodriguez's face, but she tightened her grip on the pen in her hand. "Love has turned to dust already," she said with a sarcastic sigh. "What a shock."

"As I'd suspected it would," the captain said as he clicked

open a digital report. "Even if her last name wasn't Luca, she just didn't look like your kind of woman, Hartigan."

The death glare Rodriguez shot the captain could have been used in place of the electric chair. The captain, distracted by the report on his computer screen, missed it. Ford did not. It was so unexpected and vicious that a surprised snicker escaped before he could stop it and he had to cover the noise with a fake coughing fit.

The captain looked up, confusion making a V in his otherwise unlined forehead. "Do you need to recuse yourself to go get some water?"

Ford coughed once more for good measure and pounded on his chest. "No, sir. I'm fine."

He turned his attention back to Rodriguez, whose expression had warmed by half a degree. Considering that none of the women in his life were currently talking to him—and neither were his brothers—after what happened at family lunch, that minuscule amount of warmth felt like the first day of summer.

"We have information that the Luca brothers have been busy lately," Rodriguez said. "They've been boxing up a lot of stuff and taking it to a storage building on Elmherst. We can't confirm that it has to do with the shipment tonight, but we need to find out either way."

The Luca brothers and mystery cardboard boxes. That sounded a little too familiar. "Any idea what's inside the boxes?"

"Nope, but we think there was at least one delivered to the sister's house." She paused as if to gauge his reaction. When he didn't have one, she went on: "You don't happen to know anything about that, do you?"

"No." One word. One bald-faced lie to the woman who held his spot on the organized crime task force in her hand and the captain who held the rest of Ford's career in his.

It wasn't a great plan. It wasn't a plan at all. It was pure gut reaction. Implicating Gina in anything that had to do with her brothers was not something he was going to do when he knew she wasn't guilty of a thing. Damn the regulations and proper protocol.

Rodriguez continued, "Our informant has not been inside the Luca brothers' apartment, and we can't risk his position on the inside for answers about a couple of low-level loan sharks in case it doesn't pan out. Still, we don't want to miss anything, so we need to know what's in the boxes at the storage facility or the ones possibly at Gina Luca's residence."

"And you want me to find out?" Well, that wasn't going to happen because if he showed up on her door, she'd probably let him fall through the porch again and leave him there.

"That was the idea, but if you've lost access then we can send in someone else to poke around." Rodriguez looked down at her notes. "She's renovating her house, right? So maybe an inspector for a spot check, see if there's anything suspicious. If there is, we can get a warrant for the storage unit."

All he could picture was the box on Gina's kitchen counter, the one her brothers had left and made her promise not to look in. This was the point in the conversation where it was standard operating procedure to offer up that pertinent information.

He said nothing.

And he couldn't let another cop look in that box first. If there was something illegal inside and Gina was holding it, she could be facing charges even if she had no idea about the contents. After seeing how the Luca brothers were with their sister at the bowling alley, he couldn't imagine her brothers would set her up to take a fall. Still, he had to do whatever it took to protect her in case he was wrong. If he was the one who found out whatever was inside the box, he could vouch for her, keep her safe from any fallout. There wasn't another option.

"I can still get in."

Rodriguez didn't look impressed by his declaration. "Are you sure?"

It would mean burning whatever goodwill Gina might have left for him—which, face it, was pretty minimal at this point—but he could stop her from getting tangled up in her brothers' mess. That was worth it, even if she ended up hating him for it.

• • •

Gina looked through the narrow leaded stained glass window next to the door again. Nope. She wasn't dreaming—or having a nightmare. Ford was on her porch. He was holding a white box with the red Vacilli's logo on it. He was looking a little rough around the edges. Good. He should.

"I can see you standing there," he said.

Of course he could. She was standing in front of a window. "So?"

"Please let me in." He held up the box in his hand. "I come bearing pastry and an apology."

"Really?" The man was such an asshole. Did he really think she was that much of an idiot? "You brought cannoli? That move doesn't get you in my pants anymore."

"It's not cannoli. It's rum cake."

Oh. Toasted almonds. *Shut up, Regina. Dickhead alert. Stay focused.* "That doesn't get you laid either."

He sighed and lowered the box back down. "I'm not trying to screw you, Gina."

"Yeah, you only like to screw me over." Which, while a clever retort, was both true and depressing—like a nature documentary where the little baby hippo ends up getting eaten by a pack of lions.

"Please just let me in. We need to talk."

Her natural curiosity wondering just what he was up to joined forces with that lizard brain part of herself that still responded to him with happy sighs and excited squeals. That's how she ended up opening the door before she could stop herself. *Stupid pheromones and brain.*

"At least this saves me from having to decide between burning your stuff in my driveway or taking it to your house, so you might as well come in."

Okay, so she'd binged a few days' worth of chick-gets-revenge movies this week that had given her ideas. It wasn't like she'd followed through on any of them.

"Thanks," Ford said as he walked past her.

She did not take a big whiff as he got near. She did not check out his ass when she turned to close the door. She did check out his hands as they cradled the white box from Vacilli's. He was just in her line of sight. That's all.

"You can wait in the kitchen, I'll bring the box down."

"I can get it." He started toward the stairs leading to her room.

"No." There wasn't any way in hell that she could let him into her bedroom again. "Uninvited guests stay downstairs."

She got up to the third step before his voice stopped her.

"Gina, I'm sorry." There was a raw edge to his tone that took it an octave lower, as if he was trying to keep something inside him from breaking out. "Kyle is a dickhead but he was right, I lied to get into your house. I was assigned to be here. It wasn't by choice. I couldn't let Gallo come watch over you, not after that night in the hotel."

Her grip tightened on the banister, but she didn't turn around. She couldn't.

"I couldn't stop thinking about you, and when the captain gave me the assignment, I took it. Even then I was afraid if I did that I'd break my biggest rule and get involved with someone that I couldn't. You were an assignment and a Luca—and I didn't trust myself to follow the rules when I was around you."

This was his apology? His justification? The weak man defense?

"And after the assignment ended, it was even worse not being around you. That's why I came back after I got suspended, because I couldn't *not* see you again. I thought we could move forward without me ever having to admit what I'd done. I was wrong about that, but I wasn't wrong about us."

She was shaking. Maybe not on the outside, but inside it was the mother of all earthquakes going on because, against all odds, she wanted to believe him. She wanted to have that fairy tale. And that scared her more than anything else in this world ever could.

Not trusting what would come out of her mouth, she kept it shut tight and went up the stairs to get the box of Ford's things that she'd gone to sleep staring at every night since she'd walked out of the Haringtons' house like some sort of kicked puppy.

The box wasn't heavy, just a little awkward because of the dimensions, so she was careful carrying it back down the stairs, making sure each foot was firm on one step before putting her weight on it. That made the trip down slower than the trip up—well, that and making sure her foot didn't go through the wonky step he'd promised to fix but never had. She set the box down on the table near the front door and crossed over to the kitchen, opening her mouth to let him know she was back, but the words died on her tongue.

Ford stood by the counter next to the now-open box that her brothers had left her. The one Ford had been so curious about, but—at the time—she'd pushed away any concern about that. Why would the man practically living with her be interested in whatever surprise her brothers had left for her? He probably wouldn't. But a Waterbury detective who'd been assigned to watch her sure would be interested. He'd be so interested that he'd even sweet-talk his way into her home once again to have a look at what was inside.

Despite the awfulness of the realization, Gina stood there frozen. She would have thought she would have screamed and hollered and cried and pitched the mother of all fits. Instead, she just stood there and watched him look through the box her brothers had left.

"Do you want to know what it was? That awful thing that I wouldn't tell you about at the Wooden Barber?"

He froze, his hand still in the box. There was no missing the guilt on his face or the regret—for getting caught or for what he'd done—in his eyes.

"A million years ago, in high school, I thought I was in love with a boy. He was a year older, not super popular but well known. He'd always been nice to me, said hi in the halls and asked about my classes." In half a second, she was back there at Roosevelt High, walking the halls with only a friend or two to make it bearable. She'd been the freak, the ugliest girl in class, the one people stared at but never talked to. "It's sad to admit, but in those days having someone be kind was so much for a girl like me that I'd almost died from the hope of it all." The sympathy on Ford's face was like a knife to the heart, so she looked away, dropping her gaze to the now-opened box. "One day, we were in the library together and no one else was around. He kissed me. Then he kissed me again. And again. I was so caught up in the moment that when he took my shirt off in the back stacks, I just went with it. This boy, he liked me. I liked him. What could go wrong?"

Humiliation, hot and prickly, beat against her cheeks. She wanted to run, to hide, but she refused to give into the old feelings. Instead she'd pick at that scab and prove once and for all that it couldn't hurt her anymore. That Ford couldn't hurt her.

"Then I heard the giggles. They were quiet at first, barely tickling my consciousness. Then they got louder and louder until they pierced whatever schoolgirl dream haze had enveloped me." She raised her gaze back up, needing to see Ford's face as she told the worst part, the part that made bile rise in her throat. "Pulling back from the boy's arms, I looked around. What felt like a hundred pairs of eyes stared back at me from other students who had been hiding in the next aisle over and had peeked over the top of the shelved books to watch."

All of the old emotions, the hate and anger and betrayal, clogged her throat, forcing her to take a breath before she could go on to tell Ford about the final blow.

"'See, guys, I told you,' the boy who'd always been nice to me said. 'She's a butterface, but if you can ignore how she looks above the neck, she's got a hot bod to enjoy.' Then he'd laughed. When I burst into tears, he handed me the shirt I'd so naively taken off and asked me why I couldn't take a joke." Even today the memory stripped her bare and raw. "Up until today, that had been the worst moment of my life, burned so firmly into my mind that even the vaguest memory of it made me want to puke." She inhaled a deep breath and forced herself to go on, to deliver the final fuck-you. "But this moment of finding you looking through the box my brothers had left, after you'd said all those pretty words? That's worse. You want to know why?"

"Gina, please let me explain."

"No. You don't get to lie to me ever again," she said, her voice shaking. "Today is worse than that time in the library because this time I knew better—and I let myself hope anyway. So tell me, did you find anything interesting in there that made it all worth it?"

Ford's broad shoulders flinched. Then, he turned and

faced her. "Gina, please—"

"Oh come on now, there has to be something in there." She strode into the kitchen, powered by some kind of righteous fury she didn't have control over. "Let's have a look."

She stopped at the counter next to him and pulled the first item out of the box. "A chipped porcelain horse. I gave this to Paul when we were kids because he wanted a horse so bad, but that was not in the cards for a Luca kid. He'd cried every night for weeks. It's hard to want things with your whole heart even though you know you'll never get them." A tear slipped past her iron control. She swiped the sleeve of her shirt against her cheek roughly, then sat the horse down on the counter. Next out came a dog-eared book. "*Bridge to Terabithia*. You'll have to be sure to put in your report that this has been Rocco's favorite book since our grandpa disappeared. Well, he died, but we didn't know that for sure then. But he was old enough to have had at least an idea. Still, he kept up the pretense for me and Paul for years. He was a horrible big brother that way." She laid the book down and reached in the box and pulled out a heavy scrapbook. "Now this is probably the most devastating piece of evidence of all. A family photo album." She plopped it down on the counter and flipped it open. It was filled with all the silly casual pictures that every family had. Christmas mornings. Birthday parties. Vacations. Lazy Sundays. Graduations. "As you can plainly see. I am a Luca. That's me there. You can tell it's me because even as a baby I had a schnoz for the ages." She slammed the album shut. "So my brothers left me a box with a family album, a chipped porcelain horse, and a beloved kids book. What's that going to get them? Ten years behind bars? Fifteen? Because I look at that and I figure they've got to pay for…"

She looked at the items on the counter, and her legs stopped working. Stumbling back, she reached behind her for one of the kitchen chairs. Ford got to it first, yanking it out for her. She collapsed onto it.

"Are you okay," he asked, cupping her face and forcing her to look up into his eyes. "What do you need?"

"The box. Is there a letter?" She could barely get the words out through the emotion blocking her throat. When he didn't move fast enough, the panic took over. "The box! A letter! Get it!"

He grabbed the box off the counter and reached inside, pulling out a piece of lined paper folded in half. She wanted to cry out. She wanted to scream. She wanted to pretend that damn piece of paper wasn't in Ford's hand—but it was and she knew what that meant. Her brothers were gone.

Her hands shaking, she took the letter from Ford and opened it.

Gina,

We told you we were just waiting for the right time to start over. Seeing you with Ford made us realize that you were finally ready for us to make the break. Tell your boy that if he breaks your heart, we'll find out somehow and come back to break his knees. Sorry we couldn't stay and say goodbye, but you know this was the life we'd chosen and there are some folks who might want to have a few words if they'd known we were leaving. No need to worry about us though. We've been saving up to get out for some time. We were just waiting to make sure you'd be okay, and now we know you will with Ford by your side.

Love ya sis,
Paul and Rocco
P.S.
Your boy did as much as he could. Go easy on him.

They'd finally done it. They'd been talking about leaving Waterbury for years, but it always seemed like just talk. But it wasn't. They'd done it. And the whole time they'd been waiting for her to heal, and she hadn't realized it because for so long she wouldn't even admit to herself that she was wounded.

All that talk of accepting reality, of being alone, it had been her shield, her defensive wall, because no matter what she said, she still saw herself as the world did. She was guilty of the biggest lie of them all—lying to herself. Well, that stopped now. From this day to forever, she was going to mean it when she said she loved herself just the way she was, with or without anyone by her side. She owed her brothers that much. Hell, she owed it to herself.

Butterface was dead.

She was Regina fucking Luca, successful businesswoman with friends, a home of her own, and a life that she loved.

Her heart hurt, and she had no idea if that was from missing her brothers already even though they drove her nuts, or from a bittersweet happiness that they were finally getting their dream. She folded the letter and handed it to Ford.

"Here you go." She had no idea how she managed to keep the tremble out of her voice, but she did. "You have them dead to rights on threatening a police officer. Good luck finding them. They're in the wind for good."

Ford took the letter, opened it, and gave it a quick read. The sympathy in his eyes when he lowered it and looked at her was a punch in the gut. Good thing she could take a hit.

"And what the fuck were they talking about when they said not to blame you?" Fury and hurt swirled around inside her like a tornado of misery. "What did you do?" she asked, agony burning the inside of her throat.

He held his hands up, palms forward, as if he was trying to show he meant no harm. "I tried to help."

Help? He thought getting rid of her brothers was helping? The need to lash out, hurt him as much as she ached, made her heart slam against her ribs hard enough that she was surprised they didn't crack.

"Why does that sound familiar?" she practically screamed at him, no longer even able to pretend to be calm. "Oh yeah, I remember the last time you tried to help. Only in this case instead of me worrying you were steering my clients wrong, you forced my brothers to leave."

"No." He took a step closer. "I just told them that their line of work wasn't good for their health."

"Why, because you were going to throw them in jail? After all, you had signed up for hazard duty by pretending to like me."

"You know that's not true."

"Why, because you said so? What kind of idiot am I to believe that?" She barely got the words out before she broke, the last words coming out as raw and pained as she felt inside.

"Are you okay?" He reached out for her, but she evaded his touch. "I know you were close to your brothers, that's why I tried to help."

And this is where it got them. Her screaming in the kitchen at the man she'd thought wasn't like the others, who wanted her for her. But he hadn't. He'd only come back to see what her brothers had left behind, not because he loved her the way she loved him. And that's the thought that drained the last bit of emotion from her, leaving her cold and empty.

"I'll be just fine as soon as you're out of my house," she said softly and got up and walked toward the stairs. "Your stuff's in the box on the front table. Lock up on your way out."

She didn't wait to hear whatever bullshit would come out of Ford's mouth next before going up the stairs to her room. It didn't matter what he said. She had better things to do with her life.

Chapter Nineteen

Gina had wine, chocolate, and a sledgehammer. What could possibly go wrong?

"Let's not find out. Give me the hammer, G." Lucy held out her hand.

Shit. Did I say that out loud? Gina wobbled just a bit when she turned to face Lucy head-on. She didn't weave because of the wine. It was because the fifteen-pound sledgehammer put her off balance. Really.

"I have it for therapeutic reasons. It's DIY therapy. I should totally get my own show," Gina said, only slurring a little, which was pretty good since she had a bottle head start on Lucy and Tess wasn't a drinker. "You could be my sidekicks! Do you know how to use a circular saw?"

"Of course I can use a circular saw," Lucy said, giving Gina a dubious look. "Why don't you give me Mr. Sledge, and then you can tell me all about your show idea."

That seemed like a solid plan. The stupid hammer was getting heavy, anyway. She handed it off and grabbed the almost-empty bottle of red on her way to the couch in the front room. She sat in the middle, relaxing against the Ice Knights blanket draped over the back. It was the blanket *he* had used when he came over to spy on her. The bastard. He'd defiled the Ice Knights.

She turned her head so her nose was close to the red and silver material—thank you, big honker—and sniffed the blanket. She couldn't help it. She was weak, and he had always smelled so good—especially for a big jerk with sexy green eyes and perfect forearms. "He deserves to marry someone with a Cajun Rage tattoo."

Lucy flopped down beside her and took the wine bottle from Gina, then poured herself a glass with what was left. "I don't even know what that means."

"They're a hockey team," Tess answered as she sat down on Gina's other side. "But I have no idea what that has to do with…you know."

Pressing her lips together to keep her gaze focused—she had no idea why that helped, but it did—she surveyed her friends. They were such good people. If only Lucy could get stop doing the whole scaring the shit out of guys to push them away before they had a chance to reject her thing, and if only Tess could stop getting so freaked out anytime she was around someone she found attractive that she basically forgot how to speak, they could find love. Then they'd be happy. Or they'd find someone like Ford who'd crush their hearts under his boot. But she hoped it wasn't the second one. They deserved better than someone like Ford.

"I love you two." She put her arms around her girls. "You are so sweet to have come over."

"Are you kidding?" Lucy said. "After you told us what happened with that dick-doo-wah, I snagged a couple of shovels from the store in case we needed to help you bury a body."

And that brought tears to her eyes. Maybe she *was* kinda

drunk. But still, only a true friend would help you dispose of a body. "You're the best."

"I put the two best old-school chicks-kick-ass movies in the Netflix queue I could find," Tess announced, leaning forward so she could reach her laptop, which was set up on the coffee table to click on whichever movie they picked. "*Kill Bill* or *Thelma and Louise*? Chick with a sword or driving off the cliff?"

"Spoilers!" Lucy yelled.

Gina turned to her friend. "How can that be a spoiler? These have been out for twelve billionty years."

"Billionty?" Lucy giggled and took a drink of wine.

"It's the longest unit of time ever," Gina said in the most serious voice she could manage at the moment. "I'm a wedding planner. You can trust me."

Trust me. The phrase fell out of her mouth and boomeranged on her, smacking her right in the feels. That's what Ford said she could do with him. And she had. *You're an idiot, Regina.*

"No, you're not an idiot," Tess said, sitting up and turning to face Gina.

Shit. She'd said it out loud again. No more wine for her.

"Yeah," Lucy chimed in. "Don't be mean to my friend. She's a pretty cool chick."

"I'm sorry, guys." She let out a sigh and did some fast blinks to get rid of the tears making her vision all watery. "This whole thing just brought back a lot of stuff I thought I'd gotten past. You know, I thought if I acknowledged my own undateabilty that it would make everything easier."

"But it didn't?" Tess asked.

Gina just shook her her head. The double friend sandwich hug was immediate. She really did have the best friends.

"Nope, the thing is—" she said, getting a mouthful of Tess's auburn hair as she spoke, cutting off what she was about to say.

That set off a giggle fit between all three of them that lasted through a trip to the kitchen for more chocolate and then coming back with everyone's glasses refilled—Lucy with wine, Tess with Pibb Xtra, and her with water.

"What's the thing?" Lucy asked once all three of them were back on the couch.

Gina took a deep breath and tried to think of prettier words to use, but the only ones that came to her head were the plain, unvarnished, rough-around-the-edges truth. "The thing is that this is me. Sure, I could have plastic surgery and tweak this and alter that, but I don't want to. More power to anyone who wants to go that route, but it's not for me. I don't want to get a makeover. I don't want to change my face. I just want a man who sees me and doesn't see the ugly girl. He sees *me* and he loves *me*, not in spite of my face but in part because of it." She'd never verbalized it before, but it was true, and putting the words out there lifted a weight off her shoulders that she hadn't realized she'd been carrying.

The truth was, she didn't want to be a beauty queen. She wanted to be herself, and no one could stop her from being the best her she could be unless she let them, which she sure as hell wasn't going to. "And if that doesn't happen, I'm okay with that. I like me just the way I am."

Tess gave Gina's shoulders a squeeze. "We like you, too."

"Lies," Lucy hollered, the wine obviously kicking in. "We love you—just the way you are."

"Thank you, Mr. Darcy," Gina said.

"You're quite welcome," she said in the world's worst British accent, which got the three of them giggling again.

And as inappropriate as it may have been, they continued to giggle and cheer all the way through *Kill Bill*—because some days, watching a kickass female with a sword and a bad attitude was what a woman needed to get through a heartbreak.

...

Ford stared at the beer mug sitting on the bar. He'd been sitting on the same barstool at Marino's for two hours in the middle of the afternoon and in that time, he'd watched the foamy head on his beer disappear but hadn't taken a single drink. It wasn't that he didn't want to drink. He wanted to have *all* the drinks. But he lived too far away from Marino's to walk, and in his present dark mood he wasn't sure he could stop at one or two or twenty-five, and he wasn't getting behind the wheel after that.

So instead of drinking the beer, he stared at it until the lack of condensation dripping down the outside of the mug proved the amber liquid inside was now room temperature. That had gotten more than a few comments from his brothers and sisters in blue who were playing darts in the back and checking each other out in the front. He'd ignored them. He didn't care what they thought or didn't think. None of it mattered.

After four days of being shut down every time he tried to reach out to Gina to explain, he wasn't sure if anything mattered any more.

Of course, he'd known that was a possibility when he'd accepted the assignment from Rodriguez to check out the box Gina's brothers had left. But knowing something could happen and having it actually happen were two very different things. One result made him drink a few beers. The other made him want to drink a few kegs.

The barstool next to him scraped against the floor as someone scooted it back and sat down. The flash of red hair in his periphery told him who it was before Frankie even opened his mouth.

"When Shannon called and said you'd been sitting here staring at your beer for the past two hours, I thought she was just trying to get in my pants again." He winked at the woman behind the bar, who just rolled her eyes. "But here you are, like a man about to snap and, oh, I don't know, join the police department or something."

Ford cut a dirty look at his older brother. "I *am* a cop."

"I know you are, moron. That's what makes it funny. I give you shit for being a cop. You tell me to go eat smoke. We flip each other off and all is right with the world." Frankie picked up Ford's beer and took a long drink, then grimaced and set it back down on the bar. "You are fucking up the flow of things almost as much as this shitty, warm beer."

He flipped off his brother. The idiot just laughed and clapped him on the back. Then, he threw some bills on the bar and stood up. "Come on, you're coming with me."

"Why?" Ford asked as he eyeballed his brother, not trusting where the impulsive giant was going with this.

"Because sitting in a cop bar talking about your feelings," Frankie said, making the last word sound like an infectious disease, "is not something I want to do."

That made two of them. "We aren't talking about my feelings."

Not now. Not here. Not anywhere. He was going to sit here and stare at his beer and not think about Gina Luca and how he'd fucked up the best thing to have ever happened to him. He put his elbows on the bar and laid his arms on either side of the beer mug and gave it his full attention.

Frankie snorted, obviously unimpressed. "But we will be talking about your feelings, because your head is wedged so far up your ass right now that you are insufferable even for you."

"Insufferable." Ford picked up his beer and took a swig of the lager that was so flat and warm that he immediately regretted it. "That's a big word for a firefighter."

"There you are." Frankie grinned down at him. "I knew you were lurking in there somewhere. Now get your scrawny ass up before I pick you up and embarrass you in front of your little buddies in blue."

Scrawny? What the fuck? "I'm six two."

"Exactly. Scrawny. Now get a move on, baby brother. Finian is on shift tonight, and Fallon and the rest of our lovely sisters still aren't talking to you, so that means knocking some sense into your thick skull is up to me."

Ford didn't want to go. He wanted to sit here at Marino's and glare at his shitty room-temperature beer and snarl at anyone who had the balls to try to talk to him. But he knew Frankie. He'd known him his whole life. And never in all those years had the eldest Hartigan sibling ever backed down from a single solitary thing.

His brother had two speeds: full throttle ahead and dead asleep, which meant that if his brother was all in for making Ford come with him then he really was all in. At six feet six inches tall, Frankie was big enough to throw Ford over his shoulder and haul him out of Marino's. Ford couldn't let that happen. He might be a complete idiot, but he still had his pride.

"Fine," he said, adding enough distaste to the word to make sure his brother knew his exact thoughts on the matter, and then stood up and walked out of Marino's.

If he'd thought Frankie would be any more chill when they were both sitting out on his deck looking at the grass that Finian had painstakingly planted and watered for months, then he was wrong. Frankie was even more of a pain in the ass in his own environment, where he'd pulled out every detail of the Gina fiasco with the subtlety and gentleness of a Mack truck skidding across an ice sheet and smacking into a snowman.

"So, let me get this straight," Frankie said while staring at Ford like he'd never seen a dumber human being in his life, which, since he worked with firefighters, was really saying something. "First, there was the thing at the hotel, which you fucked up."

"I didn't know Gallo and Ruggiero had set her up, and when I mentioned I hadn't been expecting her, she ran."

"Yeah, because—newsflash—chicks have egos, too." Frankie took a drink of his beer. "And then when, by the grace of some benevolent force in the universe, you get the opportunity to hang out with her again, you fuck that shit up by not being honest."

"I didn't lie, regulations kept me from being able to tell her the complete truth."

"You went to the same Catholic school that I did. Do you really think Sister Mary Helen would say that a lie of omission didn't count if it was work-related?"

"Fuck you," he grumbled and flipped his brother off.

"That's what I thought." Frankie returned Ford's middle-finger salute with one of his own. "And then, because you're not a big enough asshole already, you don't do whatever the fuck it takes to make Gina understand that you've seen the error of your ways after the disaster of epic proportions at Mom's house, and instead slink away back to your cop shop until you go over to her house under false pretenses *again* and snoop around for evidence of her brothers committing a crime."

"It was for her own good. If someone else had gone in there and found something, they wouldn't have been able to protect her against the fallout like I would."

"So, you're the hero in all of this, is that what you're saying, baby bro?" When Ford didn't answer, Frankie went on. "Because you sure as shit look like the heel to me."

"Thank you, Professor Hartigan. I wasn't aware of how

badly I'd screwed everything up."

"Well, it's a good thing she was just a piece of temporary ass and not someone who actually mattered."

The world turned red. Ford shot up and bum-rushed his brother, wrapping his arms around his waist and taking him down in a picture-perfect tackle. After that it was total chaos, complete with jabs, elbows to the ribs, and a flipped deck chair. They wrestled for control, delivering as many punches as possible before they were both laying side by side on the deck, surrounded by chairs that had been knocked over—or in one case, broken in half—and breathing so hard he would have thought they'd just tangled with a pack of elephants. Well, judging by the feel of his jaw, he might have.

"You are such a dumb fucker," Frankie said, his words sounding funny because of the right hook Ford had delivered to his big brother's mouth.

Ford was too tired and achy to sit up and smack Frankie around for the comment. "How's that?"

Frankie snorted, then let out a pained groan. "Because instead of being here trying to kick my ass—which you'll never be able to do, by the way—for insulting your girl in order to get a rise out of you so that the dim bulb above your head would go off, you should be out there begging and groveling and doing whatever it takes to get the woman you love to give your scrawny ass another chance."

Because there wasn't a damn thing he could do about what Frankie got right in that little speech, Ford focused on what his brother got wrong. Just because he didn't shop in the giganto section didn't make him a pipsqueak. He was six foot two, for the love of Mike. "I'm not scrawny."

"But you *are* wrong."

Ford opened his mouth to argue—a move that made his sore jaw ache—but he had nothing to say to that, because his oversized doofus of a brother was right. "I know." Damn it.

He hated it when that happened.

"So go get your girl, Ford."

"What if she won't listen?" His voice cracked on the last word, as though his fears had been ripped from his throat. He'd be lucky if she didn't swing that sledgehammer at him, let alone actually hear him admit what a dumbass he'd been.

Still laying down beside him, Frankie swung his arm in a wide arc, and his massive paw of a hand landed with a hard thunk on Ford's chest. Both men let out an *oof* of pain before Frankie said, "You mean the guy who bucked three generations of tradition by bypassing the fire department for the police department is scared of doing something hard? Don't fool yourself, little bro. You've got what it takes to make this happen. If anyone can beat the odds, it's you."

Ford lay there, his breaths still coming out as big puffs of air, trying to figure out what to say, because that was probably about as close to an "I love you man" and "you aren't a total dipshit for becoming a detective" as he'd ever heard from his oldest brother.

"If you ever tell anyone I just said that," Frankie said, "I'll deny it."

"All the way to the grave," Ford said with a laugh, even though it made his ribs hurt like hell, but not nearly as much as the idea of spending the rest of his life without Gina.

So, he ignored how much his entire body ached and got up, so he could go get his girl.

Chapter Twenty

Ford walked into the hotel on Bleaker Street out of breath and a little out of his mind. Okay, a lot out of his mind. He'd tried Gina's house, but she wasn't there. He'd tried Vacilli's Bakery. No dice. He'd braved Lucy's house and had to remind her that maiming was a serious offense as she put a mean-looking claw hammer down on her kitchen counter when he asked her if she knew where Gina was. Finally, Fallon had taken pity on him—thanks to intel from Tess—that Gina was working a wedding at the very hotel where they'd first met.

And that's how he'd ended up here with no fucking clue what to do next.

He didn't have to be a detective to find her once he got to the lobby. He just followed the sound of the Cha-Cha Slide to the right ballroom.

"Where do you think you're going?" asked an old lady in head-to-toe black standing next to the door like a gargoyle.

"I need to talk to the wedding planner." And he didn't have time to play good cop and chat with this old biddy.

He started to walk through, and the old woman whacked

him right in the shin with her cane. Pain ricocheted up his leg, and he stopped dead in his tracks before she took a whack at his head with that thing.

"My fool of a great grandson is in there celebrating a marriage that's not going to last past thirty days, and I know you weren't invited, so go find another party to crash."

Since hip checking an old lady wasn't on his to-do list, Ford turned and reached down deep for the Hartigan charm that had thus far eluded him his entire life. "You look like a woman who knows what she's talking about, so I'm sorry in advance for your great grandson's doomed wedding. But I only need to talk to Gina. I promise I'm not crashing."

"Don't try to soften me up, buster." The cane came down on his toe this time. "I'm beyond flattery."

His toe throbbing, Ford took her at her word and took a step back and tried another tack—honesty. "Look, lady, I messed up with the woman I love, and she's inside, and if I don't talk to her and set everything straight, then everything is going to go right to hell."

The gray-haired bouncer kept her cane on the ground and glared up at him. "Don't use that kind of language around me. I'm a lady."

"One with a cane she's not afraid to use," he muttered.

"Damn skippy," she said, using it to tap his toes with enough force to remind him of the damage she could do with that thing. "Now, I don't want to know what you did, because it's plain as day that it was total foolishness." She put the plastic stopper of her cane down on the ground, missing the inside of his foot by two inches, and leaned on the handle to bring herself to her full height of probably five foot nothing. "So what are you going to do about it?"

"Tell her I love her." That was all he had so far when it came to having a working plan.

The old lady gave him a look that screamed try again.

"Pretty words are cheap."

If he clamped his jaw closed any harder, he was going to lose his back molars. Taking a deep breath—or at least as much of one as he could through his nostrils—he looked over the old lady's head to the ballroom beyond. The lights were dimmed, but he could see people dancing, a wedding party up at the front, and a DJ in front of a huge movie screen. That was it. Everything had started with that Kiss Cam. Maybe that would fix everything, too.

"Ma'am," he said, his voice louder than he meant for it to be, but volume control had gone out the window the second time she'd gotten him with her cane. "I'm gonna do whatever it takes to get her back."

The old woman gave him an assessing look, then snapped, "So what are you doing standing out here?"

What the hell? After all that, she was just going to act like he was the one delaying everything? It had to be the wedding. People lost their minds at weddings. Not willing to waste another second on trying to unravel that mystery, he rushed inside the ballroom.

Gina wasn't near the DJ booth. She wasn't near the catering stations. She wasn't by the bridal party dais. He was getting ready to breach the dance floor, when light spilled out from the swinging door leading to the staff area. There was no mistaking that brown, wavy hair with its tendency to frizz. He'd found her.

He rushed over to that side of the ballroom and through the staff doors into a makeshift kitchen in full go mode. There were waiters and guys in tall chef hats and dishwashers carrying heavy tubs filled with cutlery and mini plates rushing around the room. And there, in the back by a woman in one of the hotel's signature black blazers, stood Gina. She was wearing that green dress again from the first night they'd met. It had made him stop and take notice. Now that he knew the woman in the dress, he appreciated how beautiful she looked in it even more.

His mouth was open to call out to her before he knew it, but he clamped his jaw shut. He'd spent the past week giving her words. That wasn't going to be enough. He needed to show her this time, and for the first time since she'd walked out of his parents' house, he knew exactly what to do.

And sadly, it wasn't going to be as easy as just getting her on a Kiss Cam again.

...

The wedding had gone off without a hitch and the reception finished early, and Gina was so glad that at least one thing in her world was turning out the way she'd hoped. She walked into her house and swept up the mail scattered on the floor under the postal slot in her front door.

The daily paper was on the top, with a huge front-page spread about how the Waterbury Police Department had stopped a shipment of heroin and arrested ten people associated with the Esposito crime family. After that it was bills, junk mail, and one blue envelope with a foreign stamp. She was about to dump it all on the foyer table when the return address on one envelope caught her attention.

George Ainsley
510 Luca Street
Nassau, Bahamas

Her fingers shook as she ripped open the envelope. After they'd taken a cruise a few years ago and had discovered Luca Street, her brothers had told way too many lame jokes about how awesome it would be to live on a street with their name. It had to be from them.

Ms. Luca,

Thank you for your interest in renting the home on Luca Street. Unfortunately, it has been occupied by new buyers. They were alerted to the real estate investment opportunity by a mutual friend you share who gave them an early heads-up about how their former circumstances were not tenable. The current owners have no plans at the moment to sell the property but should the situation in your location change, they will reconsider.

Sincerely,
George Ainsley, Esq.

Gina didn't know whether to cry or laugh. She'd recognize Paul's ridiculous sense of humor anywhere. He probably thought using the name of their old next-door neighbor and writing in code to let her know they were okay was hilarious. Chuckling despite her frustration that her brothers had gone all cloak-and-dagger on her, she relaxed for the first time in days. And once that weight was off her shoulders, something else landed in its place as she looked down at the newspaper laying on the table.

Ford hadn't just tried to help. He actually had. He'd gotten her brothers to leave before an Esposito-related drug bust went down. He'd tried to tell her, and she wouldn't listen. She wouldn't give him a chance. Even after he'd broken one of his precious rules for her by giving a heads-up to her brothers. Her lungs tightened, and she crumpled the letter in her hand. After years of not trusting people and building her walls, she hadn't given Ford the chance that he'd given her. Instead, she'd spent their time together just waiting for him to show his real self. What she hadn't realized was that he had been doing exactly that the entire time. And her? She'd been too scared to let herself believe what had been there in front of her all along.

But could she ever really trust him?

And that's when she heard the unmistakable sound of a hammer hitting wood coming from the other side of her front door. Discombobulated, confused, and really pissed off at herself, she yanked open the door and stopped dead.

...

"What in the hell are you doing?" Gina's question cut across the porch as sharp as the blade on a hockey skate.

Ford didn't look up. He thought he'd have more time to finish the project. As it was, all he had done was leave the reception and pick-up the specially sourced wood Juan had ordered that matched the original planks. He had one laid out but not secured in place. Of course, he could only last so long without looking at her.

She stood in the doorway. The tip of her nose was red, and the ruby blotch of annoyance at the base of her throat was in full effect. But she was still beautiful in her full-on warrior mode. Really, she was magnificent, and for the first time since he realized he needed to show her that he would always be there for her, he had second thoughts. The woman looked like she might just murder him, and he couldn't blame her. He stood up, careful to stand in front of the unfinished patch job.

"I had to fix it." It sounded lame but putting his feelings into words wasn't his forte.

"My porch?" she asked, suspicion thick in her voice. "You *had* to fix my porch."

"I know how much you love this house and I wanted…" The planned speech he'd been practicing in his head about how this house was her heart and how he'd protect it and care for it no matter what fizzled into nothingness. Shit. He was fucking this all up. "No," he finished, floundering for words. "I want to fix us."

"Stop right there." She held up her hand, palm forward. "I need to tell you something."

That couldn't happen. She had to hear him out. He took a step toward her, leaving his spot in front of the hole in the porch. "Gina—"

Chin trembling, she walked toward him and stepped just right on the unsecured planks. Her foot slipped, and her eyes went wide with shock. Ford could see it all happening in slow motion. She was going to go through the hole in the porch. He grabbed for her, curling his fingers around her waist and reaching with his other hand for the handrail surrounding the porch, but he missed it by millimeters. Before he could even holler out to warn her to brace herself, they were both waist-deep in the porch, the fronts of their bodies pressed together, his arm still around her waist, and their mouths within kissing distance.

"Are you okay?" he asked.

Unable to stop himself, he swept his free hand over the parts of her body he could reach to make sure, a process made difficult by the fact that there was maybe an inch between her back and sides and the pointed edges of the wood, and because she glared at him the entire time as if she was plotting his death, which she probably was. He moved his hands so they were between her back and the broken wood.

"I'm fine," she said, turning her face from his as if she could will him away.

His gut dropped. "Gina—"

"I don't want to hear it," she interrupted. "I just want to get out of here."

Ford looked around. The replacement planks of wood

were scatted out of reach across the porch and down the steps. His feet were on solid ground, but the fit with the two of them stuck in the hole together was too tight for him to leverage either of them up. The truth of it was, they were well and good stuck.

"That's not happening without help." The first glimmer of a backup plan began to flicker in the back of his mind. "Can you reach your hand in my front pocket?"

She narrowed her eyes. "Really, you want me to cop a feel?"

Yes. No. Well, not at this moment. "My phone is in there. We have to call for help."

"Fine," she said with a huff.

It took a little adjusting in how they were squeezed together, but she managed to get her hand in his pants—or at least close enough to make his dick stand up and take notice.

Cool it, Hartigan. You're not going to get another chance at this.

She bit her lip in concentration and pulled out his phone. "Got it." She angled it so the camera zeroed in on his face, unlocking the screen.

"Go to contacts," he said, working his new plan on the fly. "Hit the one that's just the number six."

"Is that your precinct number?"

He shook his head, praying silently that she'd understand what he was about to say next. "It's Frankie's station."

Her finger hovered over the touchpad. "I thought you never wanted to call them for help because you'd get so much shit for it."

"It's worth it to make sure you're okay." And it was, a million times over.

"Let me stop you there. I don't know where my brothers are, and since I don't have any other ties to the Esposito family, you can just stop trying to butter me up." She hit the contact listing for station six with a solid thunk.

"I'm not," he said, and his heart sank as he watched the pain and anger flash in her eyes before she locked everything out, including him. He knew he had to tell her the truth, though. He owed her that much at least. "I know you won't believe this, but I love you and I can't imagine my life without you in it."

She laughed. It was the broken sound of a woman who'd reached her limit. "Well you better figure out how, because I'm done with liars and people who see me as a way to get ahead in their career. I know that's why you came back. You thought my brothers had some Esposito secrets in that box."

The relief that had gone through him when he'd realized there wasn't anything related to the Espositos in that box had been so powerful that he'd nearly dropped into the nearby kitchen chair, because it wasn't until that moment that he'd realized how far he was willing to go to protect her, the woman he loved.

"I did. And I was willing to do whatever it took to make sure none of the criminal repercussions came back to you."

That got her attention. She stopped pretending to ignore him as if they weren't practically glued together and looked up at him, her expression softening.

Of course, that was the exact moment when Frankie's voice came out of his cell phone's speaker. "Station Six, Hartigan speaking."

...

Gina needed a minute to process. Heart beating against her ribs like it was getting ready for a jailbreak, she tore her gaze away from Ford—seeing him muddled her thoughts—and looked around at her neighbors' houses. No one was out, but curtains were getting moved to the side, no doubt to figure out what the commotion was on her porch.

The chest-tightening, clammy-palmed anxiety about being stared at didn't materialize, though. Even as mad as she was at Ford, there was no denying that being with him acted as a nerves minimizer.

She vaguely listened while Ford told Frankie what had happened and ordered him to get his ass out to her house to get them out. On autopilot, she hit the end-call button, unable to look away from the man who'd turned her life upside down.

"What do you mean, protect me?" she asked, trying to stay mad at him so she wouldn't feel how every hard inch of him was pressed against her and how happy her pheromones—and girly bits—were to be near his pheromones—and more—again.

"My superiors knew about the box." His hand rubbed soothing circles across the small of her back that set off a wave of awareness through her. "I didn't tell them. They wanted to send someone else to check it out."

"And you didn't want that because…?"

"If there was something illegal in the box, I didn't want it to fall back on you." The circling against her back stopped as he adjusted his stance, something that brought them even closer together than they had been before. "I wanted to protect you."

"Why?" It didn't make sense. None of it made sense. Ford always followed the rules. She'd actually seen him reading the rules for Monopoly one night instead of just playing house rules like a normal person. Her breath hiccuped as the first hint of hope started to fill her up.

"Because I love you and I know you. You wouldn't knowingly have anything to do with your brothers' illegal activities."

Of course not. It was ridiculous to assume, but how many

times had other people done just that? Ford hadn't, though. Not even that first night. She may have a problematic last name, but he'd never judged her on that. Her heartbeat sped up, and she had to dig her nails into her palms to keep from melting against him. He still was going to break her heart some day. Might as well be a clean break today.

The sounds of a fire truck's sirens could be heard in the distance, getting closer with each heartbeat. If she could just make it through the next few minutes, then she'd be free—to do what, she had no idea.

"You lied to me about my brothers, about why you were in my house." A bittersweet agony gripped her chest and squeezed tight because she he had a way of making her want to believe. She looked up at him, his face a little blurry because of the tears making her eyes watery, and then dropped her gaze. She couldn't face seeing his reaction when the truth came out. "What else did you lie about?"

"I never lied about how I feel about you," he said, reaching up with his free hand and brushing back a strand of her hair that had tumbled free.

The sirens grew louder, and she could see the fire engine in her peripheral vision, but she couldn't look away from Ford.

"The fact is, you deserve better than me. I'm the lucky one, and I fucked it all up because I was too scared of losing you to tell you the truth, to tell you that I'd fallen in love with you." He cupped her face with his large hands and forced her to look up at him. "I love your laugh, your smile, and the way you look at the world as if it's like the Victorian, just needing someone to love it." He smiled down at her, warm and encompassing, and promising so many tomorrows. "I love how you feel in my arms. I love how you make me feel every time you walk into a room. I even love being stuck in this damn hole with you, because it means that I get to see your beautiful face."

"Don't," she said, continuing to fight the hope expanding in her chest. "It's okay. I know how I look and I really am good with it now."

The sirens were blaring by now as the engine pulled to a stop in front of her house, but she barely heard them or saw the firefighters getting out. Ford was the only person that mattered.

"I do, too. You're beautiful, and I love the woman you are *because* of your face, not in spite of it." He dipped his head down and brushed her lips with his, setting off a cascade of sensations that left her breathless. "I fucked everything up, and I can't say I won't mess up again, but I love you, Gina Luca, and I'm okay with doing whatever it takes to prove that to you."

She glanced up at him, looking, really looking, at the man who'd twisted up her world and thrown it around, and realized that he was telling the truth. He loved her.

"We should probably let the fire department get us out of here now, or the neighbors will expect this kind of show every night," she said, because of course she was the woman who said the wrong thing at the wrong time. This was even worse than pointing out the open bar when he'd asked if he could buy her a drink at the wedding.

"Well, I'd heard that public declarations of love were romantic," he said, dipping his head down for a kiss but stopping millimeters short of touching his lips to hers.

Her heartbeat sped up again. At this rate, she was going to need blood pressure medication or a kiss. She knew which one she preferred. "And I'd heard they were silly."

"Whoever told you that was an idiot," he said.

"But I love him anyway," she said, meaning every single word.

Rising up on her tiptoes, she closed the distance between

their mouths, kissing him with every bit of everything she had. At that moment, there were too many everythings to be separated. There was love and hope and anticipation and, yeah, nerves, because the important things in life were always a little bit scary, but in a good way.

"Are you catching all of this, Mom?" Frankie's voice cut through the euphoria of the kiss.

Well, that and the number of people stomping across her front yard. She looked around. There were way more firefighters there than the call needed. Front and center of the crowd was Frankie, who was holding up his phone. Kate Hartigan was visible in the majority of the screen but there was no missing—event though they were in the little box on the right of the FaceTime screen—Gina and Ford with their kiss-swollen lips.

Heat rushed to her cheeks, but unlike the last time she and Ford had been kissing onscreen, it was from pure, unadulterated happiness.

"Hey Mom," Frankie said. "Let Finian know that I call dibs on being the best man at the wedding."

Gina gulped. "He hasn't asked me to marry him."

"Good Lord, Ford." Frankie shook his head. "Do I have to smack your scrawny butt around again, or are you going to get it right finally?"

"Shut up, Frankie," Ford said. "I've got this."

There wasn't a ring, and he didn't get down on one knee. Instead, they were stuck in a hole in her front porch surrounded by firefighters while Ford's mom watched on FaceTime.

"Gina Luca, I don't deserve you, but I'd be the luckiest guy in the world if you'd agree to be my wife."

Fighting back tears of joy, she let her gaze travel around the people slowly crowding in on them. Here she was, about to kiss a guy while a crowd of people watched and smiled, and that old nausea started to rumble in her belly. But then her gaze collided with Ford's again and she could see *he* was even more afraid of rejection than she was. A fine sheen of sweat had broken out on his forehead, and his eyes were literally begging her to forgive him. To love him. His lips mouthed the word, "Please," and her heart cracked open. All the insecurities she used to protect her heart from pain, barricades she'd spent decades erecting, just...melted away.

She wasn't sure she could trust her voice, so she mouthed back, "Yes."

His face lit up like she'd made him the happiest man in the world. And she believed him. His lips found hers in a hungry kiss, her arms winding around his neck, her fingers getting lost in his thick hair and holding him to her. Cheers broke out from the assembled firefighters and a few happy exclamations from Kate on the phone. They barely noticed.

Eventually Ford pulled back, his big hands cupping her face. "You don't happen to know any good wedding planners, do you?"

"I might." What a smart-ass this man she loved was.

And then before she could even formulate a thought, he kissed her again.

Chapter Twenty-One

Five Years Later…

It was total chaos in the Victorian's backyard as about twenty mini Hartigans, mini Lucas, and a smattering of other little kids squealed in glee as they ran from the bounce house to the face-painting station to the puppet show in the far corner. In the middle of it all was the birthday girl, sprinting toward the inflated castle wearing her favorite gift—a bright red firefighter's helmet from Uncle Frankie.

"Out of my way, big nose," one of the kids said, shoving Amalie Hartigan out of her place in line.

Ford jumped up from his chair on the porch and was halfway down the stairs when Amalie pulled back her right fist.

"Amalie," Gina's voice called out.

Their little girl froze, then turned to her mother with as close to an innocent smile anyone with Hartigan blood could pull off—even at three years old.

"We don't hit our friends," Gina said as she walked over to Ford's side on the stairs. "And Christopher, it's not nice to call people names. Do it again and I'll tell your mom."

The little dark-haired boy, whose fifth birthday party had been the weekend before, glanced over at his mom and then turned to Amalie, who was practically his twin in all but parentage. "Sorry."

"It's okay, let's go fly." Amalie grabbed her cousin's hand and they clambered inside the bounce house together.

Only once they were inside and giggling together did Ford let out the breath he'd been holding.

"Calm down there, papa bear," Gina said with a laugh. "That won't be the last time she gets teased for having the Luca schnoz, but I'm glad she has it."

"Even though you hated it for so long?" he asked, trying to figure out where his wife was going with this.

"I've decided that it's lucky." She tapped the tip of her nose. "It means she'll end up with the perfect man who loves her for who she really is—just like it was lucky for me."

"I'm the lucky one here." He curled his arm around her waist and brought her closer, dipped his head, and kissed the most beautiful woman in the world.

Don't miss Lucy's story!

For an early sneak peek of *Muffin Top*, turn the page!

Chapter One

Nothing good ever happened when the captain asked Frankie Hartigan to come into his cramped office at the back of the firehouse and close the door. Frankie ran the last few calls through his head. It had to be about the asshole with the Jag. They'd had a warehouse fire down by the docks, and this idiot had parked right in front of the hydrant. Really, the guys didn't have a choice but to bust the car's windows and run the line to the hydrant through there. The rich dipshit had pitched a royal fit, right up until Frankie had come over, loomed his entire six-foot-six frame over him, and asked him if there was a problem. There hadn't been. Shocker.

"Have a seat, Hartigan," the captain said as he sat down behind a desk overloaded with paperwork and manuals and—rumor had it—a computer untouched by human hands.

Frankie looked around. Captain O'Neil's office always needed its own *Hoarders* episode, but today it looked worse than usual. There was shit everywhere. The two chairs in front of the desk were stuffed with half-filled boxes, old standard operating procedure manuals were stacked four feet high up the wall, and the coveted firefighters vs cops rivalry trophy from last year's charity hockey game had the place of honor on top of the tower. Even if he wanted to sit down, there wasn't a place to do it. So, he did what he always did when he got brought in for a good reaming out: he stayed standing.

"I'm good."

The older man sat there, staring at Frankie from under two bushy gray eyebrows so fluffy they looked like they were about to take flight. "Is there anything you'd like to tell me before I start, Hartigan?"

Frankie did the walk down memory lane again and came up with only one possibility. He'd been a fucking angel lately. At thirty-three, he really must be mellowing with age. "Is this about the dipshit with the Jag?"

"Oh, you mean the one who plays golf with the mayor? The one who needs two new windows and a fresh detail?" O'Neil gave him a hard, steely glare that lasted for all of thirty seconds. "That little prick got exactly what he deserved, which is what I told the fire commissioner when he called to take a chunk out of my well-endowed ass."

"Well, that's the only thing I can think of." And if it wasn't that, then why in the hell was he in what amounted to the principal's office of Waterbury Firehouse No. 6?

"Good," O'Neil said with an ornery chuckle. "You never know what someone will confess to when you start off that way."

"You're a piece of work, Captain."

"I'm an old relic, but I'm here and I'm not going anywhere, even if they are making me archive or dump most of this stuff." He waved huge bear paw of a hand at the mess.

Frankie looked around. "Yeah, I thought it looked like more than normal."

"Well you won't be seeing it after today."

That yanked his attention back to the man behind the desk. "Are you going somewhere?"

"Nope." The captain's face lost all signs of humor. "You are."

For the briefest of seconds, Frankie wished he had taken the offer of a chair. Then, the familiar sizzle of the Hartigan obstinate Irish temper sparked to life.

He stalked over to the captain's desk and laid his palms down on it. "Are you shit-canning me?"

"Nothing of the sort. It has recently come to my attention, thanks to all of my spring cleaning efforts, that you haven't taken a leave of absence in I don't even know how long, which is totally against regulations. I can't believe human resources and professional standards haven't ganged up on your oversized Irish ass already about it. The department has gone all in on the mental wellness aspect of firefighting safety, and that includes taking your required leave to mentally refresh yourself."

Frankie threw up his arms in frustration, wishing like hell that the captain's office was big enough to pace in because he was about to go off like TNT and needed to let off some steam stat. "That's a bunch of touchy-feely bullshit."

"Agreed, but you have three weeks built up and you're taking it all as of now." The captain fished around on his desk for a minute and then pulled out a sheet of paper, handing it over. "And here's the letter from up the food chain ordering you to take three weeks immediately."

Frankie looked down at the sheet of paper like it was a death sentence.

"This sucks." The sheer boredom of sitting on his ass for three weeks was going to kill him. He was already to the point where he took extra shifts just to avoid having too many days off in the month to sit around the house he shared with his twin, Finian, and do the same shit he'd been doing since they got the place a decade ago. It wasn't that he needed the money—although, come on, everyone had too many bills to pay—but the firehouse was his life. The adrenaline. The comraderie. The going out and saving shit. It's what a guy like him was made for. "What in the hell am I supposed to do for three weeks?"

The captain shrugged. "Get drunk. Get laid. Get a hobby. I don't fucking care. Just get out of my office and don't let me see that freckled mug of yours again for three weeks, Hartigan."

• • •

Marino's wasn't a nasty dive bar, or an outlaw biker bar, or the kind of bar where when Frankie walked in all the patrons stopped what they were doing and turned to give him the stink eye like they were picturing the best way to dispose of his body. Those places would have been more welcoming. Instead, it was a cop bar. And why would a self-respecting firefighter go into such a place of ill repute? Because his poor, confused baby brother was one of Waterbury's finest, complete with detective shield and annoying habit of always following the rules. Ford did, however, have the night off and a willingness to play wingman as Frankie checked through the captain's proffered to-do list with get drunk being at the top of it.

"Can you believe this crap?" he asked, taking a drink from his first draught beer. "Three weeks."

Ford was watching the dartboard in the back, since he was up soon, but he glanced away long enough to roll his eyes at Frankie. "If you'd just taken your leave each year like you're supposed to, you wouldn't be in this spot."

Frankie flipped him the bird. "Wait, not only do I have to drink away my sorrows in this place, but you're going to tell me I told you so, too?"

"What else are younger brothers for?"

"I should have called Finn." His fraternal twin, younger

by six minutes and forty-two seconds, as their mom reminded them at every birthday, would have commiserated properly with Frankie in a real bar.

"Finn is in Vegas because he," Ford said as he shot him a shit-eating grin that made it look like he was as much of a troublemaker as the rest of the Hartigans. "Wait for it." He paused, held up a finger, and took a drink of his beer, soaking up the moment for all it was worth. "Took his leave like he was supposed to."

"I swear you were switched at birth," Frankie grumbled. "Somewhere out there is a changling Hartigan who doesn't get a hard-on for following procedure."

"You already have one brother and four sisters who are like that already. I bring balance to the force."

It was probably true.

"How about instead of feeling sorry for yourself for having all this paid time off, you do something productive like figure out what we're going to do for Mom and Dad's fortieth anniversary," Ford said. "We all agreed to pitch in and do something big for them."

"Yeah, but no one can figure out what."

The plan had been to send them to Paris for a week, before their dad came home and declared that if Frankie's mom forced him to go to one more frou-frou French restaurant to eat snails and force-fed duck livers, he was going to choose to starve to death instead. Yeah. The Hartigans were all known for being a little bit on the loudly dramatic side, with every hill being the hill they'd die on.

"I'd say with three weeks off you're the perfect man for the case, Junior," Ford said, using Frankie's most hated of nicknames.

"Yo Hartigan, you're up," someone hollered from the area near the dartboard, saving Frankie from having to smack his brother upside the head on general principle for calling him junior.

Knowing he'd been saved, Ford raised his beer in salute and strolled off to the back, leaving Frankie in unfriendly territory without a cop guide. Now, it wasn't that the cops and firefighters of Waterbury were sworn enemies, it was just that, well, there was a long-lived and healthy-ish rivalry between them, and they tended to stick to their own kind—except for the annual charity hockey game, during which they happily and enthusiastically beat the ever-loving shit out of each other in between scoring goals.

The bar got a whole lot friendlier when Bobby Marino, who was all of seventy-six if he was a day, gave up the serving duties to Shannon Kominsky. Frankie had known Shannon for years. They'd spent time together naked before and had both walked away relaxed and happy. If he played his cards right, tonight could be a repeat performance, complete with orgasms and her post-sex chocolate chip cookies. Some women liked to snuggle after sex. Some liked to talk. Shannon baked.

"Heya, Shannon," he said, giving her the half-lazy, half-cocky grin that had started getting him laid in high school.

And the grin would have worked, if she'd have seen it. Instead, she kept her gaze off of him as she picked up his beer, slid a coaster under it, and sat the mug back down. "Not tonight, Frankie."

Damn. That brush-off came brutally fast.

"What did I do?"

Now she did look up at him, and it was probably just to give him the are-you-stupid look on her cute face. "It's what you didn't do."

His expression must have been as blank as his brain right then, because she shook her head and her lips curled in a rueful smile.

"Call, Frankie," she said with a chuckle. "You never called."

Fuck. He shifted on his barstool. "I'm sorry, it's been

crazy, but I've got some time off. Maybe you and I could—"

"Honey, it's been six months." She held up her left hand and wiggled her fingers, the neon light from the Budweiser sign above the bar catching in the diamond ring on her finger. "I'm off the market."

"Damn." This was starting to happen with way too much frequency lately. Why was everyone getting married all of a sudden? "Looks like I'm too late."

"You were never in the running." Shannon leaned her forearms on the bar and brought her head close, lowering her voice as if she was about to impart an important secret. "Frankie, you're one of the best lays in Waterbury, all us girls agree."

His ego grew two sizes before the second part of her declaration registered. "You talk about me? All of you together like that?" Comparing notes? Chicks did that? Fuck, did other guys know this little factoid? Because that shit was dangerous.

"It's Waterbury. This neighborhood is like a small town when it comes to gossip," Shannon said. "But here's the deal. You're respectful. You don't promise anything you're not going to deliver. You're fun. You're honestly a good guy, but, honey, you're not the kind of guy who delivers happily ever afters." She gave him a look that walked the line between sympathy and pity. "And once you get to a certain point in your life, all of the fuck-buddy fun loses its luster and you want more, you want a forever kind of thing. You understand what I'm saying?"

Love. That's what she meant. That once-in-a-lifetime, you're-a-lucky-son-of-a-bitch-if-you-find-it thing that his parents had, that Felicia had with Hudson, that Ford had with Gina. And for him it was as likely to happen as him finding a unicorn, because he knew Shannon was right. He'd always known it. He wasn't a delivery driver for Happily Ever Afters R Us, which meant he was as likely to find it as he was to find…

"A fucking unicorn," he muttered.

Shannon's eyebrows went up in question. "What?"

"Nothing," he said with a sigh, because how did you explain a unicorn to a woman who'd just told him he wasn't ever getting one?

Shannon shook her head at him and strutted down to the other end of the bar to take some fresh-out-of-the-academy kid's order. Annoyed with the fact that the zinger she'd delivered had hit a little too close to home, Frankie turned around and perused the crowd at Marino's. Going east to west, it pretty much went cop and a badge bunny, several cops and one hot badge bunny, a group of sad-sack cops with no badge bunnies, a shitbird in a suit who looked totally out of place, and one Lucy Kavanagh, who looked like she was about to punch the guy's lights out. Now this could get interesting. Frankie got up off the barstool and strolled on over to provide the zaftig firecracker best friend of Ford's girlfriend some help should she need it.

. . .

If one more person told Lucy that she'd be so pretty if she just lost some weight, she was going to set them on fire.

All she wanted to do was sit in Marino's in peace and enjoy the jalapeño cheeseburger with a side of spicy fries and a Coke—yeah, that's right, full-calorie Coke, suck it Judgey McJudgeyPants—as her own special treat after the week from hell.

Instead, the concern troll in the shitty suit had invited himself over to let her know that if she'd only ordered a salad that she might actually walk out of the bar with someone instead of with a few additional pounds.

"And what business is it of yours what I eat?" She punctuated the question by slathering a fry in Sriracha and popping it in her mouth.

"No need to get defensive there, I'm just trying to help," said the guy—who hadn't even bothered to introduce himself or—wait for it—say hi before launching into his unasked-for monologue about *her* eating habits. "I mean come on, no woman comes into a bar alone unless she plans on walking out with someone."

Now that was just some sexist bullshit right there. Who in the hell ever said that to a guy? Answer: no one.

The truth was she was there to meet up with her friend Gina later—her boyfriend already hit the dartboard in the corner—but she'd texted she was running late and eat without her.

"Really?" She pushed her steak knife farther away from her plate so she wouldn't be tempted to stab him with it. "You don't think I might just want a Coke and a burger?"

The guy went on as if she hadn't said a thing. "I'm serious. You have a great face, if you just upped the veggies and eliminated the carbs, high-fat protein, and sugar, you'd be a solid seven instead of a three."

She eyeballed the guy who wouldn't stop flapping his gums about things that had *nothing* to do with him. He was balding and wore a bad suit that only emphasized his beer belly—and *he* wanted to give *her* tips about how to look good? Of course he did.

"And," he continued, totally clueless about how close to death he was, "I'm only rating you as a three because your face is nice and your tits are fucking fantastic."

That was it. She was going to have to kill a man in the middle of a cop bar. They better have chocolate cake in prison, but even if they didn't it would probably be worth it.

"There you are, honey," a man said just as a very large shadow fell across her table.

She looked up—way up—into the beyond-handsome face of Frankie Hartigan, who was built like a redwood tree and, rumor had it, had one between his legs.

"I'm sorry I was late for our date." He glanced over at the dipshit veggie pusher. "Is this guy giving you a hard time?"

About the Author

Avery Flynn has three slightly wild children, loves a hockey-addicted husband, and is desperately hoping someone invents the coffee IV drip. Find out more about Avery on her website, follow her on Twitter, like her on her Facebook page, or friend her on her Facebook profile. Join her street team, The Flynnbots, on Facebeook. Also, if you figure out how to send Oreos through the internet, she'll be your best friend for life.

Also by Avery Flynn…

The Negotiator

The Charmer

The Schemer

Killer Temptation

Killer Charm

Killer Attraction

Killer Seduction

Betting on the Billionaire

Enemies on Tap

Dodging Temptation

His Undercover Princess

Her Enemy Protector

Butterface

Discover more Amara titles…

Handle with Care
a *Saddler Cove* novel by Nina Croft

First grade teacher Emily Towson always does the right thing. But in her dreams, she does bad, bad things with the town's baddest boy: Tanner O'Connor. But when he sells her grandmother a Harley, fantasy is about to meet a dose of reality. Tanner spent two hard years in prison, with only the thought of this "good girl" to keep him sane. Before either one thinks though, they're naked and making memories on his tool bench. Now Tanner's managed to knock-up the town's "good girl" and she's going to lose her job over some stupid "morality clause" if he doesn't step up.

What Happens in Vegas
a *Girls Weekend Away* novel by Shana Gray

Tough-as-nails detective Bonni Connolly is on a girls' getaway in Vegas with her friends and she splurges on a little luxury, including a VIP booth in an exclusive club. That's when she sees *him*. Professional poker player Quinn Bryant is in town for one of the largest tournaments of the year. What starts as a holiday fling soon turns into something more, as Bonni learns to see the man behind the poker face. Even though Bonni's trip has an end date and there is another tournament calling Quinn's name, their strong connection surprises them both. And by the end of the weekend they start to wonder if what happens in Vegas doesn't have to stay there…

ONE WEDDING, TWO BRIDES
a *Fairy Tale Brides* novel by Heidi Betts

Jilted bride Monica Blair can't believe it when she wakes up next to a smooth-talking cowboy with a ring on her finger. Ryder Nash would have bet that he'd never walk down the aisle. But when the city girl with pink-streaked hair hatches a plan to expose the conman who married his sister, no idea is too crazy. And even though Monica might be the worst rancher's wife he's ever seen, he can't stop thinking about the wedding night they never had. What was supposed to be a temporary marriage for revenge is starting to feel a little too real…

SCREWED
a novel by Kelly Jamieson

Cash has been in love with his best friend's wife forever. Now Callie and Beau are divorced, but guy code says she's still way off-limits. Cash won't betray his friendship by moving in. Not to mention it could destroy the thriving business he and Beau have worked years to create. But this new Callie isn't taking no for an answer. He's screwed…

Printed in Great Britain
by Amazon